Under
Almond
Blossoms

Under *Almond* Blossoms

Anja Saskia Beyer

Translated by
Annette
Charpentier

Text copyright © 2016 by Anja Saskia Beyer
Translation copyright © 2020 by Annette Charpentier
All rights reserved.

No part of this book may be reproduced, or stored in a retrieval system, or transmitted in any form or by any means, electronic, mechanical, photocopying, recording, or otherwise, without express written permission of the publisher.

Previously published as *Mandelblütenliebe* by Tinte & Feder in Germany in 2016. Translated from German by Annette Charpentier. First published in English by Lake Union Publishing in collaboration with Amazon Crossing in 2020.

Published by Lake Union Publishing, in collaboration with Amazon Crossing, Seattle

www.apub.com

Amazon, the Amazon logo, Lake Union Publishing and Amazon Crossing are trademarks of Amazon.com, Inc., or its affiliates.

ISBN-13: 9781542019842
ISBN-10: 1542019842

Cover design by Plum5 Limited

Printed in the United States of America

First edition

Under *Almond* Blossoms

Chapter One

'It's just a feeling, Mum.' Milla's voice was shaky, and not just because of the potholes she was manoeuvring around on her mint-green Dutch bicycle, one hand holding the mobile to her ear while the other gripped the handlebar. As every other morning, she was cycling along this road in Berlin-Friedrichshain, lined with cafés and small shops. The wind felt cool on her pale face, but it was a mild February day, and some trees were already showing their first buds. Here and there, early yellow crocuses lightened the beds around the tree trunks.

'Feeling? What feeling? Are you saying you aren't sure?' Her mother's voice sounded alarmed. Even though she had lived in Berlin for years, her Spanish accent was still very strong.

'No, I don't know for sure any more, Mum.' Milla felt her stomach tighten as she realised her mother wasn't really listening to her. As usual.

'Well, if you don't trust him, then you can't marry him, Milla. Under no circumstances. The wedding has to be cancelled.'

Milla briefly closed her eyes in despair. Why on earth had she said anything? She was annoyed with herself. Normally, she wouldn't have confided in her; her mother never talked about feelings, let alone vague feelings. But Milla had been awake all night, getting more and more upset, and when her mother had rung to tell her that she had no idea what to buy Milla for her wedding, because she had no idea what her daughter would like – the words had just slipped out.

How could her mother suggest cancelling the wedding, as if it was an appointment at the hairdresser's or dentist's? Why did her relationship with her mother, Sarah, have to be so complicated? How she longed for a loving mother to be by her side during these weeks before her wedding. A mother she could tell everything, who was looking forward to the big day with her. But her mother appeared – as she had ever since Milla could remember – strangely detached, only absently listening to Milla's worries and never seeming to take a real interest in her life. At least, that's how it felt to Milla, and the sadness this brought was like a pain in her stomach. She thought back to her mother's reaction when, overjoyed, she had told her about the wedding plans. Sarah had seemed slightly surprised – as though she couldn't believe anyone would want to marry her daughter – then she'd smiled briefly and congratulated her somewhat stiffly. Wouldn't any normal mother have hugged her daughter at that moment? But not Sarah. Milla remembered how rarely her mother had shown her any tenderness. She had occasionally, when she'd run to her crying with a grazed knee. But even then, it hadn't really felt comforting.

Milla had been a sensitive child and had always felt that her mother didn't love her like other mothers loved their daughters. She'd wondered whether it was her fault and blamed herself, trying even harder to be a good girl and make her mother proud, but that didn't change anything either. So over the years she had learned to stop the endless ruminations about what she might have done wrong, locking her feelings away in a corner of her mind. But the worry that something was not right with her remained. She had convinced herself that families weren't that important and she could

2

be happy with a handful of good friends, but now, with her wedding on the horizon, she missed having a family. During these last weeks of preparations for the big day she was more and more aware that though she had very good friends – particularly her 'bestie', Tine – at the end of the day she longed to have a loving family around her.

Presumably these feelings would never stop, because she was thirty-six now and, by all accounts, a grown-up. But still she wanted a father to walk her down the aisle; a father who would always be there for her. But her dad had died in an accident at work when Milla was only three years old. She couldn't really remember him, and all that remained of him were photos showing a blond, friendly-looking man carrying her lovingly in his arms. How different her childhood and teenage years would have been if he had still been alive. His parents, Milla's grandparents in Berlin, had also died a long time ago, as had the ones on the Spanish side of the family. There were no aunties and uncles either, because Milla's parents were both only children.

When Milla went to kindergarten, she'd been envious of her friend Julia's loving, cheerful father and doting grandparents. When she was younger she would ask her mother for stories about her family, but, whenever she did, Sarah's eyes would fill up. Her mother rarely showed emotion and, not wanting to hurt her, Milla had stopped asking.

A cold gust of wind touched Milla's face and made her eyes water. As she wiped the tears away she noticed the letter she had hurriedly pushed into her orange bag that morning flying through the air, landing in the middle of the road. She braked sharply, just as a white van turned into the road from the right. The vehicle's wing touched her front wheel, and Milla was thrown on to the cobbled street, landing hard on her back and smashing her phone on impact. She lay for a moment in shock, the pain from the cobbles radiating through her, but before she could gather herself enough to move, the world went dark and she fell into unconsciousness.

3

♦ ♦ ♦

When Milla came to again, she was looking up into a bright sky and she could hear the birds singing. The blurred face of a very old woman with white hair hovered above her – or was it a hallucination? The old lady smiled gently at her. Milla rubbed her eyes and reached out for the loving face, but then it disappeared. Milla focused and saw a brown-haired woman in her forties kneeling next to her, accompanied by a pug. 'Oh, my God, are you hurt? Shall I call an ambulance?'

'No, no, it's alright.' Milla sat up, and her face contorted with pain. Other people stopped to look, but most of them hurried on when they saw that she was conscious.

'You must have a guardian angel,' the woman said, while her pug peed against a nearby tree. 'And that bastard just drove off! Hit and run! It was a skinny young bloke, but I don't remember his number plate.'

Milla nodded slightly and touched her aching back. Then she got up painfully and looked around. Her battered bicycle was lying by the side of the road, the letter next to it in a puddle, soaked and unnoticed. Cars drove past as if nothing had happened.

'Are you sure you're alright?'

'Yes, thank you.' Milla felt every bone in her body, but at least none were broken. She touched her long, dark curls, a nervous habit of hers, and felt something warm running down the side of her face.

'Oh, no, you're bleeding!' the pug woman cried, covering her mouth with one hand.

'It's just a few drops.'

'Wouldn't you rather ring somebody?'

Milla immediately thought of Paul. She belonged to him, and he to her. Or not? 'No, thank you. I work at the goldsmith's over there. I'll be alright.'

The pug woman looked in the direction Milla indicated. The workshop was only three shops further down the road. Its small window was beautifully decorated with mosses and birch branches as a backdrop for the gold jewellery. Shaking slightly, Milla went to the letter, picked it up from the puddle, shook the water off and put it back in her bag. Then she lifted her bike and quickly pushed it, its wheels squeaking loudly, towards the goldsmith's workshop.

The bell above the door tinkled as Milla, her knees still shaking, entered the atelier, which belonged to her best friend and boss, Tine. They had met on the first day of their goldsmith's course when Milla had arrived at the class with red, swollen eyes and slumped down on the nearest free chair. The night before, she'd caught her then boyfriend, Achim, kissing another woman and by morning she still couldn't hold back her tears. Luckily for her, the chair she sat in was right next to Tine, a small, somewhat chubby woman with short blonde hair. Tine had seemed to know instinctively that it could only be boyfriend trouble, and when the lecturer had suggested Tine take Milla out of the room to comfort her, she had stood in the bleak corridor and hugged her. This had made Milla cry even more, and she found herself telling the woman everything. It turned out that Tine also had a difficult relationship with her mother – an actress who had spent much of her daughter's childhood touring. But Tine was lucky in that her father was a friendly, jolly man who made up for everything her mother couldn't give her. And it was from him that she had inherited her warmth.

From that moment, it was clear this was the beginning of a wonderful friendship.

'Oh, dear, sweetie, what happened? You're bleeding?'

Milla's legs were faltering now, and she only just managed to stagger to one of the gilded chairs meant for customers. 'My knees feel like rubber . . .'

Tine, who was wearing bright-red lipstick, took a tissue from the box on the counter and rushed towards her friend. Carefully and gently, she dabbed at the blood, while her other hand rested on her friend's shoulder and Milla, sniffling, told her haltingly of the accident.

'I can't believe it! And the bastard simply drove off?'

'Yes, but it's nothing more than a few scratches.'

'Well, if you say so. You could have been dead. Or have internal bleeding, or broken your neck . . .'

Tine was a self-confessed hypochondriac and tended to exaggerate any medical condition. At least once a week she went to a doctor because of some imaginary illness. But it was thanks to this that a myoma the size of a hen's egg had been detected in her uterus. If it had been left just a few more months, then she might not have been able to have children. As it was, once she had the operation to remove it, she should be fine. Tine didn't have a father for a potential child yet – and she was in her mid-thirties too – but someone would turn up, Milla was absolutely sure of that. Tine was such a wonderful person it could only be a matter of time before a man noticed.

Milla smiled wanly at her friend, who was to be her witness at the wedding. 'I'm fine, just a bit shaky.'

'I'm not surprised. Stay there. I'll get a plaster. Would you like a cappuccino and some chocolate, maybe?'

'I don't need a plaster. It'll heal quicker if it's not covered. But a cappuccino and chocolate sounds great!'

Tine smiled and went to switch on the coffee machine, keeping a careful eye on her friend as she did so, as though she was expecting her to faint at any moment. Milla, meanwhile, took her mobile – or what was left of it – from the bag. But although she managed to put it together again, it wouldn't turn on. Milla couldn't help feeling a little relieved. Her mother had probably tried to ring a few times. Maybe Paul too.

While Tine was busy with the hissing milk-foamer, Milla looked at her face in the mirror opposite. As so often when she saw herself, it struck her how frighteningly similar she looked to her mother. The only difference was that Milla's eyes were almond-shaped, but their general features were very alike . . . and the older Milla got, the more similar the two women became. She touched the dried blood and the small scratch on her forehead and hoped it would be healed before her wedding in two months' time. Then she remembered her mother's words and tears filled her eyes.

Could she really marry Paul now? Of course she could. It was, as usual, her own paranoia that had aroused her suspicions, making her question whether she could fully trust him. Maybe it was bad luck, or maybe she was just attracted to unfaithful men like a bee to apple blossom: in all her three long-term relationships her boyfriend had been unfaithful. The first, Achim, had 'only' snogged someone else; the second, Benno, had cheated on her with an old schoolfriend and confessed to it; and Matti, whom she'd been with for three years, had had an affair with the red-haired neighbour from the third floor.

'You must have a brilliant guardian angel!' Tine interrupted Milla's dark thoughts and passed her the cappuccino before sitting down and giving her a sideways look full of love and empathy. Milla warmed her hands on the cup and breathed in the smell of the coffee.

'Thank you. It smells delicious.'

'Doesn't it? You don't have to work today, sweetie. Look, your hands are still shaking,' Tine said gently.

'You're so kind! And the best boss in the world. But I'll at least engrave our wedding rings, as I'm here already. I want to finish them before things get too busy.' Milla fell silent and looked sadly at her friend. 'Or shall I leave them, after that text message yesterday?'

Paul and Milla had the same phone covers, and so she had mistakenly grabbed his when it beeped with an incoming text message.

Do you have to go home straight away or are we meeting up again? That was all. Only a name. The name of the new assistant graphic designer in his office. Corinne. Of course, Paul could go for a coffee with women she didn't know. But not women with French names – Tine and Milla agreed on that. Apart from that, he hadn't told Milla, and that was the crucial point. They always told each other everything – didn't they? This 'meeting up again' said it all – or was she making a mountain out of a molehill?

After Milla had discovered the text, she'd rung Tine straight away and the friends had discussed every word of the short message. Tine had suggested she should simply confront Paul. But Milla just hadn't felt up to it.

Now, Tine hesitated for a moment and then vehemently shook her head. 'Hey, of course you should get your rings ready. But it really doesn't have to be today.'

'You're right. It's not a good idea to engrave with shaking hands. They are supposed to be perfect.'

Only their names were to be engraved in the rings. No heart, no date, nothing else. The same applied to the wedding. No wedding cake, no horse-drawn carriage, no long dress. Paul liked things simple and thought all those romantic trappings were cheesy. He was not the romantic type and had never really wanted to get married at all. But what woman doesn't want to wear a dress that makes her look like a fairy princess on her special day?

'Now, have your coffee, and then go and see a doctor. Shall I come with you? Maybe you're a bit concussed?' Tine sounded like a worried mother-hen.

'Oh, no, I don't need to see a doctor. You'll have to hold the fort here, anyway. I'll go home, lie down on the sofa, eat more chocolate and read. Okay?'

Tine nodded reluctantly.

Milla was grateful for Tine's care. Her friend would be a wonderful mother and Milla hoped with all her heart that the operation to remove the myoma would go well next week and Tine would soon meet the potential father of her children. She took another sip of the coffee, burned her tongue and again thought of Paul. In her heart of hearts, she didn't really believe he'd cheated on her. But it was a well-known fact that men often became panicky before they got married. Milla swallowed hard. After four wonderful years, a single text message she had accidentally seen on his mobile shouldn't make her so insecure, she told herself. Or was she repressing things again? Pushing any problems they had to the back of her mind, just as she did with her mother. How often had he turned his head to look at another woman, or met up with female colleagues or ex-girlfriends for sport or a glass of wine? Some weekends, Paul worked as a DJ, and he was very popular – something he enjoyed a great deal. Every now and then Milla had pondered whether he was faithful to her. But part of this, she knew, was because she found it so difficult to trust people. Her mother's coolness towards her and her lack of a loving family had left her full of self-doubt and with the nagging feeling that she was unlovable.

Was her lack of self-confidence the reason for her jealousy? Milla didn't want to be jealous, but she couldn't help it. Sometimes the feeling would just rise up within her, like molten lava, and she seemed unable to control it.

The bell tinkled, and the first customer of the day came in. While Tine attended to the older man, Milla caught sight of the still-damp letter sticking out of the top of her bag. She took it out and looked at it gratefully. Without the letter the accident could have been much worse. It had probably saved her life. She'd taken it from the letterbox a few days ago – or had it been weeks? Then it had stayed on the kitchen table, unnoticed, and only this morning she had pushed it into her bag. She read the sender's address: it was a notary in Zehlendorf. Strange. What did a notary want from her? Maybe it was because of the wedding? Had Paul secretly set up a pre-nuptial agreement? Milla looked at Tine, who was busy showing the customer several necklaces for his daughter.

Hastily, she opened the letter and read the first few lines with growing excitement.

> Dear Frau Stendal,
> Acting on a client request from Palma de Mallorca for my assistance, I have finally been able to trace you with the help of my colleagues. I do hope it is not too late. Please contact my office as soon as possible. My secretary, Frau Meierhofer, will give you an urgent appointment.
> With kind regards,
> Aaron Birnbaum.

Milla exhaled with relief. It wasn't about the wedding. But what was it about? Aaron Birnbaum – she had never heard the name. What did the man want? Why had they been looking for her? Milla was curious and grateful for the distraction from her jealous thoughts – which she hoped would turn out to be silly. Very silly.

At last the customer left and Milla showed Tine the letter.

'You have to ring them straight away,' she said, studying it with excitement.

'Can I borrow your mobile? Mine's broken.'

'Of course.' Tine gave it to Milla.

She quickly pushed in the number of the notary, turned it on to speaker and waited nervously for Frau Meierhofer to answer. A squeaky young female voice answered. 'Notary Birnbaum. Silke Meierhofer speaking. How can I help?'

'I don't know,' Milla began. 'I mean, I'm Milla Stendal, and I'm supposed to ring you.'

There was silence at the other end for a moment, and Milla and Tine looked at each other questioningly.

'Frau Stendal! It's you!' Frau Meierhofer exclaimed. She sounded excited, which made her voice even more squeaky. The friends grinned at each other.

'Yes, me,' said Milla.

They heard papers rustling, a little cough. Maybe Frau Meierhofer had a cold? Yes, indeed. She blew her nose.

'I'm sorry. Can you come straight away?'

'Today?' Milla was surprised, and Tine whispered with a gesture to her head, 'Under no circumstances. After *that* accident.'

'It's not really possible today.'

'But it has to be today.' Frau Meierhofer's voice now sounded stern. Maybe she was a good secretary after all. 'Tomorrow will be too late.'

'Ah. And why, please? What is it actually about?'

'I'm not allowed to tell you. Only Herr Birnbaum is. Please come today. It's in your own best interests.'

'To Zehlendorf?' That was a long way away from Friedrichshain. At least, without a car and with only a battered bicycle.

'Yes, to the office. Herr Birnbaum doesn't make home visits,' Frau Meierhofer said sarcastically. But then she added, 'Please.'

'Can I borrow your car?' Milla whispered. Tine, ever the good friend, nodded. And as Milla wasn't just a notoriously jealous person but also extremely curious, she agreed.

◆ ◆ ◆

The notary's office was in Prinz-Friedrich-Leopold-Strasse in Nikolassee. Milla parked Tine's little red sportster, got out and

11

looked admiringly at the richly ornamented nineteenth-century villas with their large, mature gardens. She took a deep breath, and the fresh air soothed her head, which had started to ache. She was grateful for this distraction, and although she didn't really like surprises, her curiosity was currently winning out over her trepidation.

Milla stopped in front of a pretty villa with bow windows and a lush garden boasting a tall old pear tree. 'Aaron Birnbaum, Notary' it said on the discreet brass plaque that sat beside the number 37.

Milla pressed the smooth brass bell. Nothing.

But the thick, beige lace curtain at one of the ground-floor windows moved. There was a quiet hum and the wrought-iron gate clicked open. A narrow path of moss-covered paving stones led to the house and the enormous old wooden door was opened by a young blonde woman with frameless glasses wearing a dark skirt. Her look was half expectant, half envious, Milla thought. But she wasn't sure why this young woman could have any reason to envy her.

'Good afternoon, Frau Stendal.'

'How do you know who I am?' Milla hadn't arranged a particular time for the appointment. 'I could be a bicycle courier,' she joked, pointing to her orange bag, which looked like something a courier would carry.

'I know you from a photo.'

Milla was surprised at that, but nodded anyway, as if to show she'd expected as much.

'Come in. Herr Birnbaum is with another client, but he won't be long.'

Milla sighed with annoyance. She hated waiting, and her curiosity was eating at her. Hopefully, she wouldn't have to wait long.

◆ ◆ ◆

Aaron Birnbaum's office smelled of old leather and the desk looked like a valuable antique. As for the man himself, he looked like the good uncle in a fairy tale. Alternatively, Milla thought, he looked exactly as she'd imagined the man who used to read stories on the radio would look. He had white, longish hair, glasses that sat on the tip of his nose and a sonorous, pleasant voice. Every Christmas she had asked for a granddad like that. But her mother had always shaken her head and refused to talk about her parents – Milla's grandparents. And so, for all those years, it had been just the two of them sitting by the Christmas tree. Milla remembered how every Christmas she had invented a whole arsenal of relatives – grandparents, godmothers, nephews, cousins – and her soft toys had to take on those roles: Teddy as Grandpa, the llama as Grandma . . .

'Frau Stendal, at last we have found you!'

Milla winced a bit. 'What? Yes. But I haven't been in hiding.'

Aaron Birnbaum laughed. It was a friendly, throaty, restrained laugh. 'But you have taken on a different name. Or rather, your mother has.'

Milla was confused and wondered fleetingly whether her mother might have been a spy. That would explain a lot. 'No, not really. She was always called Stendal.'

'No, not always. Only since she got married.'

'Yes, that's true.'

'And before that her name was Fuster. Is that correct?'

'Exactly. And why does it matter?'

'It matters a lot.' Aaron Birnbaum looked at her curiously. 'It is her family name, the name of your grandmother.'

Milla nodded. 'I guess so. But I never met her.' What did this man want from her? Her grandmother had died a long time ago.

'Your grandmother has wished to see you in the last few weeks.'

'My grandmother? But she died shortly after I was born.'

'Who says?'

13

'My mother.'

Aaron Birnbaum sighed deeply and looked at Milla with com-passion. Then he shifted in his creaking leather chair. It seemed that he was wincing now.

'Then your mother hasn't told you the truth.'

'What? That's not the truth?'

'I'm sorry,' Herr Birnbaum said quietly and empathically. 'Your grandmother died only a week ago. My condolences.'

Milla stared at him, stunned, his words reverberating around her head until it started to thump. A week ago? She rubbed her temples. Her grandmother had been alive all these years! The grandmother she had missed so much when she was little, who could have picked her up from kindergarten, like all the other chil-dren's grannies. Who could have taken her for an ice cream, to the museum, to the cinema?

How often Milla had watched enviously when her friend Julia was picked up by her grandmother to do the fun things that only grandmothers and granddads seemed to have time for. Milla's mother never had time for things like that. Milla had never tasted candyfloss, never been on a big carousel. As a single mother, Sarah had to work hard to earn a living for the two of them. At least that was her excuse. Quite often Milla was the last child to be picked up from kindergarten, always shortly before it closed. Twice, her mother hadn't turned up at all and Milla had gone home with the childminder to her flat. It was evening before her mother had come to pick her up. Milla suddenly remembered the fear that had flooded her at the time, that her mother would never come again. Never again. This feeling came back to her now as she realised once more that she could never trust her mother. Sarah had lied to her for many, many years.

Milla hadn't known her granny, and her heart ached at the thought that now she would never meet her. That she had been lied to by her own mother and kept from the family she had longed for hurt her more than she could say. Why on earth had her mother deceived her all those years? Why had she pretended that her own mother had died? What could have happened that a daughter would say that about her own mother?

Milla felt her throat tightening. Her hands were cold and her nose started to run. She sniffled audibly. Aaron Birnbaum looked at her with compassion. 'Your grandmother would have loved to meet you.'

'Me too,' Milla let out in despair. Why hadn't she opened the notary's letter sooner? Her thoughts were whirling around like a swarm of disturbed birds.

'Why didn't she contact me earlier?' she asked, still shaken.

Aaron Birnbaum hesitated before he answered. 'Your mother was against it. This made your grandmother very sad, but she kind of understood her daughter Sarah's reasons for it. For a long time, she accepted it. For too long, in my opinion.'

Milla looked at him agitatedly. 'My mother didn't want it? Why not? What happened between them? What could have been the reason?'

'I only knew your grandmother vaguely and, unfortunately, I don't know the background. Later, we only ever spoke on the phone. She was quite a reserved person. Maybe you could ask your mother?'

'I certainly will.' Milla looked down at her hands. She was determined to do so, but she knew it would be very difficult to get the truth out of her.

Aaron Birnbaum cleared his throat. 'Your grandmother has written you a letter.'

'A letter?' Milla looked up questioningly.

'You were her only grandchild. She has left you something. Financially speaking, it is not massive. Towards the end, your grandmother had to spend much of her fortune on a care home

15

by the sea. But she has left you what was most important to her: a small property. Her beloved little souvenir shop in the middle of Palma de Mallorca's old quarter.'

Milla was now completely overwhelmed, and her eyes welled up. Her grandmother had left her the most beloved thing she ever had. And that must mean that she, her granddaughter, was important to her, even though they had never met. For a moment Milla sensed something like an invisible family bond holding her. It felt wonderful.

'A souvenir shop?' she repeated.

Aaron Birnbaum smiled. 'Yes, in a prime position. Have you ever been to Mallorca?'

'Mallorca? Yes, of course. Who hasn't? A beautiful island.' Milla's sadness was overcome by images full of sunlight from her and Paul's holiday four years ago – the first they had taken together. They had been newly in love and, hand in hand, had drifted through Palma's old quarter, drinking *horchata*, the famously refreshing Spanish drink, in one of the pretty cafés; they had walked along the Playa de Palma in the evening, watching the sunset . . .

Milla sniffled again, unconsciously. How lovely it would have been if she could have visited her grandmother then. How she would have loved her to meet Paul, and to get to know this grandmother without having to rely on her mother's judgement. She wanted to go and confront her mother straight away. Why on earth had she hidden her grandmother from her? How could she have done that to her daughter? To her mother? Milla pressed her cold hands together. It seemed as if all the blood had drained from them.

'I am truly very sorry.' Aaron Birnbaum rearranged a few pens on his already very tidy desk. 'Maybe it will be a little comfort that you can still attend the funeral. It's in two days' time.'

'In two days?'

'In Palma de Mallorca. I'll give you the address.'

Two days? She had so much to do. There was the wedding. And work. What would Tine say? She had to make sure she was back for Tine's operation. She owed that to her friend.

Milla's thoughts were tumbling over each other, her mind in a whirl. She wanted to ring Tine now, because Tine always had an answer to everything.

'Why Mallorca?' she finally stammered. 'My mother hails from Andalusia.'

'Is that what she told you?' Aaron sounded amazed. Again, he looked at Milla with a kind of pity, and scanned the scratch on her forehead. 'Your mother comes from Mallorca. Like your grandmother. Like your whole family, going back to the fifteenth century.'

Milla stared at him. Had he really said fifteenth century?

Gently, Aaron Birnbaum continued, 'I assume you didn't know that you are of Mallorquin descent?'

'What? No, I didn't know that either.' Milla was overwhelmed. What did it all mean? What else had her mother kept from her?

'And you don't know anything about the history of Mallorca?'

'No, nothing.'

Aaron Birnbaum fell silent and just looked at her with his watery blue eyes. Then he bent forward. Only now could she see the scar on his right temple. It was in the same place as her scratch from the accident this morning. Milla's mouth went dry, as if she hadn't had anything to drink for days. She took the last sip of her coffee, but it didn't help.

Aaron Birnbaum cleared his throat and changed the subject. 'Shall we have a look at the inheritance documents now? Would you like another coffee?'

Milla nodded. She felt uneasy, and her thoughts were jumbled. Why was he changing the subject? What about this shop? Why hadn't her grandmother left her beloved shop to her daughter,

Milla's mother? Why had here been no contact between the two women, and why had she abided by Sarah's wish of not ever seeing Milla for such a long time?

'Frau Meierhofer!' Aaron Birnbaum's voice tore through the fog in her brain. She winced. The door opened immediately, as if Frau Meierhofer had been standing behind it listening. 'Frau Stendal would like another coffee, please.'

'Coming right up.'

Then he pulled a few documents from a drawer, together with an envelope. 'This letter is from your grandmother, written to her granddaughter. Only very late and by circuitous routes had she learned that her daughter, Sarah, had given birth to a baby girl.'

Milla swallowed hard and looked at him sadly. She was deeply moved, her heart was pounding and her fingers had become clammy.

'Your grandmother, Abbigail Fuster, has told me how happy she was when she heard, years ago, of your existence.' A warm, homely feeling began to spread in Milla's tight stomach. Her grandmother had been happy that she existed!

The notary pulled the letter from its envelope, adjusted his glasses and began to read it aloud slowly and respectfully.

> *My darling granddaughter. I would have loved so much to have met you, but I had to respect your mother's wish. She was against it. Please forgive her — and me too. I can't undo it, and neither can I diminish my guilt in the matter.*
>
> *But now, as my life is coming to its end, I really need to see you. I do hope this letter gets to you in time, because I don't have many days left.*
>
> *In case we don't meet, I just want to tell you that I wish for you to have a happy life and that you always follow your dreams. I do hope you will find the*

love of your life – if you haven't found it yet. You must promise me to always listen to your heart and only choose the right person, my child. It is never too late.

Mr Right, Milla thought. How could you know one hundred per cent who was the right one?

She tried to concentrate as Aaron Birnbaum cleared his throat and continued.

All I can do now is to leave you what has always kept me afloat, and I do hope that for you it will always be a safe haven as well. Please, never part with it, my beloved little shop in the Calle Montesión, which I took over with great pride as a young woman in 1956.

Until we meet, whether in this life or the next,
Your loving grandmother.

◆　◆　◆

Milla stopped outside Aaron Birnbaum's villa and stared at her grandmother's letter, which the notary had pressed into her hands with a compassionate look in his eyes. A blackbird was singing, hopping from one branch of the pear tree to a higher one. Milla felt very small in this large, overgrown garden, and what she had just heard had confused and unsettled her deeply. She stared at the envelope, her grandmother's handwriting so elegant and confident. What kind of a woman had she been? Why had there been no contact with her own daughter? What did she mean by her 'guilt'?

Milla could feel the anger that had been growing like a hard ball in her stomach expand even further. Her mother had lied to her all her life, had kept her away from the family Milla had longed for since she was a little girl. She wondered what all this would mean for her, for her future, because nothing seemed to be the same as it had been only an hour ago. To be cheated by one's own mother . . . Milla's thoughts raced and her heart ached so much it took her breath away.

One thing was clear, though: there must be a reason why her mother was not able to love her daughter as unconditionally as other mothers. Milla thought of her grandmother's words about guilt and that she had to respect her daughter's decision. She was now absolutely determined to find out what had happened: to find peace; to establish that her mother's apparent lack of love for Milla was not her fault.

She took a few deep breaths, and the cool, fresh air inside her lungs calmed her. Out here, close to the Grunewald, the air was much fresher than in the polluted eastern part of the city. It smelled of pine, birch trees and earth.

But Milla's thoughts about what to do next were gathering speed again. Should she ring Tine or Paul, as she had always done in the last few years whenever she was unsure what to do? No, she thought. She needed to be strong and decide for herself what was right for her now. She had to listen to her gut feeling, and that told her she needed to confront her mother.

Her grandmother's letter had sounded so loving, so warm and full of understanding, that Milla couldn't imagine what had driven her mother to pretend all those years that she had died. Her own mother!

Head pounding, Milla made her way towards Tine's car. Suddenly, a blackbird flew close over her head and, shocked, she ducked away. As she gazed after the bird, a shiver went through her, even though the early-afternoon sun was shining quite brightly now. What was the family secret that her mother had been hiding from her?

20

Milla sat in a corner of the Anita Wronski café by the water tower near Kollwitzplatz. The café offered a variety of delicious cakes; Milla loved the apricot and almond crumble best. Normally, she would have attacked the cake, first pulling the crumble from the top, then the almonds, and only then devouring the rest. But today she had lost her appetite and just stirred her cappuccino nervously – already the fourth one today. No wonder her sensitive stomach was rebelling. Chronic gastritis, the doctor had diagnosed a few months ago. But Milla wondered whether all the small emotional scars her mother's strange behaviour, year after year, had left her with, had made her stomach lining extremely sensitive.

Milla looked at her watch again, but even the second hand seemed very slow. It annoyed her every time her mother was late, but today she wasn't just annoyed: she felt furious. She hadn't mentioned on the phone why she wanted to meet up, and it was only worry about Milla's relationship with Paul that had made Sarah consent to leaving her flat in Kreuzberg to come to the area where Milla lived.

Milla had left home when she was only eighteen because she and her mother had argued all the time. Since then, Sarah had rented a small flat in Kreuzberg and lived a very reclusive life, surrounded by her old-fashioned furniture and ornaments. Milla had stopped visiting her because she couldn't bear the smell of lavender and scented candles that pervaded the flat, so now mother and daughter always met in this café or, very occasionally, at Milla's apartment. But since Paul had moved in with her, they both preferred the café, because Milla had had enough of her mother's nagging about what a bad housewife she was. Sarah invariably found fault with something – at least, this was how it seemed to Milla.

'*Now* what have you done?' Milla's head turned at the sound of her mother's distinctive Spanish accent and resentful tone.

Milla glared at her. 'Me?' she uttered, wondering wildly where on earth she could begin.

'Well, a man doesn't cheat when he's happy in a relationship.' Sarah was a petite woman in her early sixties, with shoulder-length dark hair. She sat down and, with a flourish, took off her lilac jacket embroidered with dark roses. She always wore bright-red lipstick. Sarah loved colourful, extravagant clothes; Milla didn't.

'Paul isn't cheating on me, Mum. I've told you. I simply have a funny feeling, but let's not talk about that.'

'A funny feeling? That says it all.'

Milla took a sharp breath and tried to remain calm. 'I wanted to talk about something else,' she said with a grave face.

Sarah gave her an irritated look. 'And what is that?'

'I want to know why you've lied to me. Why you never told me that our family is from Mallorca. That my grandmother wasn't dead,' Mila spat.

Sarah swallowed hard. She understood. The word 'wasn't' said it all. Her right eyebrow twitched. Despite her dark complexion she suddenly looked pale. She started to breathe heavily, rubbed her sweaty forehead and put a hand on her heart.

'Which means . . . that she has died?'

'For you, she died a long time ago,' Milla hissed. 'But why? I don't understand all this, Mum.' Milla's voice was getting shaky. But she didn't want to cry in front of her mother and reined herself in, pressing her lips together as she looked at the other woman. 'How could you do this to me?'

Sarah stared back at her and shook her head but didn't say a word. The news seemed to upset her, probably more than she herself would have thought possible.

'What can I get you?' The waitress, a small red-haired woman with a round face, stood by their table and looked at Sarah impatiently. A baby at the table next to them began to cry and his mother took him from the stroller and held him lovingly in her arms.

Sarah mumbled, 'I . . . er . . . a cup of tea, please.'

'What kind of tea?'

'Anything, something calming.'

'Camomile?'

'Yes, I don't mind.'

'Okay.'

Milla took a sip of her cappuccino and shot a challenging look at her mother.

'How do you know?' Sarah asked quietly. 'Have you secretly been in touch with her?'

'No.' Milla looked at her mother incredulously. 'Why have you lied to me? What about my grandfather? Is he still alive?'

Sarah shook her head, tight-lipped. 'No, he died a long time ago.'

'And why should I believe you? You've deprived me of my grandmother. And you know how much I would have loved a granny. How could you do that to me?'

Sarah looked at her as if she'd been struck by an arrow. She took a deep breath. 'I only wanted . . . I wanted to protect you,' she replied quietly. 'How could you ever understand?' Then she hastily started to put her jacket back on, missed one sleeve and cursed in Spanish under her breath.

'I don't understand anything. And that is why you're going to stay here and tell me everything.'

Sarah, one arm in the jacket, rose sharply and turned away, just as a baby at another table started to cry very loudly. Milla tried again, this time more gently. 'Mum, please. Why do you hate me so much? . . . What have I done wrong?'

Sarah stopped short. She turned around and sat down again, looking upset. She was visibly struggling for words. 'I . . . don't hate you, Milla! You haven't done anything wrong. It has nothing to do with you. Oh, my God, is that what you've thought all these years?'

Milla could only nod sadly, as painful memories from her childhood came up again. Like when she was standing in the door crying because her doll had broken and her mother just turned around and continued with her ironing.

'I'm so sorry,' Sarah whispered, her voice brittle.

Surprised, Milla looked at her. She had never seen her mother so upset. 'What, Mum? What exactly are you sorry for? Please tell me.'

The mother at the next table had managed to calm her baby by walking him gently up and down, humming.

'That . . . that I haven't been better . . . than her. And I was so determined to be a good mother . . . but I couldn't. I've been a failure as a mother.'

'Better than who? Grandmother?' Milla wanted to know.

Sarah only nodded wordlessly, lips firmly pressed together.

Milla was confused. She needed to know more, because this had to do with her. 'What do you think she did wrong?'

Sarah took a deep breath but just shook her head sadly. 'She . . . she didn't love me. Her own child. I've always felt that . . .'

Milla realised her mother was close to tears. 'But why couldn't she?' Milla felt as though she'd been punched in the stomach. She knew exactly how her mother had felt.

'I don't know, Milla. I don't know.'

'You don't know?' Milla kneaded her hands. Should she really believe this? 'Have you never asked her?'

'No.' Sarah was still breathing heavily. 'I couldn't.'

'But if you had known, maybe . . . maybe there was a reason, and maybe it would have made things easier for you.'

'And if there wasn't?' Sarah replied quietly. She stood up, squeezed past the mother with the baby and fled the café.

The waitress brought the camomile tea, her eyes following Sarah with a puzzled look, and told Milla that she still had to pay for it. Milla nodded, watching her mother leave. Why did she still have the feeling Sarah wasn't telling her the whole truth?

◆ ◆ ◆

Milla left the café in a trance. A dark cloud had obscured the sun and she shuddered. A woman pushing a stroller stopped to carefully rearrange the blanket covering her baby, blocking Milla's way. Milla stopped and waited impatiently. She just wanted to be home, in her flat; her nest. She suddenly felt a deep longing to be held by Paul and be comforted. But then she remembered that he would be late back from work tonight, for whatever reason. A pain shot through her. Could she really trust him? Her mother's words echoed in her ears. 'Now what have you done? A man doesn't cheat when he's happy.'

Had she not invested enough in the relationship? Not made him feel that he was the most important person in her life? Maybe he thought she couldn't love unconditionally. And maybe that was true.

It was shortly after four in the afternoon and Kollwitzplatz was busy with mothers and children on their way home. Milla, too, wanted a child, and had persuaded Paul to agree that they would begin trying for a child after the wedding. But suddenly she was gripped with the fear that she might turn out like her mother. That she would try to make things better but wouldn't be able to. As she hadn't experienced a mother's love, would she able to love a child as a mother should?

Tears came to her eyes as she noted how tenderly the mothers around her treated their little ones. It came to her then that she had to solve the family mystery if she wanted to be able to show her love for her future children. And to do that, she needed to go to her grandmother's funeral. There would be old friends and acquaintances who she could ask about her grandmother. Maybe they knew something that would help her to explain her granny's detached behaviour towards her daughter.

◆ ◆ ◆

She strode past the playground and turned into Kollwitzstrasse, where she and Paul lived in a three-bedroom apartment in a newly renovated old house. She ran up the stairs to the third floor, unlocked the door and listened. 'Paul? Are you there?'

As she had expected, no reply. Milla took off her jacket and stood still. Putting one hand on her stomach, she checked: it was tight and rumbling. The flat smelled of Paul. Of his aftershave, his unmistakable scent. Like a lost child Milla stood in the middle of the hall and breathed it in, her thoughts racing.

If she was going to make it to Mallorca in time for the funeral, she needed to start preparing now. Quickly, she went to the bedroom to find her passport and start packing.

She opened her wardrobe door, wondering what to take. It would be early-spring weather in Mallorca. Didn't the almond trees blossom around this time of year? She felt a surge of excitement at the thought of being on the sunny island with its sea of blossom. She took two dresses from the wardrobe, then paused as she spotted the T-shirt she had been wearing when she first met Paul. It had been at the atelier, and he'd wanted to buy a necklace for his mother's sixtieth birthday. Milla's T-shirt had a 'Be Cool' logo, and Paul said that he liked it. They'd started chatting.

The next day he turned up again; this time he urgently needed a pair of earrings for his sister. The day after it was a watch for himself, and Milla had jokingly asked why he didn't simply buy the whole shop. It would never have occurred to her that this good-looking man was seriously interested in her. Milla wasn't bad-looking, but Paul was definitely out of her league. That, at least, was Milla's opinion – and her mother's. Paul had asked her out for a coffee and they'd met in one of the many cafés in Friedrichshain after work. For five hours they had talked and laughed, and for the first time Milla felt completely at ease with a man. On all her previous dates she had felt uneasy, as though it was hard work. But with Paul she felt light and carefree.

A short time later Paul introduced her to his large and slightly chaotic family, but here, too, Milla felt very much at ease. Paul and Milla; Milla and Paul. Their friends soon started to consider them a dream couple, because they managed to be very close and yet somehow remain independent of each other. Particularly Paul. He went out nearly every night, met his friends for cards, to watch football or play badminton. Milla tried to accept this, even though she sometimes asked herself why he wouldn't rather spend time with her. But she consoled herself with their long weekend lie-ins followed by an extended breakfast and then maybe an amble through one of Berlin's many flea markets. Everything was just fine: so fine that Milla, when he spontaneously proposed, had said yes without thinking.

But now the doubts had surfaced. Only weeks before the wedding.

'What are you doing?' Suddenly she heard Paul's voice behind her. She hadn't heard him come in. His light brown hair was cut into a floppy fringe and his green eyes looked at her questioningly. He really was good-looking. As soon as her mother met him, she'd told Milla, 'You always have to share a tasty dish.'

'I'm going to Mallorca the day after tomorrow.'

Paul looked at her in surprise. 'Are you going to leave me, just weeks before the wedding?' He tried to make it sound funny, but his voice was serious.

Milla examined him closely. For the last few months he'd been going to the gym regularly, as well as jogging a few times a week, and now his jeans sat loosely on his narrow hips. He looked even better for the weight loss. Milla wondered for a moment whether she deserved this man and whether this was the right time to confront him. Why was he back already, even though he'd said he'd be home late? Had his colleague with the French name let him down? Milla felt like having a proper row but didn't have the belly for it.

Instead, she just answered sadly, 'No. Something has happened.'

'What is it?'

'I . . .' Where to start? 'I went to a notary today who had managed to track me down. I've had a grandmother all these years, but she's died now, and her funeral is in two days.'

'Oh.' He sounded surprised, 'A granny? And you never knew about her?'

'No, but you know I always wanted one.' Milla looked at the floor miserably, and he came towards her to give her a hug.

'I'm so sorry, my love.'

How good it felt to be held by him, especially now. Gently, he let her go, then pulled her to the bed, and they lay down, cuddling up to each other. After a few minutes he asked, 'What I don't understand is why you didn't know anything about her.'

'Well, my mother has lied to me all these years. She pretended that my grandmother had died.' Milla swallowed hard. 'And that was true for her. But she hasn't told me why.'

'Strange. But your mum *is* a bit strange, we all know that.'

'But we don't know why. And I have to find out the reason.'

'She's just like that. Forget it. You can't change a person.'

'No, but maybe I can understand her better. And that could change quite a lot for me.'

Paul wasn't convinced and took a careful breath. 'Forget it, you don't need her love. You're a grown-up now and you have *my* love.' He kissed her. Milla smiled uncertainly. Did she? 'What else did the notary say?'

'That my mother's family is from Mallorca, not Andalusia. And that I have inherited a souvenir shop on Mallorca. In Palma, in the old quarter.'

'That's crazy! How fantastic!' Paul was beaming at her. 'A rich granny on Mallorca! What more could you want?'

'A rich granny on Mallorca who is alive.'

They looked at each other. Paul's thoughts started to wander. 'A souvenir shop. I recently read that more than nine million tourists visit Mallorca every year; four million Germans alone.'

'So many?' Milla tried to stall him. 'But the shop won't be worth a lot, anyway.'

'Think about it. A property in the middle of Palma's old quarter? You're a rich woman now.' Paul smiled at her.

'Really?' Milla felt uneasy. 'My grandmother didn't want me to sell the shop.'

'What? What else could you do with it? Have trouble with tenants all the time? Milla, don't be stupid. The property prices over there, in such a prime position, are probably fantastic. You have to sell it.'

Milla just nodded, lost in her thoughts of the upcoming funeral, hoping to find people who had known her grandmother and her secret.

'Will you come with me?' she asked. 'It's the day after tomorrow. I need to look for flights later.'

'The day after tomorrow? I'm sorry, I can't. I have a meeting with one of our most important clients.'

Milla smiled sadly and sat up. A meeting which would certainly include Corinne. But she didn't say this out loud. 'I thought so.'

'But I'm sure your mum will go.' He tenderly moved a strand of hair from her forehead and looked into her eyes.

'Mum? I'm not so sure.'

'But why? She was her mother, after all.'

'Yes . . . well . . . for her, she died a long time ago. Something very bad must have happened. I've no idea what, but I might find out when I'm there.'

'You should ask her to come. I'd prefer it if you weren't all alone over there. Also, it would help to make sure nobody cheats you when you begin the process of selling the shop. It's best if you start all that straight away.'

Milla nodded silently, took her old mobile, into which she had inserted her SIM card, and wrote a text message to her mother. Then she turned towards Paul and looked into the warm, green eyes she had fallen in love with at their first meeting.

'I'll ask her, but I bet she won't come.' Milla pressed send, but wasn't surprised when she didn't get an immediate reply.

◆ ◆ ◆

That night she tossed and turned, unable to sleep as she looked at Paul, in a deep sleep next to her, and asked herself how much she really loved him.

The next morning at work she tried, together with Tine, to sort out her still-confused thoughts. As they worked on a piece of jewellery, they went through what they knew so far.

'What if I don't find out what my grandmother did to my mother?' Milla asked, a worried look in her eyes. 'In which case . . . I don't want any children. Because it seems to be a family tradition – this coolness; the detachment. I don't want to do this to my future children.'

'Ah, sweetie, you really are exaggerating. You'll be a fantastic mother, whatever has happened,' Tine replied, shaking her head. Then she added more quietly, 'And hopefully me too – at some point.'

Milla looked up and smiled at her friend. 'Your op next week will be fine, Tine. Don't worry. Will you promise me?'

Tine nodded and forced herself to smile, but her eyes betrayed her anxiety. 'Okay, but you have to promise me that you won't allow yourself to be so easily undermined. You're good enough as you are. Otherwise, I wouldn't love you so much.' They smiled at each other, and Tine sent her an air kiss.

They turned their attentions to their work, but Milla was still unsure and restless. 'But . . . what if Mum is right after all and I'm unable to be truly close to a man? And Paul will find that with another woman?'

Tine, who was engraving a silver ring, stopped and took a deep breath. 'Sweetie, stop talking like that! We have no proof, only one dubious text. That he goes out for a drink with other women is pretty shitty . . .' She smiled. 'But we're grown-ups and know that men need their space. I'm sure Paul isn't cheating on you with someone who's more lovey-dovey. *Hello?* He wants to marry you. When a man plans that, he has made his decision.' Then she added jokingly, 'Men are able to do that, unlike women. Make a decision.'

Tine's positive words had a good influence on Milla, and she pulled herself together and tried to look at everything in a brighter light. The glass was half full, not half empty. It was entirely up to her how she decided to view things. 'You're right: Paul loves only me, and I will find out what made my grandmother the woman she apparently was. And then the ice around my mother's heart will melt, and the ice queen will realise what a wonderful, lovable daughter she has.'

'Sorted.' Tine grinned, relieved. They smiled at each other again.

'Coffee?'

'Coffee.'

◆　◆　◆

Milla sat in the taxi, disheartened. She had waited in vain to hear from her mother, but now, as she made her way to the airport, she realised that she would be going to Mallorca on her own to attend the funeral. As she had booked an early flight, she'd chosen to go by taxi so she could sleep half an hour longer. After all, she was rich now, so Paul had claimed. Or would be very soon.

Berlin Tegel airport was already very busy, even though it was only four o'clock in the morning – practically the middle of the night. Milla sleepily climbed out of the taxi, which had stopped in front of the terminal. The friendly Indian driver smiled at her. 'The night is black and heavy, but love always lights the darkness,' he said. 'An Indian proverb.'

Milla smiled at him. 'That sounds lovely.'

The driver nodded. 'It's nice when you smile.' After a pause he continued, 'The smile you give will come back to you.'

Touched and grateful for his kind words, Milla gave him a generous tip. The taxi had been worth the money, and she felt much better now. Hopefully, she would find a trustworthy property agent who could arrange the sale of the shop. Milla had never been very good with money matters.

Despite it being so early, she had put on full make-up because she wanted to look good at the funeral. There wouldn't be time to stop at the small hostel she had booked. Maybe there were other distant relatives who would be pleased to meet Abbigail's long-lost Berlin granddaughter. Again, Milla smiled. She hoped so much to be welcomed with open arms.

She checked her mobile once more but, as expected, there was no news from her mother. Milla tried to fight it but, as always, her stomach clenched with pain.

As she was wheeling her case into the airport, she stopped and watched a family with a number of colourful suitcases and bags. The woman was Asian, and together with her African husband they had three children, all particularly cute. The youngest waved to her; Milla smiled at him, and the smile came back. Encouraged, she walked on, looking for her gate number.

There were queues everywhere; people jostled and pushed, and for a moment Milla felt overwhelmed. Where did she have to go now? She realised that over the last few years she had relied on Paul, who always seemed to know where to go. Maybe she ought to stay here, in Berlin? Maybe it would be better if she didn't find out about her family? The sale of the shop could certainly be arranged from here. Milla hesitated, remembering how much she had spent on the flight, the hostel and the taxi. Then she recalled her grandmother's loving letter and inwardly shook her head. She had to find out what had happened. She would manage it by herself. Confidently, she marched towards the large noticeboard. Then suddenly she stopped, unable to believe her eyes. There was her mother, wearing a knee-length red coat, a flowery trolley case by her side, her hair fastened into a stern bun and her mouth painted with red lipstick. She was studying the noticeboard, looking upset, and then she saw Milla. Milla swallowed hard and walked towards her, trying to smile. But this time the smile didn't come back to her. Blast the Indian proverb, Milla thought. Instead her mother said impatiently, 'Look at that! Do the greedy pilots have to strike today, of all days?'

'No, please, no!' That couldn't be true. Milla followed her mother's eyes and saw the notice. Her flight was delayed by an hour. Of all things. Why couldn't things just go smoothly, for once? Now there would be little time to get to the funeral; they would probably only arrive towards the end.

'But we've paid, and we'll wait.' Her mother had always been very money conscious; working at the cheese counter in a supermarket, she didn't earn much. Without a word she pulled her suitcase towards Gate A09. Milla followed her glumly, deeply regretting having asked her to come.

Chapter Two

As the plane approached Mallorca, Milla could see the sea of blossom covering the island in the late-February sun. She could also make out the many hotels everywhere. It seemed as if the number had increased even in the four years since she was last there. In the fifties, when her grandmother was a young woman and opened her little shop, Mallorca had probably still been totally unspoilt.

While they had waited in the queue at the gate, and on the flight, the mood between mother and daughter had remained reserved. Sarah appeared dejected. She confessed to Milla how difficult she had found the decision to embark on this journey into the past, and that she had only decided to come for Milla's sake, assuring her again that she had only ever wanted to be a good mother. 'But what mother doesn't want that?' she had sighed.

At last the doors of the plane were opened and Milla and her mother, together with countless other tourists, were released into the mild spring air. The sun warmed Milla's face and she took a deep breath. At the end of February the almond blossom was in full swing, accompanied by fresh green shoots and spring flowers.

The sun seemed to be shining much brighter than in Berlin, and Milla wondered why her mother hadn't moved back to this beautiful sunny island after her husband died. Milla would have grown up on Mallorca, close to her grandmother, and the rift between the two women might have healed – if they had only tried. Her whole life would have been completely different. Milla wouldn't have met Paul and wouldn't be getting married now – at least, not to him. Fate was a funny thing. What else did it have in store for her?

Due to the pilots' strike, they were two hours late. Hopefully, if they could hire a car quickly, they would still make it to the end of the service and meet some of the mourners. Milla and Sarah rushed to the baggage carousel and waited impatiently for their luggage, neither exchanging a word with the other. When their bags finally appeared, they grabbed them and quickly walked to the car-hire desk. Milla cursed when she saw the long queue. Why had she forgotten to book one when she bought her flight? It would have saved them time now.

Although they barely spoke, Milla could see how dejected her mother was, but her stomach was fluttering with tension and excitement and she didn't have the strength to comfort her mother as well.

By silent agreement, they each stood in a different queue, and as Milla waited her tension rose. If they arrived too late for the funeral would there be a wake? If there wasn't, then there would be no one she could question. What would they do then?

She prayed that the queue would move a little faster, but the clocks on Mallorca seemed to move at a different speed. The people in front of them had clearly come for a holiday and chatted and joked while the staff at the desks took their time. It seemed to take an eternity, and it slowly dawned on Milla that if they didn't get out of here soon, then they would definitely miss everybody who might have known her grandmother.

Finally, they set off in a little Seat Ibiza: Milla at the wheel, her mother sitting silently next to her, her face inscrutable. The beautiful Mediterranean landscape rushed by in a blur of purple flowers and lush greenery. It was clear they had missed the funeral and so there seemed little point in rushing to the cemetery outside Palma, because all the mourners would have left.

'I want to go to the hotel straight away,' Sarah said abruptly. 'Not to the grave. We can do that tomorrow or the next day.' Sarah had booked to stay for six days, Milla for only four.

'Okay.' Milla needed some space and was glad that her mother had booked a different hotel. It was also situated in Palma's old quarter and only a few minutes' walk from Milla's hostel.

She stopped in front of her mother's hotel. 'Do you want to come and have a look at Grandma's shop?' she asked, hoping her mother would decline.

To her relief, Sarah shook her head and replied quietly, 'She's left it to you, after all.'

Milla looked at her mother, aghast. Was Sarah angry that she hadn't inherited anything – after all that had happened?

'You don't seem to have had the best of relationships. And not knowing anything about that, well, then I don't understand it either.'

Sarah was standing next to the car now, one hand on the roof to steady herself. She was breathing heavily and seemed to be thinking.

'Mum, please tell me at least something about your time here.' Milla gently tried to get her mother to talk. 'What kind of a person was Grandmother . . . what made her tick? What did she love?'

Sarah stared at her, visibly fighting for words. 'Come to my hotel with me. We'll have a cup of tea together and I'll tell you about her.'

'All right. Let me find somewhere to park and I'll be with you in five minutes.'

Chapter Three

Palma de Mallorca, 1956

Twenty-nine-year-old Abbigail, a young Spanish woman with fashionably short hair, stood proudly in front of a small shop in the Calle Montesión. The shop window was a bit dusty, but that didn't diminish her happiness. The property was situated on a small street in the middle of Palma's old quarter. The bright Mallorquin sun illuminated everything beautifully. Next to Abbi's shop on the right was a place selling petticoats; to the left a bakery. The cobblestones were very hot and dust motes shimmered in the air. It was busy, and among the many Mallorquins there were already a few enthusiastic tourists, who loved quirky Palma with its trams and one-way pavements. Here, the cars drove on the left-hand side of the road, unlike in the rest of Spain, and tourists had started to flock to this beautiful, unspoilt island. Abbi hoped that soon more and more people would come.

Noah Fuster, Abbi's father, was a tall, slim man with thick, dark hair and bright-brown eyes. Together with his short, chubby wife, Esther, he walked along the little street towards his daughter and hugged her lovingly. As she was only five foot five, she had to stand on her toes to put her arms around his neck. 'Papa, Papa, thank you so much for the shop. Can I marry you?' She grinned mischievously, cheek to cheek with him. Her mother gave them an amused smile.

Noah grinned, flattered. 'I think your mother would mind, my child. That's what I'd hope, anyway.'

'Would you really?' Abbi looked at her still-beautiful mother and smiled. Esther pretended to be cross. 'Oh, yes. I'll never find another man as good and generous as your father.'

'All you have to do is grant a woman her dearest wish, and she's yours for ever,' Noah joked. Abbi's mother had recently got one of those expensive new electric mixers from Germany for her kitchen, and Abbi, after years of begging and cajoling, had got the shop.

Abbi opened the door and the family entered together. Until recently, it had been a cobbler's workshop, and it still smelled of leather and tannins. Abbi looked around her little haven, speechless, and then twirled around a few times so that her petticoat flew up. This had been her wildest dream – her own little shop, to do something on her own, not dependent on her parents and later, maybe, on a husband. Whatever was considered normal by other girls of Abbi's age – getting married, having children, cooking, washing and cleaning and being pretty for a husband – had always felt alien to Abbi.

Instead she'd had the brilliant idea of opening a souvenir shop, here in the middle of Palma's old quarter, and she wouldn't budge. She had confidently explained to her father that tourism was about to take off. German people especially had started to come to this original, unspoilt island with its deserted beaches and lovely cafés. Abbi had done her research and discovered that each year they expected approximately a hundred thousand tourists, and the figure was growing every year. Noah couldn't help being impressed by his daughter's plans.

The old cobbler, a friend of the family, had retired, and Noah had been looking for a new tenant for his property. For weeks on end Abbi had tried to persuade her father to let her open a shop in it and, in the end, she had succeeded. Noah couldn't deny his – by now, only – daughter anything, for which his wife often criticised him. But after the loss of their other daughter, Rachel, this was not surprising.

Abbi, too, mourned the early death of her sister, but tried to hide it from her parents, and every now and then she exploited her new status as the only child. Not in a calculating way, because that wasn't her nature, but out of a kind of hurt. Because during the time of their deepest grief her parents hadn't paid much attention to how Abbi was feeling but had struggled to get through the days without collapsing with grief. It had been eleven years since Rachel's murder, but what are eleven years when you have lost a beloved child?

Since then, Abbi's mother had put on a lot of weight, while her father, a well-known solicitor, had lost many clients. He simply hadn't been able to concentrate on his work, because all he could think about was his daughter Rachel, his little angel. The tragedy was over, but not the memory of it.

In 1945, one week before the end of the war, sixteen-year-old Rachel had come across a young blond man in a dishevelled Nazi uniform while collecting mussels on the beach. He was lying in the sand on Cala Figuera, a beautiful bay in the south-east of the island, an empty bottle of red wine next to him. Noah, who was accompanying Rachel, had walked ahead around a rocky outcrop, out of sight. Then he heard a gunshot. Running back, he found Rachel's bleeding body in the sand. The Nazi officer had run away. A man who had observed what had happened told him the officer had asked Rachel whether she was Jewish. The girl apparently had just looked at the man and kept silent. The next second, the officer pulled his gun and shot her. Noah had described to Abbi and her mother only once how his child had been lying there, her gentle, innocent face paler than pale. The sand beneath her and the water which lapped up every now and then had turned red. His words were etched in Abbi's brain; she could never dispel those pictures from her mind. Abbi had been eighteen then, and suddenly had to grow up. She had learned that anything could happen, and became nervous and anxious when she came across any kind of hostility. She had sworn that if she should ever be the target of discrimination she would fight. Because all humans were equal.

Since that day, Abbi's family had avoided the beautiful bay, almost as if they were worried it could happen again if ever they went there.

In the years after Rachel's death, Abbi had tried hard to be perfect for her parents and to make them laugh again. But it wasn't always easy. She thought that maybe if she could make a success of the shop it would make her parents happy again and impress her successful, beloved father. But it was the fifties, and Noah had instead hoped Abbi would find a suitable husband – yet she wasn't really interested. For a woman her age not to be married was considered an anomaly. Maybe men didn't like her confidence and independence. Generally, they were looking for someone to run their house, rather than a partner. Abbi often openly criticised her mother for treating her husband like a king. Every night before she served her husband his dinner she would dress up and put on make-up. She even helped him to take off his shoes. For the young, rebellious Abbi, the thought of behaving like this seemed impossible, and it was why, early on, she had resigned herself to becoming an old maid. She would rather be free and independent than serve a husband. That was her life plan. Now she wanted to use all her energy and creativity on the renovation and running of her shop. She was sure it would make her feel safe and happy.

This was probably the reason she hardly noticed the blond young man with dark blue eyes and a hat who watched her through the shop window, which was now immaculately clean. *A tourist, of course*, she thought, because of his blond hair. She liked his reticence. Most Mallorquin men were more forward. When he kept coming back over the next few days, smiling at her through the shop window, at first she pretended to be very busy and didn't look at him at all, but soon she couldn't resist the lure of those dark blue eyes. Smiling to herself, she unpacked some ceramic mugs with a 'Palma de Mallorca' logo and put them on the shelves. She offered a wide range of souvenirs and, though her neighbours wondered why such a pretty young woman wasn't married yet and had her own shop, the tourists were curious and came in droves and her souvenirs sold like hot cakes. Her customers were mostly German, but also from Sweden and Britain. Was this man German? She hoped not.

Again Abbi stole a glance at the shop window and saw that he was shyly smiling at her, which made his cheeks dimple. Abbi was looking him straight in the eyes and involuntarily smiled, too, but immediately turned her head away in embarrassment. With irritation, she felt a strange tickling in her belly. She had liked his gentle smile very much. His eyes were warm and friendly, like her father's. He had high cheekbones and was slim, as far as she could remember after only a few seconds looking at him. But she knew, even if he was Swedish or Finnish, how it would end. Young men always wanted only one thing: a woman who would do their housework and who didn't have a job of her own. What was it she had recently read in a magazine? 'A woman only has two questions in her life: what to wear and what to cook.' This attitude might be widespread – but it didn't apply to her.

41

She glanced over once more, but he had disappeared. *Shame*, she caught herself thinking, then became cross with herself that she hadn't smiled back at him again. She started to unpack a box of tea towels embroidered with the words 'Palma de Mallorca'.

Humming a Spanish song, she went through them, checking the embroidery, which had been done by some friends of her mother. The women had worked very meticulously. She looked up as the bell above the door tinkled. Four young men, Mallorquins in short jackets, came in and looked around curiously.

'Well,' said one of them, his hair dark with pomade and obviously the ringleader of the group, 'where is the old cobbler?'

'He's retired. It's my shop now.'

'Your shop?' He laughed, looking her up and down disparagingly. 'A woman and a shop? That'll be the day. You belong in the kitchen.'

'But I'm here, as you can see,' Abbi replied briskly.

'That's a real shame,' he said threateningly.

Abbi remembered where she had seen the guy before. He had been in her year in school and even then had always stared at her from a distance.

He grinned at his friends. 'We'll have to show her what she's supposed to do, eh?' The other men laughed.

Abbi watched them warily. 'I definitely know one thing,' she countered. 'I never want to be dependent on an idiot.'

'Ha,' he laughed. 'You're a real wild cat, aren't you?'

He took a step towards Abbi, and she hissed, 'Leave my shop – at once.'

'Why should we? We're your customers.' He grinned. 'And the customer is always king.' His hand went through his hair, the pomade sticking to his fingers. One of his teeth looked brown and rotten. 'Or shall we spread the word about how you treat your customers? Typical for your lot. Bah!' He spat on the floor in front of her. On the clean floor of her beautiful shop, directly in front of her feet! Abbi's blood began to boil and she wanted to spit back at him. But she was terrified and trying not to show it. Her hands were trembling, and she pushed them under her red and white apron, swallowing back her spit.

'Well, if you're customers, you'll want to buy something, won't you?' She still sounded angry and provocative. 'Now, what would you like? Oven gloves? Or does Mummy still make your dinner?'

Pomade laughed. 'Yes, as it should be.' But rather than leaving he took two more steps towards Abbi. His mates grinned, and the voice of the ringleader sounded threatening when he hissed, 'I don't want oven gloves, I want something different, *chica.*'

Abbi instinctively backed away, but the shelf with the ornaments blocked her way and she was trapped. Her hands behind her back felt the cold porcelain. Cups and plates were clinking.

Frantically, she tried to figure out how to get rid of the gang. Then the doorbell rang again, and the attractive blond man with the hat came in, looking worried.

'Hello. Is everything alright? Do you need help?' he asked in broken Spanish with a German accent, even though he could clearly see that things were not alright. But that was probably the best strategy. The gang looked questioningly at their ringleader, who now, taken aback, adjusted his collar. 'Piss off, German!' he shouted at the blond man, and looked at Abbi challengingly.

'You'd better watch your mouth!' The blond man looked at Abbi questioningly.

'Thank you, I'll be alright. These gentlemen were about to leave,' she said bravely.

'Were we?' the ringleader asked his mates, but they didn't respond, waiting for his orders. But seeing that the German was now rolling up his sleeves, his expression angry, and Abbi had grabbed a broomstick she could use as a weapon, he clearly thought better of arguing further.

Pomade grinned at Abbi. 'Ooh, I'm getting really frightened now. You've got a great protector here. A German clown. He won't help you, though, will he?' With that he left the shop, his friends following. The bell chimed loudly as the door shut behind them.

Abbi breathed a sigh of relief as the tension left her, and she smiled gratefully at the stranger. From his accent and his broken Spanish she had recognised that he was German. Oh, why couldn't he be Swedish?

'Thank you. That's never happened before. Well, not like that, anyway.'

The man nodded and smiled warmly, his eyes calm and reassuring. 'And it will never happen again.'

'What can you do about it?' Abbi laughed. 'Will you stand guard outside my shop?'

He smiled at her again, his expression friendly and open. No man had ever smiled at her like that.

'Yes, if necessary.'

How courageous he was! For a moment the world seemed to stand still. The two of them looked into each other's eyes and were enveloped by a sense of closeness and belonging.

'What's your name?' He broke the spell.

'Abbi. Well, Abbigail, really. And yours?'

'Johann. And I like confident women.'

Chapter Four

Milla stared at her mother, who was looking upset. They had been sitting in the lobby of Sarah's hotel for a while now. In the large brown leather armchair underneath an artificial palm tree, her mother looked even more fragile than usual.

Milla tried to make sense of what she had just heard. So many questions were racing through her mind, but before she could voice any of them Sarah rose abruptly. 'My dear, I'm tired. Getting up so early isn't easy for me. I'm going to have a rest now. After all, we have a few more days together.'

Milla nodded absently and stayed seated. Still numb, she stared at the artificial palm tree, its leaves covered with a thin layer of dust. She thought about her grandmother and the story she had just heard. Abbigail seemed to have been a clever young woman and very modern for the conservative fifties, when being a woman mainly meant being a mother and doing the housework. The awful early death of her sister, Rachel, must have been traumatic for her. Was that possibly the reason why she had been so cool towards her daughter? Milla couldn't believe it. The loss of a sister alone would not turn a happy young woman into a cold mother years later. She had also been able to fall head over heels in love, like Sarah had just told her, with this attractive German. Was he maybe her grandfather? No, she knew from Sarah that her grandfather was Spanish and called Baruch. Milla remembered the strange name very clearly.

Lost in thought, Milla rose. At least she felt a bit closer to her grandmother now. She knew that Abbigail must have been a confident woman, because to run her own shop in the fifties was a very unusual thing on Mallorca – as it probably had been in Germany. It was a time when most women looked after the house, the children and their husbands. *How awful*, Milla thought. *That wouldn't have suited me at all.* She was, again, very glad to live in the twenty-first century.

A large group of English tourists, with fat beer bellies and cans of lager in their hands, rushed into the lobby. They smelled strongly of alcohol and sweat, and Milla quickly squeezed past them towards the exit. Once outside, she took a deep breath of fresh air. Then she looked around for her car. Damn, where in this maze of small streets had she parked it? She had no recollection of it at all. Was it over there? No, that one had a different number plate. Had it been towed away already? Milla's sense of direction was like that of a mole above ground. Why hadn't she memorised the name of the street? Or taken a photo with her mobile of the location, as she usually did?

With rising panic, she searched one little street after another, trying to remember their names. But they all looked the same to her. After a few minutes she came across a street sign: Calle Montesión. That rang a bell. Of course! Her grandmother had mentioned it in her letter! The souvenir shop she had inherited must be somewhere around here. Nervously, Milla looked at the small shops lining the street and started to rummage in her handbag for the letter. Yes! It was 53 Calle Montesión.

Quickly, she walked down the street towards number fifty-three. There it was – and right opposite was her car! Abbi's heart was pumping. What a coincidence! Her grandmother's shop; her inheritance. And somehow fate had led her towards it! Again, there seemed to be an invisible family bond holding her, guiding her.

The shop window looked like it had not been cleaned for a while, but it was surrounded by a climbing plant with purple flowers, so it still looked inviting and charming. Aaron Birnbaum had explained that her grandmother had spent a long time before her death in an old people's home. Obviously, nobody had looked after the shop during this time.

The shops to the left and the right of it looked newly renovated and inviting, and there were lots of tourists milling around. On the right was a café called Coffee & Books, and on the left a bakery selling the typical Mallorquin *pastelerías*. Delicious! Milla loved Spanish pastries: *ensaïmades*, almond cake . . .

She stepped closer to the shop window and tried to look through the dull pane. But all Milla could see was a yellowed piece of paper stuck to the window saying 'Closed due to illness' in a spidery hand. Grandmother must have lived in the home for quite a while. How awful, Milla thought, to be all on your own at the end of your life in an institution, without any visitors – not from the only daughter, nor the only grandchild. Hopefully, she'd had lots of friends, but friends couldn't replace a family. Milla's heart was aching. She just couldn't understand why her mother had broken off contact with Grandmother so radically. What on earth could have happened?

Frantically, Milla rummaged in her handbag for the key that Aaron Birnbaum had given her, but she couldn't find it and it dawned on her that she might have left it at home on the kitchen table. She rooted through her handbag again. As usual, it held a mixture of things: hand cream, her make-up bag, chewing gum, a half-melted chocolate bar, two tampons, a lipstick. She knelt down and emptied the bag on to the pavement. Some tourists watched her, grinning, and one woman smiled knowingly. But the key wasn't there.

Milla looked around feverishly, contemplating what to do now. Spotting a large rusty nail in a corner, she quickly put all her belongings back into the bag, got up and looked at the lock. It was old and ornamental, like something in a horror movie. Milla hesitated, but she didn't have a choice. She was, after all, the legal owner of the shop. Reluctantly, she picked up the rusty nail and probed the lock. When she heard a click, she felt encouraged and tried again. Just as the lock finally gave way, a strong hand grabbed her shoulder from behind.

Aghast, she stared into the dark eyes of a Mallorquin man in his forties who spoke angrily and very fast in Spanish. Luckily, her mother had talked to her in Spanish regularly, so Milla had learned the language easily. It came in handy now. He obviously thought she was breaking in and was threatening to call the police. A few sensation-seeking tourists and neighbours stopped to stare.

Milla tried to reassure the man in Spanish and to explain that it was all a misunderstanding. She told him that she had left the key to the shop in Germany. The onlookers moved on. With a sceptical look, the man let Milla go. Stepping back, she couldn't help noticing how handsome he was: the dark hair falling across his forehead made him look very dashing.

'You are German?' he asked in passable German. On Mallorca, probably everybody knew a smattering of the language.

She nodded, slightly miffed. Her shoulder was aching. What had the man been thinking? 'Yes. And I am the owner of the shop.'

'You? The owner? Anyone could claim that!'

'But I am not anyone,' Milla countered.

Then it seemed to dawn on him. 'Well, I expected that, sooner or later, relatives who have never before cared for Señora Fuster would turn up to claim the shop.'

Milla felt hurt. 'I never knew her.'

'As I said. Families don't mean anything to you lot any more. But when it comes to inheriting, you're here like a shot.'

Milla was offended. 'What would you know?' She tried to defend herself. 'I would have loved to know my grandmother, but I only found out from a solicitor the other day that she had been alive all these years.'

He looked at her incredulously and, frowning, turned around and walked the few metres over to Coffee & Books. Then he stopped and turned around again. 'Has your solicitor also told you that somebody is interested in buying the shop?'

'Yes, he has.'

He pointed to Coffee & Books. 'That's my café. And I would like to buy Señora Fuster's premises and extend into it. I have made a good offer already.'

'Indeed?' Milla replied, and remembered Paul's words about being cheated. 'I'll make enquiries as to whether the offer is good enough.'

He stared at her wordlessly, then nodded a goodbye and went back to his shop. The delicious smell of coffee wafted out on to the street.

Well, that was just great. Should she have been a bit nicer? He was her neighbour, after all, and he had obviously known her grandmother. Milla took a deep breath. Strangely, her heart was pounding hard. She would love a cup of coffee right now. But definitely not from his café.

Milla looked at the door to her grandmother's shop, which was standing ajar now. Inhaling the musty, stale air, she entered gingerly. Once in, she looked around with a growing fascination. The dusty shelves were probably from the fifties and were stocked neatly with typical Mallorquin souvenirs. There was an old till on the counter, which was clad with typical Mallorquin tiles. Everything looked old-fashioned, but lovingly decorated. In a corner was a coffee machine: an old model with a filter.

This was it then, her grandmother's haven from when she was a young woman.

Milla had her back to the door when she heard something creaking. Startled, she turned around. A very old woman peeped around the door, apologised quickly in Spanish and started to retreat.

Milla rushed towards her and called to her in Spanish. 'Wait, please wait!'

The old woman stopped. Her salt-and-pepper hair was constrained in a bun on the top of her head, and she was wearing black, like a widow. Her back was bent and she was walking with the aid of a stick.

Milla smiled at her. 'Did you know the owner of the shop?'

The old woman's eyes looked at her sceptically and shyly. Then she nodded. 'Abbigail. May she rest in peace.'

Milla nodded gravely. 'I'm her granddaughter, from Germany.'

The old woman looked at her, alarmed. 'Germany?' Then she came in and closed the door.

'Well, I never knew all these years that my grandmother was still alive, and I would like to know more about her. Maybe you can help me?' The old woman hesitated, shaking her head. Milla added quickly, 'Can I offer you a cup of coffee?' But even as she said it, she knew that there was no way there would be fresh coffee in this shop.

'Well, then.' The old woman paused. 'Next door at Leandro's the coffee is very good.'

Milla cursed inwardly. What had she landed herself in? But she couldn't pull out now; if she did, she would never learn anything about her grandmother.

'Really? But I've just had . . . a bit of a row with him.' Again her mouth was quicker than her brain.

The woman smiled. 'I'm not surprised. Leandro is a very emotional man. But if I were young again, I think I would like him.' She grinned. 'Big emotions, passion, romance – that's Leandro, and that's what we women want, after all, isn't it?'

Milla could only stare at the old woman, lost for words.

'Come on, he doesn't bite. I'll invite you.'

Reluctantly, but not sure how she could possibly refuse, Milla agreed. The old woman nodded in satisfaction and hobbled out on her stick. Milla followed her uneasily to the shop next door.

As soon as they entered Coffee & Books, Milla felt warm and comfortable. Whether it was the delicious aroma of coffee and cakes or the cosy, inviting atmosphere, she didn't know. But the feeling irritated her. Looking around, she had to admit that the guy had good taste – or a good interior designer. Velveteen sofas invited the customers to sit down and read, quiet Spanish music played in the background. Some young tourists were sipping *café con leche* and studying a map of the city. There were even e-readers to borrow. Milla loved the concept of such a shop/café, and it was obviously popular. No wonder, then, that he wanted to expand.

Milla hadn't spotted him yet – to her relief.

'Well, no empty tables. I'm sure we'll find another café,' she said, trying to lure the old woman away.

But the old woman shook her head vigorously. A young couple was just leaving, and she made for their table like a shot. 'They serve the best Mallorquin almond cake here.'

Milla resigned herself and followed her. At that moment Leandro appeared from the kitchen, saw the two women and walked towards them with a broad smile. He was wearing denims, a black T-shirt and beautiful black shoes Milla hadn't noticed before.

He greeted the old woman with a kiss on both cheeks and Milla with a *Hola*.

'Hi.' Milla blushed and quickly hid her face behind the menu. The old woman ordered a coffee and almond cake. Milla mumbled, 'Same for me, please.'

Leandro went to pass on the order to the young waitress at the counter, smiling curiously at Milla. Milla tried to ignore him and turned to the old woman, who had established herself in an armchair. She seemed to have relaxed now, at the prospect of coffee and cake.

'You have no idea how glad I am to have met somebody who knew my grandmother. My name, by the way, is Milla Stendal. My mother's maiden name was Fuster.'

The old woman nodded. 'I know. My name is Eli.'

'Eli, what else do you know? I mean . . .' Milla wasn't sure where to start without frightening the old woman away. 'Please tell me about her.' Any information could give her a piece in this jigsaw puzzle.

The young waitress brought their coffees and cake, and, while eating and drinking, Eli told her that Abbigail had been her best friend. 'Do you have a best friend?' she asked Milla.

'Yes, I do. Her name is Tine.'

'Well, then, you know how important a best friend is.'

'Too true.' Milla nodded with a smile. But she wasn't quite sure what Eli was after.

'Abbigail and I, we were very pretty . . .' Eli mused. Milla stared at the old woman's bad teeth and the hair sprouting on her upper lip. 'Why are you looking at me like that? In the fifties I was indeed beautiful and slim,' old Eli said, and grinned mischievously.

Milla found it difficult to picture a young, beautiful woman in old Eli's face, but confirmed to her that she could easily believe it. What life does to you . . .

Eli began, like many old people, to tell her quite insignificant stories from her past which had nothing to do with Milla's grandmother.

Initially, Milla listened carefully, but then she insisted on hearing more about Abbigail. By then, though, Eli had finished her almond cake, which indeed was delicious, and now placed her coffee cup back on the table. With the help of her stick, she scrambled to her feet.

'You're going already?'

'I can't – I can't talk about the past,' Eli whispered, shaking her head.

Milla sighed. What was it that Eli couldn't talk about? What did she know? She tried to persuade the old woman to stay longer, but Eli wanted to leave. The memories were upsetting her too much. Maybe once she had slept on it, they could meet again tomorrow? 'You'll be around for a few more days, won't you?' Eli wrote down her phone number on a piece of paper and hobbled out.

Milla sat back with a sigh of disappointment. Then her glance moved to Leandro, who was just settling the bill with a young tourist. Was he flirting with her, or was it – again – Milla's interpretation? She thought of Paul, of how she missed him and how she hoped that her suspicions were unfounded. She would find out once she was back in Berlin.

Milla went to the counter to settle her bill with the young waitress, but Leandro appeared next to her and looked at her searchingly. 'Eli always talks rubbish,' he said.

'What?' Milla was bemused. What did he know?

'You want to pay?' He changed the subject.

'Yes.' With trembling fingers, Milla rummaged in her purse.

'Fourteen euros, please.'

She pressed a ten-euro and a five-euro bill into his hand. 'Keep the change.' Their hands were touching. Quickly, she withdrew and took one more look into his handsome, open face. Then she turned and left the shop.

◆ ◆ ◆

Milla lay on the narrow bed in her hostel, feeling tired and confused. Her eyes were fixed on the painting on the opposite wall. It pictured a typical Mallorquin landscape with white and pink flowering almond trees. In the foreground was a couple, hand in hand, with their backs to the viewer.

She thought of Paul, whose hand she loved to hold in the mornings. Was it really him she missed, or was it the stability he gave her? Milla had learned a lot about her family today, but nothing yet that would explain or even give a clue as to why her grandmother's relationship with her mother had been so strange.

Milla took a selfie with her smartphone, in which she looked tired and old, and wondered whether to send it anyway. Then she looked at the painting, took a photo of it, added the caption, *That's us*, and sent it.

No reply. Where was he? Normally, he replied straight away. Milla tried hard to suppress her usual jealous thoughts and instead reflected on the day so far. This man, Leandro, seemed to be so different from Paul. Paul was always easy-going and didn't like romantic gestures and big passion. He liked life to be casual and steady. Leandro appeared much more serious. But could he be faithful? And Paul?

Recognising that she felt attracted to this Leandro and that she was thinking about him so much annoyed Milla. She loved Paul, after all – or was she not able to love anybody deeply? How was it possible to even have a shred of feeling for another man if your love was true? She remembered her grandmother's letter and her advice to decide on the right man. Milla shuddered.

Feeling restless, she got up and looked into the noisy old fridge in the corner, but it was empty. No minibar. Then she remembered the chocolate bar in her handbag and hungrily devoured it. It was no comparison to the delicious almond cake, but she had forgotten to buy food, and right now she didn't feel like taking one more step.

Exhausted, she sank back on to the bed, thinking of almond cake and Leandro. He wanted her shop, but she wasn't sure any more. Should she really sell it? Her grandmother's beloved shop?

Her phone buzzed with a WhatsApp message from Paul. *Hi darling, been jogging. Nice picture. Everything okay?*

Hmmm. Jogging? She wrote back. *It's okay. Very exhausting. Do you miss me?*

Of course. And you me?

She stopped briefly. *Yes, me too. Goodnight.* Suddenly she didn't feel like telling him about her day, her grandmother. It was as if she wanted to keep the story to herself. Strange. All of a sudden she felt like an ally, a good friend, of Abbigail, who apparently also had to keep a secret. A secret Milla didn't know. Not yet.

Milla decided to ring Eli first thing in the morning. Her flight back was in three days and before then she had to find out more about her family, about herself.

◆ ◆ ◆

Milla woke up the next morning with the Mallorquin sun in her face. It was already half past ten. She hadn't slept that late for a long time. Breakfast was over, and she planned to buy some *ensaïmades* on her way to her mother's hotel.

Soon she was dialling Eli's number, but nobody answered, not even an answerphone. Damn. Why hadn't she asked for her address? Or arranged another meeting? Maybe the old woman didn't hear the phone ringing, or was out all day? Annoyed with herself, she wondered what to do now. Time was short, and there was no one else she could ask about her grandmother. Leandro certainly wouldn't know anything about her mother when she was a little girl or a teenager. But even if he had, she'd rather avoid him. Milla didn't trust her feelings any more and didn't want to risk her relationship with Paul. She tried to concentrate on what to do. Best to meet up with her mother and ask her about Eli.

◆ ◆ ◆

Milla and her mother were sitting on the sunny Plaza Mayor, eating *tostadas*.

'Well, have you met anybody interesting yet?' Sarah asked.

How could she know about Leandro? 'What do you mean?' Milla replied tetchily.

'Well, somebody you could ask about your grandmother. Who else? That's the reason you're here, after all.'

Ah, that's what she meant! Milla nodded. 'Yes, a woman called Eli. She suddenly turned up in Grandmother's shop, an old friend of hers. Do you know the name?'

The waiter turned up with two bottles of mineral water. He smelled of cheap aftershave and smiled charmingly at the two women, probably wondering whether they might be two more female tourists looking for sunshine and a bit of fun.

After he'd left them, Milla tried again. 'It seems that for a long time Eli was Grandmother's best friend. You must know her.'

Sarah looked at her and, judging by her expression, she certainly had known Eli, but then she shook her head. 'No, I don't know her.'

'Mum, what's the matter? I can see that you're lying.'

Sarah seemed upset and took a sip of her mineral water. Fighting for words, she finally started haltingly. 'Your grandmother . . . she hadn't had any contact with Eli for a long time. Eli doesn't know anything.'

Milla pricked up her ears. What didn't Eli know? She tried to remain calm. 'What was it she didn't know, Mum?'

Sarah made a dismissive gesture. 'Well, the way my mother treated me. Her own child.'

'How do you know?'

'That's what I think.'

'Mum, you don't break with an old friend just like that.' Milla thought of Tine and how nothing would force them apart – nothing. That's what she hoped, anyway.

'Milla, what if you find out that your grandmother was just a heartless, evil woman?'

'Nobody is like that by nature. And she wasn't either.' But what if Milla was wrong?

'How can you be so sure?'

'Because of her letter. It sounds loving and friendly.' Milla felt as though they were talking about two very different people. But why? She realised her mother was stonewalling. 'Do you know her surname? Eli's, I mean. I have to find out where she lives. She isn't answering her phone.'

Sarah hesitated. 'I don't remember . . . but it'll come to me . . .' Sarah really did seem to be trying to recall the name.

'Shall we go to the beach?' Sarah asked suddenly, and smiled at Milla encouragingly. It was quite warm now, for this time of year, even on Mallorca.

Milla looked at her in surprise. Her mother rarely suggested they do anything together. This is a very special spring, Milla thought. In every respect.

'Please come to the beach with me,' Sarah said. 'We have a lot to catch up on. And the city beach, Ca'n Pere Antoni, is supposed to have changed quite dramatically. I'm sure I'll remember Eli's surname before long.'

It was a nice offer, and Milla all of a sudden felt closer to her mother. 'How is the beach supposed to have changed?'

'Well, it was always a bit dirty and crowded, but apparently it's been cleaned up and is much more attractive. That's what I read somewhere, anyway. And we can walk over, so you don't need to look for a parking place.'

'Alright.' Milla smiled at her mother. She couldn't care less about fashionable beaches at the moment but was happy that her mother had suggested it. Maybe she would indeed remember Eli's surname. And she could Google her address on the beach anyway. 'But I want to go back to the shop later.' She had remembered that she needed to put a lock on the door. Hopefully, she wouldn't meet Leandro . . .

Milla smiled secretly to herself when she realised she was in the same position as her grandmother, young Abbi, with her friend Johann. They both needed to try and distance themselves from men who might not be good for them.

Ca'n Pere Antoni was busy with tourists and Mallorquins looking for some downtime in their lunch hour, or after sightseeing in the city. Milla and Sarah took their shoes off and walked over the cool sand. Out at sea, an expensive-looking super-yacht was passing, and gentle music drifted over from the fashionable Nassau Beach Club. The smell of grilled langoustines wafted over from a restaurant on the promenade. 'Hmm, delicious. Shall we go there?'

Sarah smiled easily for the first time since they had arrived on the island.

Milla hadn't been on holiday with her mother since she was sixteen, and now, at thirty-six, she was beginning to like it again. In the shadow of a modern, quite ugly block of luxury flats, they talked about how beautiful the island must have been in the fifties. Despite the development around them, it was lovely to dig her toes in the sand and watch the world go by. The beach was great for a quick respite from the city, but when Milla had visited four years ago they had always gone to more beautiful coves around the island to swim.

Now she walked down to the water and turned her jeans up. The cool waves lapping at her feet felt wonderful. In Berlin there were only lakes, and the temperature at this time of the year was markedly cooler. Milla closed her eyes and relaxed, but not for long. Time was moving on. Her flight home was in three days.

'I've got it!' Sarah called to her. 'I remember Eli's name.'

'What is it?' Milla ran towards her mother.

'Pomar. That's what I think, anyway.'

'Thank you, Mum!'

Milla straight away tried to Google the name, but the internet signal was very weak and kept failing. Impatiently, she put the mobile back into her pocket.

'Let's go and find a better Wi-Fi connection. Are you coming?'

'Where to?'

'First to Grandmother's shop. Maybe I can link up with next door's Wi-Fi.'

'Oh, no.' Sarah vehemently shook her head. Mentioning the shop seemed to trigger something. But what?

'Mum, please help me,' Milla said gently. 'I feel that you know something. And that Eli woman is also keeping something from me.'

Sarah stared at her, clearly struggling with her thoughts, and then she couldn't hold back any more. 'You don't know Mallorca's history at all, do you?'

Milla tried to recall the information she had gleaned from the travel guide and the internet, but she remembered nothing except recommendations for beaches and restaurants. She didn't have a clue what her mother meant. 'No, please tell me.'

Sarah took a deep breath. 'Well, you'll find out sooner or later. This particular part of Mallorca's history goes back to the fifteenth century. It was the time of the Inquisition, and everywhere Jewish people were forced to convert to Catholicism. And because Mallorca is an island, everybody knew which families were descended from Jews. They were called *xuetes*. Originally, it is said to have meant "pigs".'

Milla stared at her mother, stunned. 'Pigs?'

'The *conversos* only started to call themselves *xuetes* from around the seventies onwards, and then in a confident and provocative manner. For a long time they had been treated with hostility, with discrimination; were spat at. And here on the island there was no escape, not even in the middle of the twentieth century. That's why your grandmother was threatened in her shop. Because we have Jewish roots.'

'We? Our family too?'

'Yes, we are the descendants of converted Jews. And Mallorquin society didn't allow a *xueta* to marry a non-*xueta* until the fifties; nor did the *xuetes* allow marriage outside their community. But it's not relevant to us any more, Milla.'

Milla tried to understand what she had just heard. Did it really not matter any more? She couldn't make sense of it but understood now why young Abbigail would never have been allowed to be in a relationship with a lovely man like Johann. How awful!

Chapter Five

Mallorca 1956

Abbi was still living with her parents, as was the custom for young, unmarried women. She loved the flat in the centre of Palma that Noah had bought for the family after Rachel's death. The old house on the outskirts had reminded them too much of Rachel: her lovely laugh, like bells ringing; the colourful hairbands she would leave somewhere in the garden or tied to shrubs.

Abbi particularly loved the roof terrace, where she could sit in the cool evenings, drinking home-made lemonade. They grew mint up here, a special ingredient of her favourite drink.

Her parents spent most of their evenings inside the flat, and each night, before she went to bed, Abbi would go up to the roof to look at the vast, star-studded night sky. Up here, the whole world seemed to be hers, and she always felt a deep longing that there might be more to life than what Noah and Esther showed her.

Tonight, the stars appeared even brighter than usual – at least, that's how it seemed to Abbi. She was excited; and her heart beat faster still when she thought of her encounter with the handsome Johann. But she tried to repress the feeling. A German man! Her father would go mad! She hadn't told her parents anything about the incident with the gang of men and their threats. Her mother had a weak heart, and Abbi wanted to spare them the worry.

Her mother had prepared a *paella* for dinner that evening, and for pudding there were almond biscuits. Abbi had been secretly collecting recipes of dishes and cakes containing almonds and often casually asked her mother for them. Many had been handed down from her grandmother, or even her great-grandmother. Once she had enough recipes, she planned to compile them into a book, submit them to a publisher and present the book to her parents as a surprise. It was her main goal in life: to be a good daughter and to make her parents happy, despite their hardships. This stemmed not only from Rachel's terrible death, but also because, as *xuetes*, her parents were frequently discriminated against, even though the war, which had caused the latent anti-Semitism to flare up again so tragically, had been over for a good few years. On this island, everybody knew who was a *xueta*, and there were always stupid people who held on to their ridiculous prejudice. Once, Noah had received a threatening letter. He had tried to keep it secret from Abbi, but she'd overheard her parents discussing it in the kitchen. Another time, his office's letterbox had been soiled. But today had been the first time Abbi had experienced it herself. She tried to persuade herself that Pomade and his gang had just wanted to intimidate her for other reasons, but she knew that wasn't the case.

Abbi took another sip of her lemonade and looked up to the starry sky. Again she realised she was thinking of Johann. Part of her hoped never to see him again, because she didn't want to bring shame on her family. But a bigger part of her longed so much for him that her heart ached. If only he would come to her shop in the morning, just to talk! Johann looked like an educated man; maybe he had been to university. And Abbi, who always wanted to know everything, loved to have interesting discussions. As a teenager, she had talked a lot to her father, but that all stopped after

Rachel's death – everything had changed then. Abbi missed their conversations, especially as most men weren't interested in talking to women.

Luckily, though, Abbi had Eli, her best friend, whom she had known since school and who lived just a few streets away. Her family, too, was descended from converted Jews, and although she couldn't discuss politics with her, she could talk about anything else. Eli loved to dress in the latest fashion and often flirted with men. She wasn't married either, but her reason was that she couldn't decide whom to accept. She was very pretty, with her short, dark hair and her slim figure, and lots of men were interested in her. The current fashion of full petticoats and cinched-in waists suited her beautifully, and Eli got enough money from her parents to buy new clothes all the time.

They were due to meet for coffee the following morning, and Abbi was eager to talk to her about Johann. After all, who else could she tell?

◆ ◆ ◆

'How romantic!' Eli commented the next morning when Abbi told her about Johann and how he had saved her. 'A real hero.' They were sitting in the café where they always met before work, just near the small tailor's shop where Eli worked.

'Well . . .' Abbi grinned. 'But it was really me who chased the men away with my broomstick.'

Eli laughed. 'I can see that! But tell me, will you meet him again?'

'I hope not,' Abbi replied sadly.

'Oh, come on, you must. Is it just because he's German?'

'Just? You know, Eli, what that means for my family.'

Eli nodded thoughtfully, pursing her bright-red lips and taking a sip of her *café solo*. She knew the whole history of Abbi's family – not only about Rachel's tragic death. Abbi's grandmother, Noah's mother, had been forced to work for a Nazi officer stationed on Mallorca who had happened to taste her almond cake. He had ordered Abbi's grandmother to be his home help and cook. The man had often ranted about how difficult life had been in Germany, having to round up all those Jews and put them on trains like cattle to send them to the camps. He had complained about the fact that so many had tried to escape, making their jobs even more stressful.

He hadn't realised that this Catholic woman was a *xueta*. When he found out he was outraged and disgusted and gave orders to have her deported immediately to Germany. Before she left, he gave his soldiers permission to do whatever they wanted with her. Noah had wanted to spare Abbi the details of what that meant, but she could well imagine what her grandmother had to endure. Miraculously, though, Noah's mother had managed to escape and survive the war, although her experiences had left her quiet and withdrawn. Abbi remembered how, when her grandmother taught her embroidery, her skilful hands were marked by numerous scars, which Abbi could only guess had been caused by burning cigarettes.

Eli interrupted Abbi's dark thoughts. 'Well, your parents have to realise that not all Germans are like that.'

'Do they?'

'Yes.'

'But still. He's not one of us.'

'My God!' Eli took her last sip of coffee and looked over to the tailor's shop where she worked. A short, skinny man was looking at her sternly with raised eyebrows: she was late. 'I have to go now, but I want to tell you one thing. When you told me about that

Johann, you looked like a different person. What if he's the right one for you? What if your heart can't stop racing just with him?'

'Ah, Eli!' Abbi laughed to dispel her worries, although she had thought the same. 'He cannot be my Mr Right.'

'How will you know if you don't get to know him better? And if he's not, you can cry on my shoulder.' Eli smiled, kissed her on the cheek and ran into the tailor's shop.

When Abbi looked at her reflection in the window of the bakery next door, she saw the traces of Eli's red lipstick on her cheek. Lost in thought, she wiped them away. Eli was right: she needed to find out more about Johann, or she would regret it for the rest of her life. That much was certain.

◆ ◆ ◆

'It just cannot happen!' Abbi repeated this sentence like a mantra. For one thing, Johann wasn't Jewish, and on top of that he was German! Even if he was her perfect partner a hundred times over, her father would never allow the relationship. And she couldn't disappoint her beloved father.

Abbi had opened her shop, like she did every morning, but caught herself looking out of the window for Johann every so often. She made herself a cup of coffee and was just taking in the delicious aroma, her eyes closed, when she heard his gentle voice right behind her. Immediately, she got goose bumps. In his rudimentary Spanish, which sounded very funny to her, he said: 'Good morning. Can I buy a cup of real coffee here?'

She turned around. There he stood, smiling at her. God, those eyes! Blue as the sea that she loved so much. 'No, you can't buy coffee here. But I could make an exception and offer you a cup.'

The smile! The dimples! 'Because I saved your life?'

'Ha!' She laughed. 'I think I saved yours. If I hadn't grabbed the broomstick, those guys would have beaten you to a pulp.'

'Maybe.' Amused, he looked around the shop. Abbi lowered her eyes and poured him a cup of coffee. 'But it must remain our secret that coffee is free here, otherwise all the other tourists will want one too.'

'I understand. Thank you. But I'm not a tourist.'

'Really?' Abby's heart beat faster. She had feared that he might leave the island in a week or two, like all the other holidaymakers.

'No, I'm living on Mallorca at the moment.'

'Really? Since when?' Abbi asked eagerly. If he'd arrived with his family before the war, it could mean he was Jewish. That would be good. Very good. If it had been after the war, he could be an ex-Nazi trying to escape revenge and punishment.

He hesitated. 'Does it matter?'

Abby shrugged, pretending not to be interested, 'No, of course not.' But she was watchful. 'And how do you like Mallorca?'

'It's a beautiful island. So unspoilt, and it's kind of a shame that more and more tourists are thinking the same.'

'Well, it's good for my shop.' Abbi pointed to her souvenirs. He nodded, but his gaze didn't move from her. Abbi tried to avoid his eyes and rein herself in. She hardly knew him, after all. 'Have you finished your coffee?'

He emptied his cup. 'Yes, thank you.'

'Okay, because I have to get back to work.'

He looked around the shop. There were no customers. Abbi pointed to a few parcels on the counter waiting to be unpacked. He handed the cup back and, as their fingers touched, it went through Abbi like an electric current. She stepped back.

Then he asked abruptly with a serious expression, 'Can I invite you for a coffee in return soon?'

Abbi nodded, overwhelmed. Johann smiled, turned around before she could think twice, and left the shop.

You stupid cow, she scolded herself. But her heart felt as if it was turning somersaults.

◆ ◆ ◆

'Are you coming, Abbi?' Esther called. She had made her special dish, *bacalao* – salted cod with potatoes and green beans. As a good housewife, she always cooked a proper midday meal for the family. Abbi's shop was within walking distance, so she always went home for lunch.

'Coming!' she replied. Abbi was sitting in her room in front of the mirror, brushing her short black hair and staring at her face uneasily. Tonight she would meet Johann. She hadn't had the courage to decline his invitation yesterday when he suddenly turned up at the shop to ask whether she would have time today. He had looked at her with eyes full of yearning and love – or was she imagining it? Could he really love her, even though he hardly knew her? What was he expecting? Eli had advised her not to be awkward or stubborn, because no man would like that in a woman.

'And what about you?' Abbi had answered.

Eli liked to play hard to get with men, but she thought that was something completely different. 'Men like it when they have to conquer a woman. But they don't like those who are constantly answering back.'

'Ah,' was all Abbi had said, thinking that Johann surely had to be different. At least, that's what she was hoping.

'Abbi?' She heard her father's deep voice calling from the kitchen. 'Food's on the table.'

Quickly, she backcombed her hair a little and rushed downstairs. Noah looked at her, annoyed. 'What's the matter with you, child?'

He knew her very well. While Esther was plating up, she, too, scrutinised their daughter. Abbi tried hard not to show how nervous she was about her date, but didn't quite manage it. Her spoon fell to the floor with a loud clang.

'What is it?' Noah barked at her. Abbi remained silent.

'You're looking very pretty?' Esther probed in a motherly way.

Abbi felt caught out. 'I'm going for a walk later. I'm meeting someone.'

'Oh, she's courting!' her mother trilled. 'And it's obviously someone she likes.'

'How do you know?' demanded Abbi.

'Well, when you brush your hair so nicely before going out?' Esther smiled knowingly. Okay, Abbi thought, let them think she was meeting a man. But they must never know that he was German.

'And when will we meet him?' Noah wanted to know, tucking into his fish dish. 'I hope he is one of us. You know that anything else would mean problems.'

Abbi went pale and mumbled a kind of 'yes' while she bent down to pick up the fallen spoon. 'I hardly know him myself, and most probably I won't like him after a while. You know me.'

'That doesn't matter. I need to meet whoever is taking my daughter out. Is he picking you up?'

'No, we're meeting in a café.'

Noah and Esther exchanged a glance, and Esther tried to reassure her husband with a joke. 'Noah, let her be. She'll drive him away, anyway, with her cheekiness.' She winked at Abbi.

Gratefully, Abbi smiled back. She could always rely on her mother. Esther was in a very traditional marriage, but something inside her, deep down, was also quite rebellious. And she allowed her daughter to express this, while denying it to herself. 'I've made an almond cake for pudding. A very old recipe from my great-great-grandmother.'

'Can you tell me about it tonight? I have to go soon.'

'Of course, my darling.'

Abbi thought it might be a good idea to include the recipe in her planned cookbook. She finished her meal quickly, eager to get back to the shop. She could hardly wait to meet Johann again. Abbi hadn't told her parents that Johann would pick her up at the shop, otherwise Noah would have turned up so he could meet him. And luckily her parents hadn't asked which café they were meeting at – because Abbi didn't know herself where they were going. Somehow, she was sure it wouldn't be an ordinary place.

That afternoon as she sat in her shop the minutes seemed like hours. The morning had been quite busy – a few German tourists had asked for sightseeing tips, an English woman had broken a cup. But this afternoon, Abbi was bored as she sat and read the newspaper – something she normally loved, but today her thoughts were all about Johann.

Finally, the clock struck seven o'clock. He would be here soon. Abbi was getting increasingly nervous as the time ticked towards eight, when they had arranged to meet. She glanced in the mirror again – yes, her hair looked fine. Abbi started when the doorbell rang. '*Hola*.' His familiar voice made her heart race. 'Am I too early?'

She turned around, smiling. Yes, it was a bit early. Johann was wearing a black, rocker-style leather jacket and looked very attractive. 'Maybe a bit, but it's not very busy today. I'll just close the shop now.'

'And that's okay?'

'Yes, sure. After all, I'm the boss.'

He looked at her, visibly impressed. 'Oh, I thought you were an employee.'

'No.' Abbi's smile seemed to be developing into a permanent fixture. But she couldn't help it. Nor did she want to.

'Good, let's go – we'll have plenty of time then.'

'Where are we going?'

'You'll see.'

Abbi loved surprises. She locked the door and followed Johann. And then she saw him: Pomade was hanging out on the street opposite the shop, with two men from his gang. They all grinned at her tauntingly.

'They're back,' Abbi whispered.

But Johann had spotted them already. 'You'd better leave this woman alone. Is that understood?' he called over to the men.

Pomade laughed mockingly, chewing his gum. 'You're keen on her, aren't you? But beware, she messes around with everybody.'

The other two laughed, and Pomade gestured to them to go. Outraged, Abbi looked at Johann. Oh, God, what would he think of her now? There was no point in reassuring him that the opposite was true. That she was still a virgin, at nearly thirty years old, something that Eli time and again teased her about. But Abbi didn't want to go to bed with just anybody. She was waiting for her Mr Right, and if he wouldn't come, she'd rather do without.

'That . . . isn't true . . .' she stammered.

But Johann only put his hand on her arm reassuringly and said, 'Shh. Do you really think, Abbi, that I believe those idiots?'

He had called her by her name! His warm hand on her arm relaxed her. 'No. I'm sure you can see right through them.' She couldn't think of anything else to say, she was so angry. How dare that Pomade treat her like this? She had never encountered anything like it. Still shaking, she followed Johann through Palma's old quarter.

'Would you like an ice cream?' he asked with a smile. 'Maybe it'll make you feel better.'

Did he sense how shaken she was after what had just happened? 'Yes, please. I love almond ice cream.'

'Me too.' Their eyes met again.

As Johann's green Vespa sped along the coastal road, Abbi's skirt fluttered in the wind; her back-brushed hairdo, which she'd taken such care over, was being held in place by a scarf, spoiling it somewhat. But she didn't mind. Instead, she clung tighter to Johann's waist, enjoying the feeling of his strong muscles and the way his hair tickled her face. She breathed in his scent, trying to decide what it smelled like: it was fresh, but also spicy, with a hint of leather from his jacket.

Abbi had never been on a scooter before and, initially, she'd been a bit anxious, but the fear was soon replaced by a wonderful, liberating feeling of being carefree and happy, even though she knew that her father would go mad if he could see her now – and her mother would certainly faint. She started humming a song, nestled her head between Johann's shoulder blades and enjoyed the wind in her face.

If it had been up to her, they would have gone on for ever, with no destination, but after about half an hour Johann slowed and turned off towards a lovely little cove near the Hotel Riu. Part of the beach was shaded with a bamboo roof and there were deckchairs and changing rooms for the guests. A sign said, 'This is a country of high morals. Bikinis not allowed'. If anyone was caught wearing the fashionable new beachwear, there would be a fine to pay, and the Guardia Civil normally kept watch. But now, towards evening, they were alone.

Johann switched off the engine and helped her from the Vespa. He had brought a large bag, and once they had found a lovely little

71

spot close to the sea, he spread out a blanket. The sand was very soft and dotted with shells, remnants of the last high tide.

Abbi, who loved food, looked in amazement at the selection Johann unpacked from his bag: tapenade with pine nuts; pickled samphire; sun-dried tomatoes in olive oil; a *fuet* Mallorquin, a hard-cured sausage; *sobrasada*, a soft meat paste; and a local cheese.

'You're crazy!' Abby laughed. 'This is far too much!'

'I know.' He looked amused. 'I just wanted to get it right.'

What a lovely man, Abbi thought, her heart fluttering.

As the sun lowered in the sky, colouring it orange and red, Abbi and Johann sat next to each other, looking out to sea. Johann told her in his funny Spanish way about his geology studies. She had been right; he had gone to university. This gave Abbi a slight shock. If he'd gone to university in Germany, he couldn't be Jewish. Abbi knew that, under Hitler, Jews had been forbidden to go to university. He must have been a Nazi, then. Or at least his parents would have been.

The thought made her heart sink. But hope bloomed again when Johann told her how he and his friends had agitated against the Nazi regime. He was no Nazi, then, but had been in the resistance movement.

Johann told her how helpless he and the other students had felt. They had distributed leaflets against the regime, but it hadn't made much difference. 'We knew we were a small minority and that there was no chance of changing the regime.'

'But you tried, unlike many others. That was very courageous.'

'No, it wasn't. We should have assassinated him, the monster, but we were not brave enough to do that.'

Abbi saw in his face how ashamed he was, and her heart melted. He was such a sensitive person.

'It was terrible to watch how the people were rounded up and shot in broad daylight. Once I saw a nine-year-old boy, the same age as my brother. He just stared at me with his big, terrified eyes, but I couldn't do anything. Or rather: I *didn't* do anything.'

Johann closed his eyes. He was trembling slightly. Abby swallowed hard and put a hand on his arm. Although there had been rumours in the Jewish community, as many people had been deported from the island, it wasn't until the war ended, when she was eighteen, that she had first heard of the millions of murdered Jews. Her father had been crying when he told her, and Abbi had been too shocked to say a word. How could anyone commit such cruelties to their fellow men? About six million Jews had lost their lives under the Nazi regime. Men, women, children – whole families – had been exterminated in the camps.

Johann continued haltingly. 'We hid two families and supplied them with food as well as we could. But that was all we did without risking our own lives any further. Well, we didn't have the courage to do more.'

The only sound now was the quiet lapping of the waves on the sand.

'It sounds like you risked a lot,' Abbi said quietly. 'You can be very proud of that. I mean it.'

'But . . . I still feel guilty . . .'

Gently, Abbi continued, 'I've thought about this a lot. And I can't tell what risks I'd have taken or whether I would have been that courageous if I'd had to live under Hitler.'

Johann shrugged and stared into the distance. Then he picked up a shell and started to dig a hole with it, but he couldn't get deeper because the fine sand kept on filling the hole.

Abbi watched him. 'How come you weren't drafted?'

'A friend of my father, a doctor, signed me off as an epileptic. Presumably, my father had made use of other contacts as well.'

'Your father? How did he manage that?'

'He was a pastor, secretly heading a kind of resistance, but without risking his family. But let's talk about something else.'

Abbi nodded and inwardly sighed with relief. No Nazi – but not her lot either. Abbi knew that her father would never accept him into the family as her husband. *What am I thinking?* she told herself off the next moment. She had met Johann only a couple of days ago and was already thinking of marriage! But Abbi had never been so attracted to a man before. And on top of that, she felt close to him. As if she'd known him for years. He looked at her, and so close to the sea his dark blue eyes seemed even darker, making her stomach tighten. *Please, take my hand*, her heart was begging, but Johann was quite shy. He turned his head again, and looked out at the water, seemingly deep in thought.

But he likes me, I know it, Abbi rejoiced.

'How did you get to Mallorca?' she asked, hoping that he would not have to leave again soon.

'I came here by plane – a Douglas DC-4 with four engines,' he told her proudly. 'That was a few months ago. Do you know the plane?' Abbi shook her head. 'It's going to transform tourism,' Johann continued excitedly. Abbi liked it when he beamed at her like that. 'We flew over the Alps, three thousand metres high. I saw all the tallest peaks. But my ears hurt terribly from the pressure.'

'How wonderful,' Abbi said longingly. 'I've never been on a plane.'

'You must do it someday.'

'I'd love to. Weren't you afraid?'

'No, it's fantastic! You feel totally free.'

'I guess so. And you work here?' she probed.

'Yes, as a geologist. I'm researching the history of the Mallorquin mountains. With a few colleagues, of course.'

Abbi was impressed and relieved. 'You'll stay here for longer then?' she continued.

'At least for the next six months. It's a limited contract, but maybe it will be extended.'

He smiled at her, and Abbi smiled back and leaned her head against his shoulder. They were quiet then, sitting happily in the cooling evening air, watching the waves and the sun.

Mallorca 2016

With her thoughts racing, Milla stood in the Calle Montesión in front of her grandmother's shop. She reflected on all the things her mother had told her about her family history, dating back to the fifteenth century, and her grandmother as a young woman, who, even in the middle of the twentieth century, had been racially harassed. Was that the reason Sarah had been so cool and detached with her daughter? Had her grandmother turned into a bitter and hard woman because of the discrimination, and had she passed this bitterness on to her daughter?

Milla couldn't really believe this. It couldn't be the whole reason. When Sarah had told her about Abbigail's first love affair, Milla had sensed how emotionally sensitive and empathetic her mother could be. She had been so moved as she told Abbigail's story that she'd had to go up to her room to lie down when she finished. So Milla didn't know yet how this forbidden love affair had ended. But she was very curious to find out.

Still lost in thought, Milla took out her mobile and tried to connect to the free Wi-Fi in Leandro's café. Yes, it worked. Quickly, she Googled the name Eli Pomar, but there were only entries on younger women, judging by the photos and blogs. The old woman seemed to have disappeared completely.

Milla gave up and took the little padlock she had bought that morning from her handbag. Many tourists were now crowding the Calle Montesión. A tall man trod on her foot and didn't even seem to notice. He looked at her, nonplussed, when she cursed at him, then walked on without a word. When she, still angry, looked in the other direction, she saw Leandro not far away, watching her. He was standing outside his café, holding a cup. Then he glanced at the padlock in her hand.

'Has your grandmother's shop been open all this time?'

'I'm afraid so,' Milla said ruefully. 'I hope nothing has been stolen.'

'I hope so too. The fifties furniture is very fashionable now. I would want to buy everything inside as well.'

'And who says that I'll sell the shop to you?'

He calmly returned her glance. 'Any reason why not?'

'Well, my grandmother's wish was that I keep it. Even though we never met.'

He took a sip of coffee. 'You live in Germany. What do you want with the shop?'

'I don't know yet.'

'Okay, how about if I rent it from you? How much would you want?'

Milla shrugged. 'I don't know yet. I haven't made a decision.' She stepped towards the door and tried to fit the padlock, but under Leandro's scrutiny, she was nervous and clumsy. She glanced at him briefly, flushing as she noted his slightly amused grin.

'Can I help you?'

'Definitely not.' Milla was astonished at how hard her voice was; this man really knew how to annoy her.

At last she managed to fit the padlock and turned to face Leandro. But he was walking towards a slim, pretty, long-legged brunette who could have been a model. She kissed Leandro on the lips, and then they went arm in arm towards his shop. Milla stared after them, her mouth slightly open. The woman, looking back, noticed her and asked Leandro who she was.

'She is . . . the granddaughter of Señora Fuster. She's inherited the shop.'

The woman let go of Leandro's arm and walked gracefully toward Milla.

'I'm Diana, Leandro's girlfriend. My condolences.' The beautiful brunette shook Milla's hand and looked at her sympathetically.

His girlfriend, Milla thought with a shock. How disappointing. But she tried not to betray her feelings.

'Thank you. Did you know my grandmother too?'

'No, not really. I only saw her three or four times before she had to move to the home. A very nice old lady.'

Milla nodded sadly, even though Diana couldn't really have known whether her grandmother was a nice person or not. But she pricked up her ears when the old people's home was mentioned. 'Do you know which home she moved to?' Why hadn't she asked anyone before? she wondered.

'It's the El Castellot. We call it the palace. There are many Jews and German expats among the residents. There are also Spanish aristocrats, professors, actors – whoever can afford it. It's not cheap.'

'Come on, let's have a coffee,' Leandro jumped in. He put his arm around Diana's slim waist and led her into the café, glancing back briefly over his shoulder at Milla.

Milla, confused and alone again, decided she would drive out to this old people's home if her attempts at finding Eli failed. She would more than likely meet people there who had known her grandmother.

Her thoughts went back to Leandro. Why didn't she just sell him her shop? What made her feel so annoyed at him? And why was she hurt by the fact that he was in a relationship – as she was herself, after all? The deep disappointment Milla felt confused her tremendously.

She thought of Paul and realised she hadn't heard from him all day. But she hadn't contacted him either. There had been a time when they texted each other every hour or so. Messages of longing, of love, of reassurance. Was it normal that, a few years into a relationship, these things faded, or was it a reason to worry? They were planning to get married and spend the rest of their lives together, after all. How would the marriage change their relationship, their love for each other? So many marriages buckled under the pressure of everyday life. Would theirs too? Could she find the stability she had always craved in a marriage with Paul? Would she find it in herself? Without knowing who she really was?

Paul had always taken life and love quite casually, something she had liked very much in the beginning. But, as time had passed, she had wanted more and more to have a family with him and had hoped he would propose. When he finally asked her to marry him, she hadn't hesitated. Then she had quickly told her friends and, together with Tine, had found a wedding venue – a small club, that wouldn't to be too romantic or tacky for Paul's taste. Paul didn't want a big do; he had once told her that his idea of a perfect wedding was to go to the registry office, have a curry afterwards and then go dancing. Maybe he had been overwhelmed by the fact that she had started planning her wedding in detail immediately after his proposal. What if Paul was finding everything too much now? What if it was all happening too quickly?

Milla caught herself wondering what sort of wedding Leandro would have. He seemed more a man of passion, of romance and high emotions. He probably knew for sure what love felt like. With Paul, Milla often wasn't sure, but perhaps that was because she herself had received so little love from her mother. No one had ever talked about feelings at home. Milla sighed. Her mother was certainly trying, but even so, she wasn't sure she was capable of showing her the sort of love she had always craved.

She pulled herself together and looked over to Leandro's café; she could see Diana through the shop window. She turned quickly away and walked along the Calle Montesión, pushing through the crowds of tourists, who, freshly showered and dressed for an evening out, were meandering along the street, looking for suitable restaurants. Suddenly she realised she was very hungry. She checked her mobile. Nothing from Paul, but there was a message from her mother. *Fancy fresh seafood in la Parada del Mar?*

Milla's mood lightened. Maybe her mother would relax enough over a nice meal and a glass of wine to reveal more about her grandmother's story, which in turn would hopefully provide the key to why her mother had been so cold and detached towards her all these years. She prayed she would. Because she was convinced the secrets her mother kept held the key to her own ability to love.

The Parada del Mar at 244 Avinguda de Joan Miró was well known for its fresh seafood and fish, and its competent, friendly staff. One had to choose the fish, mussels and shellfish at the counter and then it was freshly prepared in the kitchen. Milla, as usual, found it difficult to decide what she wanted, and a skinny German tourist behind her was getting impatient. Her mother didn't find it easy either. Did Milla get it from her, this indecisiveness?

Finally, they ordered, and were given a number and shown to their table. The food had to be collected at the kitchen counter as soon as their number was called. In the meantime, Milla tried again to contact Eli, but in vain. Over a glass of red wine she told her mother about the home where her grandmother had lived until she died. Sarah listened, but didn't comment. Milla wondered why her grandmother had chosen an old people's home known to house so many Germans. Sarah offered the explanation that Abbigail had loved Johann so much that the language would have reminded her of him.

Milla thought about it and wanted to know how the story of the two lovers had ended. Sarah, shelling a *gamba*, shrugged regretfully. 'A good question,' she said. She didn't know.

'Not even whether Johann is still alive?'

'No, sorry.'

'Mum, why don't we go to this home tomorrow? Maybe we can find out something, a lead, something that might explain things?'

'Oh, Milla.' Sarah sounded exhausted and melancholic. 'I don't think I want to go there. Is that okay with you?' She took another sip of wine. 'I'd rather go to her grave tomorrow morning. And then have a long siesta. This trip is taking it out of me more than I expected.'

'Of course, Mum. We'll go to the cemetery, and afterwards I'll drive to the home.' Milla finished her wine and smiled at her mother. At least Mum wanted to visit the grave with her.

The next morning they drove to the cemetery outside Palma. Milla enjoyed the journey, admiring again the island's beautiful landscape. Almond trees with their white or pink blossoms, orange and lemon trees still in fruit, olive trees with their silver leaves and black trunks, and tall cypresses. Milla tried to imagine what life must have been like here in the fifties. Without mass tourism, there would have been a lot more fruit farming, and Palma had expanded quite dramatically since that time.

Her mother remained silent and Milla let her be, even though she found it difficult to bear. Her stomach tightened, as it always did when she was tense. Soon they would be standing at her grandmother's grave; she would be closer to her than she had ever been before.

After parking the car, the two women asked a man in the office how to find Abbigail Fuster's grave, and he indicated where they should go. As they walked along the broad middle avenue between the graves, Milla tried to decipher the names on the headstones.

'Over there, I think, by the almond tree.' Milla's heart was beating faster. There were very few flowers and wreaths on Grandmother's grave, and it looked a bit abandoned. There was a wooden cross with Abbigail Fuster's name and the dates of her birth and death. Milla swallowed hard. She felt overwhelmed and suddenly very close to her grandmother. She would have loved to take her mother's hand but didn't dare.

'I knew it,' Sarah said quietly.

'What did you know, Mum?' Milla looked at her.

But Sarah only shook her head defensively. 'That she was an evil woman. Otherwise, there would be more flowers on her grave.'

Milla couldn't believe this after all she'd heard about the clever, friendly young woman Abbigail had apparently been. 'Rubbish. There just weren't many people her age left to come to her funeral.'

Sarah sighed, stepped closer to the grave and arranged the few flowers in their holders. One stem had half broken. Milla knelt next to her mother and took her hand. It felt cold. After a moment, Sarah took the broken flower and gently put it on the mound of earth.

'How are you feeling?' Milla had to ask.

'Terrible,' Sarah replied quietly. 'It's so final. Now you'll never learn anything about her past, Milla. Why she was like that to me.'

'Oh, yes, Mum, I will. Don't give up yet.'

Milla was surprised at how emotional her mother was. Sarah took a handkerchief from her bag and blew her nose, then she looked at Milla with tears in her eyes. 'I'm such a terrible role model! Please forgive me.'

'No, you're not.'

'Let's go. Could you take me back to the hotel, please? I'm not feeling very well. You can go on to this old people's home on your own.'

'Okay.' Milla watched a little bird hopping on the mound of earth, probably searching for a worm, then looked at Sarah. Her mother had not been able to forgive her own mother, and now she was visibly suffering. Sarah's reaction to her mother's death had driven home to her just how little time she might have to put things right between them.

The El Castellot was situated on a rocky outcrop of the Santa Ponsa coast with a fantastic sea view. It was surrounded by several acres of lush park with flower beds, shrubs and palm trees, dotted with numerous shaded seats. There were also two swimming pools for the aged residents. Everything was immaculately groomed, as were the old women and men Milla saw when she walked up to the house. They were dressed elegantly, jewellery and all; the ladies predominantly in pink, lilac or beige, the men in suits. She could tell immediately that it was a high-end old people's home. The El Castellot consisted of several buildings with modern apartments, and the main house was in the typical Mallorquin style. It looked like all the residents enjoyed a lovely view of the sea or the park.

Milla took a few deep breaths, feeling moved. Her grandmother had spent her last years here, without her family, but not alone. One could stay in El Castellot's sheltered living initially and later move to the care unit until the end. Milla spotted a young nurse, her long hair tightly braided. She asked her in Spanish where to go for information about a deceased resident.

The friendly nurse explained the way to the main house and told her to ask for Aina Garcia.

Aina, a small, slim Mallorquin woman in a brown trouser suit, looked elegant and professional. She showed Milla to a room with a long wooden table and chairs covered in vintage-looking fabric, surrounded by white shelves lined with books. It looked like a library.

She spoke German, but with an accent. 'Please, take a seat. Here our residents can read or connect to the internet. There are two laptops for them to use.'

'How thoughtful,' Milla replied with a smile. 'It's all very lovely for the residents.'

'Thank you.' She looked at Milla questioningly. 'So, Abbigail Fuster was your grandmother? Can you prove this?'

'I . . . have a letter from her. It's been given to me by the notary. But it's back in my hostel.'

'Okay, I believe you. I have to ask, because we have a few celebrities residing here, and sometimes media people turn up, pretending to be relatives.'

'I understand. But what would press people want to know about my grandmother?'

'I don't know.' Aina Garcia smiled briefly.

Milla feverishly tried to think what to ask this woman first, scolding herself that she hadn't thought of some questions beforehand or developed a strategy.

'How can I help you?'

'I'm afraid I don't know,' Milla burst out. 'But I'd like to talk to nurses or other residents who knew my grandmother.'

Aina Garcia nervously looked at her gold watch. 'Well . . . Abbigail Fuster didn't have much contact with the other residents.'

Shocked, Milla looked at the other woman. 'Really? In such an institution?'

Aina Garcia seemed to consider. 'Well, yes, there was some contact with two of the residents.'

'What do you mean?'

'One had been a well-known dancer in Berlin in the thirties. Jewish. The other is German, a former Nazi officer. For a long time, those two didn't want to have anything to do with each other. They would leave the room when the other was present. Your grandmother decided to bring them together. And it worked, to a degree.'

Milla was impressed. Her grandmother had, in this upper-class old people's home, tried to bring a Jewish woman and a former Nazi officer together. How strange and brave! The more she found out about Abbigail, the more she liked her.

'Can I speak to them, please? On their own. Please, it's very important to me . . . and to my mother. I don't know much about my family history and it would help me a lot.'

Aina Garcia hesitated, took some pearly-pink lip gloss from her bag and applied it. 'I'll ask them whether they are prepared to talk to you. That's all I can do for you.'

'Thank you so much! I'll wait outside on one of the seats. Okay?'

'Yes, alright.' Aina Garcia got up to go, but then she turned back to Milla. 'You know that Señora Fuster left the remainder of her fortune to El Castellot? The money enables us to take in people who otherwise couldn't afford it.'

'No, I didn't know.' Milla was amazed. 'I've inherited my grandmother's souvenir shop, and that is more than enough for me. It's fine by me that she left her money to you. She must have been very happy here.'

Aina Garcia smiled and sighed with relief. She appeared more relaxed now.

Milla sat under a palm tree, fidgeting. She looked out at the glittering sea and took a sip of the *café solo* a waiter had brought out to her. The El Castellot was a nice place to spend the last years of your life. If one had the means. Abbigail had only kept her beloved shop so she could leave it to her granddaughter in Germany. A granddaughter she had never met. Why?

Milla turned as she heard a deep, gravelly voice behind her. 'Hello. Are you Frau Stendal?'

Milla nodded at the tall, elderly gentleman with white hair wearing a dark blue suit that looked a bit like a uniform.

'Yes. I'm Abbigail Fuster's granddaughter.'

The white-haired man smiled sadly. 'My name is Franz-Xaver Schuller. Ex-officer. But for the last fifteen years I haven't been proud of that.'

Milla was surprised. 'And before, you were proud?' she retorted hastily.

'Yes,' he replied in a firm voice. 'Until she made me see things differently.'

'Would you please sit down?'

He was probably well over ninety years old, and he sat down awkwardly and seemingly with some pain.

'What a wise, fabulous woman she was, our Abbigail,' he began. 'I do hope you're like her.'

Milla laughed. 'I can't tell, because I never met her.'

'That's a shame, my child.' He shook his head then swatted away a fly. 'She loved me, you know.'

Milla was touched and didn't know what to say.

'No, not like you might think. In a modest way, but I sensed that in her. Whenever she was with me, she turned into a young girl.'

'How lovely! You knew each other quite well, then?'

'Yes, yes. Whatever that means. You only know about another person by the things they say to you. I didn't have to tell you that

I was a Nazi officer, did I? If I hadn't, you might have thought me a nice old man.'

Milla nodded, slightly intimidated.

He continued, now more emotionally. 'But I will have to deal with that myself. That I was taken in. That I was such an ambitious young man, who loved giving orders. After the war, I emigrated to Mallorca. Nobody knew me here, and for a long time I didn't tell anybody about my dark past. But, as I got older, I simply had to speak out. Do you understand? It was like a heavy weight on my heart, a rock, and I had to get rid of it. But that wasn't possible.'

'I think I understand,' Milla said quietly.

'Where in Germany are you from, child?' Herr Schuller asked. His hands were trembling slightly.

'Berlin. And you?'

'I'm from Berlin too. East or West?'

'West Berlin. Why are you asking?'

'Well, the Stasi officers from the East, they tortured people in the prisons too. And they are all still walking around free.'

'That's right,' Milla conceded. 'I've been to the Stasi prison in Hohenschönhausen. It's open for visitors. Those torture chambers – dreadful. But can one really compare?'

Schuller nodded sadly, and Milla thought that he was a very sensitive old man. What could she ask him in order to find out about her family's secret? 'So you didn't find my grandmother awful and bitter?'

He looked at her, his clouded, light blue eyes puzzled. 'Abbigail bitter? No, child, quite the opposite. She had suffered a lot. And at the bottom of her heart she was an angel. A virtual angel.'

'What was it she had suffered?'

'She never talked to me about it.'

'Did she ever talk about why she didn't have any contact with her daughter?' Milla held her breath, hoping for an answer.

Schuller looked at her thoughtfully. 'She had a daughter?'

'Yes. Otherwise I wouldn't exist.'

'Of course.'

Milla recognised that Schuller was embarrassed by his fading memory. 'She never mentioned a daughter. But maybe to her friend here, Bescha Baum. She was a well-known dancer in the thirties. Abbigail always wanted me to go out with her. Me, with a Jew! But I found her much too skinny.'

Milla couldn't help smiling. 'I'm hoping to have a chance to talk to Frau Baum later. But is there anything interesting you can tell me about my grandmother? Something that might explain why she hadn't had any contact with her daughter for so many years?'

Franz-Xaver Schuller shook his head. 'No, I'm sorry, child. It's terrible when one doesn't know anything about one's own family, isn't it?'

Milla nodded, tears filling her eyes. She would have loved to tell this old man everything – about how awful it felt to wonder whether your own mother loved you unconditionally. She put on her sunglasses, which she had pushed up on her head, and blinked the tears away.

Awkwardly, Herr Schuller got up. 'Please excuse me. At this time, I always take my coffee in my room, on my own. I get tired quite easily, you know. I'm ninety-five, after all.'

Milla rose and gratefully took the old man's hand. 'Thank you very much. You've helped me. At least I know now that, deep in her heart, my grandmother was a good woman.'

Schuller nodded, trembling slightly, and then, leaning heavily on his stick, went back to the main building.

Milla exhaled. What had she expected? That here in El Castellot her family secret would be served to her on a silver platter? She went for a little walk in the park, looking forward to meeting Bescha

Baum. A nurse had told her that the old lady would be ready to talk to her in half an hour.

Bescha was a petite old lady, dressed in white. She appeared very fragile, as if a little gust of wind could blow her over. She was wearing an elegant white hat to protect her skin, which was like parchment, very thin and wrinkly. Her make-up was a little over the top, the lipstick leaking into the wrinkles around her mouth. Her smile was rather reserved. 'I haven't had much fun in my life,' was one of her first sentences. 'My career ended with the arrival of that pompous midget.'

Milla was at a bit of a loss at that and didn't know what to say. Finally, she just nodded, as she was honestly moved, and waited for the old lady to continue. Bescha Baum must have been well over ninety. Her accent was upper class and she was very articulate. 'But I don't want to complain. I'm alive, and that's what's important.'

Milla nodded again then dared ask her first question. 'I was told that you knew my grandmother, Abbigail Fuster?'

Bescha Baum looked at Milla sadly. 'Yes, and I miss her very much.'

'Did she ever tell you why she didn't have any contact with her daughter?'

Bescha Baum considered the question, frowning, which created even more wrinkles on her forehead. A light breeze slightly lifted the rim of her hat. Bescha held on to it with her slim, graceful hand. 'She never understood her daughter.'

Milla's concentration sharpened. So her grandmother must have talked about Sarah? 'Why didn't she understand her daughter?' she probed. 'What do you think she meant?'

Eagerly, she waited for an answer, and recalled that she herself had always had the feeling that her mother didn't understand her.

'The girl – well, your mother, I suppose – wasn't very close to her. For whatever reason. A different person, a different character.

I've never really understood it. She made decisions that Abbigail wasn't happy with.'

'What kind of decisions?' Milla was holding her breath.

'Well . . .' Bescha hesitated, searching for words. 'Sarah wanted to move out at eighteen, away from her mother, to go to Germany, to Berlin, to marry a German.'

Strange that her grandmother would have been against this. Milla remembered that she, too, had moved away from her mother at eighteen. 'But Grandmother had been in love with a German man as well. Surely she could understand that?'

Bescha nodded. 'Yes, but it had only brought her unhappiness.'

The more Milla probed, the more Bescha Baum closed up. She deflected questions, resorted to small talk, and Milla didn't find out anything else about her grandmother. Instead, Bescha told her that she had danced at the Munich national theatre, at the Berlin opera, on many world-famous stages. Her bright, sparkling eyes betrayed how much it had hurt her to have to give up her dream of a dancing career – just because she was Jewish. Finally, she had emigrated to America and, eventually, married a millionaire. But, even with all her money, she couldn't buy back her dream. Because on the ship to New York she had met an attractive man who had flirted with her and seemed to care about her. But it had been a cruel game. He turned out to be a Nazi, who shot her in cold blood in the right foot, right in the open on the ship's deck.

Chapter Six

Mallorca 1956

Abbi had treated herself to a pair of light-yellow capri trousers – the latest fashion – and was very proud of them. She had seen a picture in a copy of *Constanze* magazine that a German tourist had left in her shop. Her parents hated the trousers and found them completely unsuitable for a young woman, but rebellious Abbi had her way. She wanted to look pretty for Johann. For the last two weeks they had been meeting in secret, and her heart still skipped a beat whenever she saw him. So far, they hadn't even kissed, but it was in the air . . . Maybe it would happen today?

They saw each other most days after closing time and when Abbi could find a plausible excuse for her parents. But they were slowly getting suspicious. Noah wanted to meet the young man who had apparently stolen their daughter's heart, even though Abbi tried hard not to show how much in love she was when she was at home. She reassured her parents she was only meeting up with Eli, who had boyfriend trouble, or with a good friend who was helping her with the accounts and giving her urgent advice about the shop.

Noah didn't believe her because, up until now, she had been managing to run her shop on her own perfectly well. So Abbi had to invent more lies about how this friend knew a few tricks about saving money. When Noah heard the word 'save', he couldn't resist, so he stopped probing – and because his wife asked him to.

'Let her be,' Abbi had heard her mother say one evening in the kitchen. 'Otherwise, we might lose her as well.'

And there it was again, like a slap in the face: the memory of her beloved sister, whom she missed so very much. Abbi often remembered the time that Rachel had tied lots of colourful ribbons into her hair, as if she were a doll. When Abbi went to school with them and a few boys laughed at her, Rachel had defended her.

The passing of the years had made the pain less sharp, but Abbi still missed her sister terribly. The wound simply wouldn't heal. Sometimes Abbi found to her horror that she couldn't clearly remember Rachel's face any more. When that happened, she quickly took out a photo and tried to memorise the beloved features yet again. In her shop, too, was a photo of Rachel in a drawer, because the thought that she might forget her sister one day was one of Abbi's greatest fears.

Abbi was conscious of how much her parents were still grieving for Rachel, and always would be. She was also aware that she mustn't add to their worries. But she knew, too, that she couldn't replace Rachel. It was *her* life, after all – and it was all ahead of her – and *her* feelings. That society expected her – well, would force her – to marry a man of Jewish descent, seemed unbearable to her. These were modern times! Even so, Abbi hated lying to her parents about Johann. Every day, she tried to forget him, to distance herself from him, not to go to their dates, to rip her feelings for him from her heart. But something inside her drew her irresistibly to him, as if towards a magnet.

Tonight, she was determined, she would live. For Rachel. She would kiss Johann, because he was obviously too shy and reticent to take the first step. But that was also what she loved about him, that he gave her time and didn't rush her. Did he sense that she was still a virgin? She had only ever kissed two men before. Abbi wondered whether she herself was awkward and shy. She must ask Eli about this – whether it was she who was doing something wrong. It was strange that Johann didn't even hold her hand.

Abbi tried to calm down. She *did* feel that he liked her. But was he as desperate for her company as she was for his? Johann knew by now that she was a *xueta*, because she had told him. He had assured her that it didn't matter to him. Of course not. But it did to her.

After she had closed the shop, they were to meet at the Plaza de la Reina, by the fountain. Her parents never normally went there, so the young couple met there often. Abbi stared at the clock on the shop wall, but today the hands didn't seem to move at all.

At last it was nearly eight and Abbi had cashed up, hung the 'Closed' sign and locked the door from the outside. Turning around to walk to their meeting, she saw Pomade and four of his friends coming towards her, grinning tauntingly.

Abbi tried to walk past without looking at them, but the five men started to follow. They kept their distance, but Abbi could hear their laughter and whispering behind her. The hair on the back of her neck was bristling. What could she do? Who could help her now? Johann, who else! Abbi walked faster; her pursuers did too. Finally, after what seemed an eternity, she arrived at the Plaza de la Reina, where Johann was already waiting by the fountain. He immediately realised what was going on and walked quickly towards Abbi, taking up a protective stance in front of her and telling the men that he would inform the police if they didn't stop harassing the young woman.

With mocking laughter, Pomade told Johann that he should feel free to make himself a laughing stock. He could walk wherever he wanted. But then he whistled to his mates, whispered something, and the five went off.

Terrified, Abbi looked at Johann. 'What do they want from me?'

'They want to frighten you, and they have succeeded.' He embraced her tenderly. Abbi breathed in Johann's unmistakable scent, and her heart skipped a beat. They had never been so close to each other. Johann felt right. Yes, he was her Mr Right. Even though it seemed the wrong moment, their faces moved towards each other. Abbi felt his soft, full lips, sensed his breath mixing with hers, loving the feeling as his tongue gently played with hers. Never before had a man kissed her so lovingly and respectfully and yet with so much passion. It had to be love. The love of her life, that she and Eli had fantasised about so often. Maybe Eli hadn't felt this before, and maybe no one on this planet had experienced this ultimate love. Abbi was conscious how lucky she was, but in the next moment she felt guilty again. She was betraying her parents, possibly even endangering them, and she knew if they ever found out she was meeting Johann, she would make them unhappy.

Breathing heavily, Abbi pushed Johann away and shook her head. 'No, no, we can't!'

'But why?' He looked hurt, waiting for an answer, but Abbi couldn't give him one. Did he know so little about the *xuetes* on Mallorca? She felt furious, but she didn't know what to do with her intense feelings. 'My parents will have problems, because you're not a *xueta* . . .' That was all she said. She couldn't mention marriage yet, after all. What was she doing? She flushed, turned around and ran off.

'What's the matter? Abbi! Please wait!'

Abbi sensed his disappointment, but he didn't follow her. Tears were running down her cheeks as she ran through the old town. Some tourists coming towards her wondered how this beautiful girl could be so sad, living in such a beautiful place. But for Abbi the picturesque streets were blurred by tears. Finally, she stopped and sat down on a doorstep, her mind whirling as she wondered what she should do. She couldn't live without Johann any more. And she didn't want to!

As the sun sank, Abbi calmed down and suddenly realised that she was cold. She got up, wiped away her tears, shaking the dust from her yellow capri trousers. Her backside would be grubby. She had to go home. Her parents would be worried about her, and that was the last thing she wanted.

As she was taking a shortcut through a dark alleyway, she heard mocking laughter, and out of nowhere Pomade and his entourage appeared. Terrified, she stared into the darkness, straight into Pomade's eyes, which were illuminated at that moment by the striking of a match. He was grinning as he lit a cigarette. 'There she is, our little whore.'

Abbi turned around and started to walk away fast. But Pomade's hands grabbed her and pulled her into a dark entrance. He pressed her tightly against the wall and she could smell his sweat, the cigarette smoke and his bad breath. She saw his rotten tooth.

'Let me go! Let me go!' she shrieked as loudly as she could. Pomade put his hand on her mouth and held her so tightly she could hardly move. Abbi was struggling like a caught rabbit and tried to bite his hand, but the dirty bastard was stronger than her. Then she remembered a scene she had once read in a book, a kind of self-defence trick for women. It was quite gruesome, but it would force the attacker to immediately seek medical attention in order not to bleed to death. As Pomade pressed hard against her, his hand between her legs, Abbi drew on all her courage and in desperation grabbed his right ear at the top and tore down hard on it. Blood splashed all over them. Pomade shrieked but let her go. His minions stared, horrified, at the blood and his ear, which was hanging down now. Abbi didn't hesitate; she ran for her life.

◆ ◆ ◆

Still trembling, Abbi lay in her bed, listening to the wind rattling the shutters. There was a thunderstorm approaching and the rain was already drumming on the roof. To explain the scratches on her face and hand, she had told her parents she'd fallen off a ladder in the shop. Though it had been late, Esther had seen to the wounds, but hadn't dared ask further questions. Noah, Abbi could see, clearly didn't believe a word. His lips were quivering. But he didn't seem able to endure the truth and didn't ask any further questions before he went to bed.

Abbi was awake for a long time, because as soon as she closed her eyes she saw him again right in front of her – the rotten tooth. The bleeding ear.

For hours, she tossed and turned, and only when the first birds began their morning chorus did she fall into a dark, unsettled sleep.

The next day in the shop was long. Each time the doorbell rang Abbi jumped, fearing it would be Pomade. But it was only tourists looking for a pretty present to take home from this beautiful, sunny island.

As usual, that evening Johann was waiting by the fountain. Abbi saw that he immediately realised what must have happened, and his face clouded with rage and helplessness. But Abbi denied that Pomade and his minions had anything to do with her injuries, so there was nothing he could do.

'I only want to help you,' he said, trembling with anger.

'You're helping me best when you don't do anything.' Then she took his hand, even though the slightest touch pained her. 'Please, Johann, I want it to stop. My family has suffered so much already . . .'

'Does it really have to do with the fact that you're a descendant of Jewish converts?' His face went ashen. 'That can't be true! We live in the twentieth century!'

'I know.'

'How long has it been going on?' His voice cracked.

'Since shortly before we met. But I think I've shown him that he can't treat me like that.' She looked at him intensely with her dark eyes. 'Please, let it be. Otherwise things will get much, much worse.'

Johann met her gaze, his eyes full of love and pain. 'Abbi, I can't bear that somebody hurts you and gets away with it. It shouldn't be allowed, and you know it. The war is over. There should never be any anti-Semitism. It's vile.'

Johann embraced her again, and she let him. Then he shook his head. 'Abbi, you have to fight back, and I'll help you. I'll give you space. I don't know what these brutes have done to you, but I'll let you be for a while.'

'Thank you, Johann,' Abbi replied, crying. She pressed her head on his shoulder, breathing in his scent, and knew that he was the right man for her. The love of her life, who understood her and with whom she felt a closeness she'd never thought she'd experience. This knowledge hit her hard as she thought again of her poor parents, who would be harassed if she married him.

Over the next few days Abbi secretly met Johann on the beach in a beautiful cove where they could sit and talk without being disturbed. Out in the open, in the shade of a pine tree, Abbi's wounds healed quickly. Johann held her hand constantly and every now and then stroked her cheek – that was all. He gave her space, as he had promised, and Abbi was hugely grateful for it. What a lovely, sensitive man he was, so different from the Mallorquin men she knew. For hours, they talked about everything under the sun. Abbi had developed the habit of asking the tourists who came to her shop carrying a newspaper or a magazine whether they had read it. Often, they wanted to get rid of it and gave it to Abbi, who devoured every scrap of information. And soon she decided that, considering how many German tourists came to her shop, she would learn their language.

Abbi was ambitious and learned quickly, and Johann helped her. He assured her that he had never met such an intelligent and open-minded woman. He wasn't keen on women whose only goal in life was being a mother and housewife, like most females he knew. Not that he was against marriage – quite the opposite.

When he said this in his loving way Abbi's heart skipped a beat. She was wondering what he would say next. Would he propose to her here, in this secluded bay, sitting on the sand? The thought alone drove her nearly crazy. Her heart was yearning for him, but she knew that she would have to say goodbye to her parents if she married him. And that wasn't possible for her – ever! To prevent him saying anything further about marriage, she jumped up and ran laughingly towards the water, stripping off her dress as she ran, ignoring the cool air. At one point, she nearly tripped over her petticoat, got up again and ran on in her underwear.

Looking back, she saw Johann, who seemed stunned, but then, like her, he stripped off to his underwear, and together they ran into the cold sea, shrieking with laughter and splashing water at each other. After a while they swam towards each other and joined in a tender, but increasingly passionate kiss.

Chapter Seven

Moved by the story Bescha Baum had told her, Milla drove back towards Palma, a journey of only twenty-five minutes. The Mallorquin landscape, with its noble cypresses and the Mediterranean vegetation dotted with buildings, flew past, the shining sea on her right. Her thoughts were racing. Her poor grandmother had been molested by this Pomade. How brave she had been to fight back like that! Milla wondered whether in such a situation she would have had the nerve to do the same. She often lacked courage, and she didn't like that trait in herself; she decided that she needed to change it. Everybody can change, after all.

When her mobile beeped, she was glad of the distraction. A text from Paul: *Have you lost your mobile? Do I have to worry? Xxx*

Milla's stomach tightened because she realised how little she'd thought of him in the last few hours. Her grandmother's story had taken up all her head space – and so had Leandro. How could that be? Milla checked with herself. Her wild jealousy of Paul's French colleague had died down. After everything she had learned in the meantime about the terrible attack on her grandmother, she realised that her problems at home were comparatively trivial.

What remained was uncertainty and a shaken confidence in the man she was going to marry in a few weeks. Involuntarily, Milla thought of Leandro again. Why did he always stare at her so strangely with his dark, hot eyes? This very passionate man she felt so attracted to, even though she tried to deny it. She compared herself to Abbigail and her Johann. They were not allowed to be with each other either. Milla was about to marry, she loved Paul, and Leandro loved Diana, that beautiful woman. Milla had to put this man out of her mind!

But judging by her fast pulse she guessed that it wouldn't be easy. Hadn't she always dreamed of something like this? To get palpitations at the sight of a man? A man capable of strong emotions who, like her, was looking for the one and only, the all-encompassing love? When she thought of Paul, her heart didn't miss a beat. Was that normal after a few years? But with Paul it hadn't raced at the beginning either. Their relationship had always been easy and relaxed; they got on well, liked each other's company, and they were good together. Paul certainly loved Milla, but how deep his feelings were for her she didn't really know. He didn't like talking about emotions, or maybe he simply didn't want to. Milla realised now how much she wanted this in her heart of hearts. Rarely had he declared his love for her.

She swallowed hard, because at this moment she realised she was questioning her whole life. And if she wanted to avoid that, she had to avoid Leandro and sell the shop. On impulse she stopped the car to ring some estate agents, and two of them agreed to meet her later at the shop to view the premises.

She was excited at the prospect, but also upset. She would certainly meet Leandro again, but maybe it would be for the last time. Before she met the estate agents, though, she wanted to tell her mother about the harrowing things Schuller and Bescha Baum had told her about her grandmother. Time was running out. Only two more days. Two days to find out more about those lost years and her family's dark past. Two days to get a bit closer to her mother.

When she found her mother in her room, she told her about what she had discovered. Sarah was shocked, and both women had tears in their eyes.

'Oh, my God, and only because of her Jewish ancestry. Unbelievable. Thank goodness she managed to escape,' Sarah whispered, staring into the distance.

'Maybe this disgusting man was also mad at her because she had her own shop, in times when women should be in the kitchen.'

Sarah shook her head silently and went to open the window, bringing the sounds of the city and the scent of food from the restaurant beneath the hotel into the room.

Milla took a deep breath. 'Let's go outside, Mum. I can't breathe in here.' Milla always needed to move to feel alive. 'And anyway, I have to be in Grandmother's shop in an hour. I have an appointment with an estate agent. I've decided to sell.'

'Really?' Sarah didn't seem too interested.

'You haven't seen the shop at all yet. Will you please come with me?'

Sarah hesitated, but then she forced herself to smile at her daughter. 'Okay. I'll come.'

Milla smiled. Things were progressing, albeit slowly.

Ambling through the small streets and alleyways of the old quarter, passing numerous souvenir shops, restaurants and bars, both women were quiet, lost in their own thoughts. Eventually they found themselves in the Plaza de Cort in the historic centre. From here they went on to the Calle Palau Reial and then on to Calle Almudaina, a small street behind the historic town hall.

It was quieter, as mostly locals lived here and there were only a few shops. An old Moorish archway stretched across the street, a sign that the Arabs had left their influence during their time on

Mallorca. 'The archway is part of the old ramparts, built by the Moors,' Milla read on a sign.

How much this city has seen, she thought. She had read up on the history of the Arabs on Mallorca, but nothing about the *xuetes*. That it now should be part of her own family's history made everything more fascinating.

Sarah, as if she had guessed her daughter's thoughts, turned to her and said, 'But no matter what faith people have, one thing they have in common: they always think that what they believe is the right thing.'

Milla agreed. 'That's so strange. But one thing I don't understand: if a faith is not practised, like in Grandmother's case, why were they still discriminated against?'

Sarah shrugged and sighed. 'I don't understand it either. That's the reason I didn't tell you. I didn't want you to become afraid.'

Warmth flooded Milla at this. Her mother had wanted to protect her! You only do that if you love your child, don't you? She looked sideways at Sarah.

It was high time for Milla to learn more about the faith of her Jewish ancestors, and also, she needed to try to understand her cool, detached mother, who had become so emotional since they had come here. Milla was both delighted and touched to see it.

She would learn more about the Jewish faith once she got back to Berlin. Involuntarily, she thought of Paul, wondering whether her Jewish ancestry would change in any way how they would get married. Did she even want to marry him, though, after all she had experienced here on Mallorca? She needed more time. Then she thought of Leandro. And of the appointment with the estate agent.

Holding a cup of coffee, Leandro was standing outside his shop in the sun as Milla and her mother walked towards the shop. His dark eyes lit up – or was that just Milla's wishful thinking? Milla held his gaze and noticed a slight smile playing around his lips. Maybe he was not as good-looking as Paul, who could easily work as a catalogue model. But the way Leandro looked at her so passionately made her forget Paul. Leandro seemed well grounded, at ease with himself, as if he always knew what he wanted.

'*Guten Tag*,' he greeted them in German, his eyes sparkling.

Sarah looked at him curiously, and Milla hoped that her mother wouldn't notice the rollercoaster of her feelings.

'*Guten Tag*,' Milla answered quickly, dropping her gaze and searching for the key in her handbag. Naturally, she couldn't find it.

'Who is that?' Sarah asked. Leandro clearly heard her and smiled.

'That's the owner of the shop next door,' Milla explained.

'The owner of the shop next door. Sounds exciting.' Leandro held his hand out towards Sarah.

Yes, it is, Milla thought and introduced him to her mother. They shook hands.

'My condolences.' Leandro addressed Sarah and assured her what a lovely neighbour Señora Fuster had been.

At last Milla found the key. 'Got it!'

Sarah only nodded and turned to follow her, but then a dark-haired man of about sixty came out of Leandro's shop carrying some empty boxes. He had obviously just delivered something. Sarah stopped as if she knew the man from somewhere. Milla gave her a puzzled look. Leandro thanked the man in Spanish and ordered more almonds for the next week.

Now the man noticed Milla and her mother, gave Sarah a friendly glance and asked, 'Leandro, don't you want to introduce me to these charming ladies?'

'Of course. They are Señora Fuster's relatives. Her daughter and her granddaughter from Berlin.'

The man shook hands with Milla, then with Sarah. He looked deep into her eyes and introduced himself in German. '*Ich bin* Jesús Fernández Jiménez. My condolences.'

'Thank you. But I'm not too upset. My mother had broken off any contact with me a long time ago,' Sarah explained. Milla swallowed; she was amazed at her mother sharing this information with a stranger, but Jesús seemed impressed by Sarah's openness. They chatted a bit in Spanish about Palma, while Milla and Leandro stood beside them in silence. Every so often Leandro would glance sideways at her, but he didn't say a word.

'Mum, I'll go inside, okay?'

'What? Yes, of course.'

Was her mum flirting with this Jesús? Sarah seemed a changed woman. Milla had never seen her mother so relaxed and open. She had to smile. It was lovely to see her so happy. She would have to ask later whether her mum had met this man before.

When Milla entered Abbigail's shop, she shuddered, remembering the abuse her grandmother had endured. Suddenly she was no longer sure whether she wanted to sell the shop at all. There must be a reason why Abbigail had left the shop to her. What had she wanted to tell her? Was it meant to reconcile mother and daughter?

Sarah came in now and cut off Milla's thoughts. 'Shame, he never asked me for my number.'

'Mum!' Milla smiled at her, nonplussed.

'What?'

'Did you know him from before?'

'No. What makes you say that?'

'Well . . . it looked like it.'

103

Sarah shook her head and said dreamily, 'What a man! I would like to meet him again, but if he doesn't want to . . .'

'He's probably married,' Milla tried to comfort her mother.

Sarah was smiling. 'You're right. Fate's against it. I'll let it go.' Then she looked around the shop in amazement. 'Nothing has changed here. After all these years!'

'Really? You recognise everything?'

Sarah nodded. She looked very moved. 'I grew up as a shop kid, you know. Mother insisted on working despite the fact she had a child to look after.' Milla sensed the resentment, the disappointment, the longing for some love.

'Well, I couldn't stand it either to be just a mother and housewife, without any outside work.'

'But it was the custom then. Other mothers wanted to be with their children. My mother didn't.'

'Mum,' Milla gently protested. 'When a mother wants to go to work it doesn't mean that she doesn't love her child.'

'You're right.' Sarah managed a smile. 'There must have been another reason.'

Milla looked at her searchingly, because she still couldn't quite believe that Sarah didn't have a clue. She still sensed that her mother was hiding something from her.

'And where is the estate agent?' Sarah tried to distract her.

'He should be here soon. Thank you for coming. You know that I'm not very good with money matters.'

'Then it's high time to learn, at your age.' Sarah smiled, but her expression was slightly critical, and Milla was pleased that the two of them could share a joke. Sarah was right. It was high time. For a long time, Sarah, as a single mother, had seen to Milla's financial matters, and then came Paul. Milla didn't like to be dependent, but money didn't really interest her. That was also the reason why she had rejected Tine's offer last year to become a partner in the goldsmith's atelier. She just hadn't dared to take the step. She didn't have the pluck to have her own shop. Had it been a mistake? After all, her grandmother had gained a lot of strength and confidence from running her own business.

A tall, stout Mallorquin man in an ill-fitting suit swept in, sweat on his forehead, breathing heavily. 'Hello, Señora Stendal. So this is it, the little property.' He spoke in Spanish.

Little property? Milla didn't like the man and the way he tried to talk her grandmother's shop down. '*Hola*, Señor Gomez. This is my mother.'

He offered them his sweaty, hairy hand. Milla secretly wiped hers on her jeans afterwards. Sarah didn't seem very happy with the man either. Mother and daughter exchanged a quick glance. Señor Gomez asked a few questions about the property, wrote a few things into a grubby notebook, and Milla succeeded in saying goodbye to him as quickly as possible with the promise of a phone call.

Sarah suggested they have a coffee in the café next door and eat some almond cake, but Milla tried to put her off. 'What is it? Do you like the owner too much, sweetie?' After she'd only briefly scrutinised her and Leandro, Sarah had hit the nail on the head, as only a mother can.

'What on earth makes you think that?'

'I have eyes to see. But why not? You could make Paul a bit jealous. Maybe he will come to his senses then?'

'I've told you I'm not sure whether Paul is cheating or not.'

Sarah looked at Milla apologetically. 'I don't mean to be critical, but Paul is a very attractive man and . . .'

'You've said enough.' Sarah had had some negative experiences with men in the last few years, but that didn't mean Paul was bad as well. Milla noticed that she was suddenly defending her fiancé.

She had probably misjudged him and loved him as much as one should love one's future husband. But the uncertainty remained . . .

'Sorry, Mum.'

'It's okay. Let's go over there. I need a *café solo* and I'm hungry.'

Milla followed her mother to Leandro's café. She couldn't avoid facing her feelings and needed to sort out her mixed emotions before the wedding. Because walking down the aisle with this uncertainty would be terrible.

The café was very busy. The coffee machine hissed, and any tourists who were not reading were chatting. There was pleasant background music, and the room smelled wonderfully of coffee. Milla looked around, and spotting a seat by the window she went over, surreptitiously looking around for Leandro, but he was nowhere in sight.

'What's going to happen now with you and Paul?' Sarah wanted to know as soon as they were settled. Normally, Milla would have appreciated her mother's interest in her life, but today she didn't want to talk about her feelings.

'Shouldn't we think about why Grandmother was . . . like that to you?'

Sarah sighed. 'I don't know. How often do I have to repeat it? She had experienced very bad things. But that applies to so many people, particularly in the war. And they still loved their children.'

Milla nodded thoughtfully. 'I think in many families the grandparents weren't able to feel or express intense feelings after what they had suffered, so their children in turn found it hard, too. It's not surprising. Just think of all the people who survived the concentration camps, who experienced nothing but atrocities and cruelties. I read a book by a concentration camp survivor who said that afterwards they found they couldn't feel anything. They were numb.'

'That's terrible.' Sarah swallowed hard. 'But my mother lived on Mallorca, and my grandmother once told me that Abbi had a pretty carefree childhood despite the war and Rachel's death. And afterwards it was alright too, apart from the discrimination and abuse. Maybe it was the murder of her sister that changed her so drastically.'

'I really need to find this Eli. She and Grandmother were friends since primary school, and she's hiding something from me. I suspect she deliberately isn't answering her phone.'

Sarah nodded, then waved to the young waitress to order *café solo* and almond cake for the two of them.

Milla pulled out her mobile and dialled Eli's number for the umpteenth time. Again, no reply. 'Something's not right.'

Then she smelled the delicious aroma of freshly brewed coffee – and the unmistakable scent of Leandro. When Milla looked up she gazed straight into his eyes as he was leaning forward to serve them their coffee. His face was very close to hers. Obviously, he had insisted on serving this table himself. 'Two *café solo*, two almond cakes, ladies.'

'Thank you.' Milla lowered her gaze to the cake, which looked delicious, topped with candied almonds that glistened in the light.

'You knew my mother,' Sarah said to Leandro. 'Do you know anything about her that could be of any interest to us?'

Amazed and grateful, Milla looked at her mother. Sarah seemed to be becoming more and more open with people, and to be on Milla's side. It felt so good to have a mother like that!

Leandro seemed to think, and then smiled, first at Sarah, then at Milla. 'It depends on what you're interested in.'

'What do you think, Milla?'

Leandro was still standing next to Milla and looked at her challengingly, although she thought she detected a hint of longing in his expression. Or was she imagining it again? She felt his breath.

'I . . . I don't know really what I'm looking for. An explanation why . . .' She stopped and realised she could hardly tell this stranger about the lack of love in her family. Leandro looked into her eyes, and just at that moment beautiful Diana entered the shop. Milla recognised immediately that she was a woman tortured by jealousy. If she had seen how Leandro had bent down to Milla and looked her in the eyes, then it wasn't surprising. She felt sorry for Diana because she knew that corroding feeling too well.

'Your girlfriend is here.' She pointed to the door.

Leandro turned around and greeted Diana with a kiss on the cheek. Diana, who was wearing a dark blue trouser suit, looked stunning.

The tall brunette greeted Sarah and Milla with a forced smile. 'Hello, I'm not intruding?'

'No, no, Frau Stendal has just asked me about her grandmother, Señora Fuster.'

'Ah!' Diana didn't sound convinced.

Leandro put his arm around her slim waist and said goodbye to Sarah and Milla. 'I'll let you know if I remember something that might interest you.'

'Thank you,' Milla said, her stomach tightening as she watched Leandro and Diana walk away arm in arm.

'You didn't tell me he was in a relationship,' her mother said reproachfully.

'I haven't told you that I have any feelings for him either.' Milla tried to defend herself. She needed to stop obsessing about that man. It could only lead to heartache.

'Milla, in matters of the heart we both have a few things to learn.'

Milla's mobile beeped. It was a text from Paul. *Have to talk to you. Will you be in your hostel soon?*

Milla felt as if she'd been struck by lightning. Paul needed to talk to her? Hopefully not about his colleague Corinne. Again she was overwhelmed by the all-encompassing, painful feeling of jealousy. Did he intend to end their relationship by phone? Milla thought of all the preparations for the wedding, the shame of everything. Suddenly she realised she had more feelings for him than she had thought only half an hour ago.

'Has something happened?' her mother asked. She sounded genuinely worried.

'No, Paul wants to talk to me in a while. I'm quite tired anyway. We can discuss what to do tomorrow, okay?'

'Of course. I'm tired too.'

On the way to her hostel Milla bought a *pa amb oli*, a baguette with tomatoes and olive oil. Nervously, she entered her little room, which smelled slightly musty, sat down on the bed and tried to calm down as she ate her sandwich. When she felt ready, she dialled Paul's number with trembling fingers.

After what felt like far too many rings, he answered. His voice sounded tense, and Milla realised she was breathing heavily. She was sure he wanted to end the relationship; she sensed it.

'Milla, at last. What have you been doing all day? Why haven't you rung me?'

'Oh, there's so much to do,' she answered evasively. She didn't feel like telling him all the things she had learned in the past three days. It was more important to know what he wanted. 'What about you? What did you want to talk to me about?'

He cleared his throat. 'Well . . . er . . . I have such a funny feeling . . .'

Involuntarily, Milla had to grin, because the sentence seemed somehow familiar. But this was a serious situation. 'What is it?' she whispered.

'I don't know . . . you're . . . so far away.'

'Paul, I'm only in Mallorca for four days. That's all.'

'That's all?' His voice sounded quite uncertain. What did it mean? Was there no reason for her to worry? Was it him, worrying about her? 'Since you . . . since you heard about your granny, it feels as if you've changed.'

'Well . . . I think that I have changed. I mean . . . there was so much to take in that I hadn't known before. The fact that I'm of Jewish descent, and all the other stuff about my family . . .'

'Eh? Jewish descent?'

'Yes, but I'll tell you all about it when I'm back in Berlin. Okay?'

'*Claro*. And . . . it has nothing to do with us? I mean, the fact that you never ring?'

For a few seconds Milla didn't know what to say. She thought again of Leandro, whom she had only met because her grandmother had left her the souvenir shop, and suddenly her mind cleared. She certainly didn't believe in the supernatural, but . . . could it be that her grandmother had wanted to bring her and Leandro together?

'Milla? Are you still there?'

Oh, God! She still owed Paul an answer. Quickly, she said, 'It has nothing to do with us, Paul.' Then she bit her lip. Now she was lying to him! 'And you? You haven't called much either. What have you been doing?'

'Me? Well, I meet up with friends. I mean, I go out, so I don't have to hang around in our flat all by myself.'

'Friends?' probed Milla. Women with French names – but she didn't say that.

'Doesn't matter. You've only been away for three days, and we're behaving as if you've been in Australia for six months.' He laughed his familiar, deep-throated laugh that she loved so much. 'But you're back tomorrow night.'

Milla swallowed and made an instant decision. 'Paul, I can't come back tomorrow.'

'What? What do you mean?'

'That I'm not coming back yet. I'm going to change the flight.'

'And your work? Tine won't like it, will she?'

'No. But she'll understand. You too?'

Paul hesitated and seemed to think. Then his voice sounded happy and light-hearted again. 'Of course. Stay until the weekend. That'll be enough time, won't it?'

Was he happy now to be alone for another few days? Milla's stomach tightened again. 'Yes, I'm sure it will.'

'Okay. Must go now. Sleep well, good night.'

'You too,' Milla answered, and hung up. And only now it dawned on her that he hadn't once told her that he loved her.

Lost in thought, she dialled Tine's number. WhatsApp was a blessing, as Milla's budget wasn't huge and phone calls to her friend were usually quite long.

'Hey, sweetie!' She heard Tine's happy voice. Milla, as usual, was flooded with warmth when she heard her friend's voice, and now the two women talked about all the latest news, why Paul had sounded so strange on the phone and all that Milla had found out about her grandmother.

It was a long talk, because Milla had to tell her everything, even the smallest detail – with one exception: she left out her mixed feelings about Leandro.

Tine was amazed and delighted that Milla had discovered so much already.

'What about the ice queen?' Tine wanted to know.

'Well, I have a feeling the sun here has started to melt her heart a bit.' Milla smiled.

'Really? That's fantastic!'

'Well, only a little bit . . . You know Mum. One never knows when she'll pull the shutters down again.'

'She'll be okay when she finally gets to know why her mum has always been like that to her . . . you'll find it all out.'

'I hope so.' Milla sighed and then said, 'Tine . . .?'

'What? No, let me guess. You've met a fantastic guy.'

Milla laughed, but it sounded quite artificial because she felt caught out. Why hadn't she told her friend about Leandro, when normally they told each other everything?

'Trust you to say that! No, I want to ask you something.'

'Go on.'

'Do you think I could stay a few days longer? Would that be okay in the shop?'

Silence. Tine now sounded a little disappointed. 'You've forgotten my operation, haven't you?'

'What? No!' But Milla had to concede that for the last day or so she really hadn't thought about it. 'I'll be back by then. Only three more days. Okay?'

'Really?'

'Yes. Promise!'

'Alright then. And what about the hot guy? You can't deceive me. I'll be your bridesmaid, Milla. No matter who you marry.'

'Don't be stupid! There's nothing to tell.' But Milla's voice was cracking a bit. Tine seemed to hear it. 'Milla Stendal, I know you very well.'

Oh, no! Milla feared to say out loud what was going on inside her head. 'He's not an option. Has a girlfriend. Happy now?'

'What? Oh, shit! Trust you to find a way to make yourself unhappy in only three days.'

Milla liked Tine's dry sense of humour but tried hard to change the subject. 'I'll have to rebook my flight now. Hopefully, it's not too expensive.'

'Okay. My skin is wrinkling already, as I'm in the bath reading a book about a great, all-encompassing love affair which, for me, only ever happens in novels.'

'I'm sure it'll be real for you soon, sweetie.'

'We'll see. If I survive the operation. Phew, my fingers look like a very old woman's. Must go now. Kiss-kiss. Love you. True love only happens between girlfriends.'

Milla laughed. 'Too true. Love you too.'

Milla rang off. Three more days. Three days to uncover her family's secret, get closer to her mother and choose the right man.

Once she had rebooked her flight, Milla snuggled under the covers and dropped off before she could have another thought – totally exhausted from all that had happened that day.

◆ ◆ ◆

Milla woke early the next morning, and when she looked at the picture on the opposite wall the carousel of her thoughts immediately started to spin. Hadn't she sent a photo of it to Paul? Two lovers, hand in hand under blossoming almond trees. Did she really love him? Could she marry him when another man was dominating her thoughts? Leandro shouldn't have sneaked into her mind like that. But even if she was developing deeper feelings for him, there was no point. He was in a relationship with Diana and obviously only playing with her, Milla. Was she imagining the passion and longing in his gaze when he looked at her? Or did he look at every attractive woman like that? She sighed, annoyed with herself. Tine was right. She was on course for making herself very unhappy. Some women had a talent for that.

Frustrated, Milla pulled the duvet over her head. Not even the bright sunshine streaming through the shutters could lighten her mood. What would her grandmother have done? she wondered suddenly. Her courageous, open-minded grandmother.

Milla had a sudden flash of insight: Abbigail had followed her heart, despite the circumstances being stacked against her. And that was the only right way.

Milla threw off the duvet, squinted into the bright sunshine and got up. She would work out who was the right man for her. She owed that to her grandmother. Hadn't Abbigail advised her to do exactly that in her letter? Milla dug out the letter from her handbag, read it again, and once again felt warmth flooding over her. She felt she knew her grandmother better now. How much this woman had suffered, but how happy she also must have been to meet the love of her life, even if it hadn't lasted long.

An idea came to her then. She decided to go to Leandro and, with the excuse of maybe selling the shop to him, invite him on a little excursion to the beach. It wasn't warm enough for swimming yet but talking was much easier on a short walk by the seaside. She wanted to get to know him better and find out more about her own feelings for him. If she didn't, she might regret it for the rest of her life. Maybe she would also find out more about her grandmother.

She went to the bathroom, applied a bit more make-up than usual and put on her jeans and a figure-hugging yellow top. With her dark curls and the light tan she had acquired since she'd been here, the colour suited her and, looking in the mirror, Milla liked what she saw. Diana was slimmer than her, but Milla had an attractive, more athletic figure. A day on the beach sounded tempting after all the trips during the last days. She just hoped Leandro could be persuaded – after all, he could enjoy Mallorca's beauty every day. Afterwards she would meet her mother.

◆ ◆ ◆

Nervously, Milla stepped into Coffee & Books, which was bustling with customers enjoying breakfast. As she breathed in the delicious aroma, she looked around for Leandro, disappointed to see he wasn't there. What if it was his day off?

'Excuse me, is Leandro in?' she asked the young waitress, a dark-haired student, who shook her head.

'No, I'm wondering where he is myself.'

'Does that mean he's due in?'

'Yes. And normally he's very reliable. Maybe he's ill.'

'Ill?' Milla said worriedly.

'Won't be serious. And he always rings in when he's ill. Can I give him a message?'

'Er . . . no, thank you.' Milla's thoughts were racing. She didn't have much time left. 'I know this might sound strange, but could you please give me his phone number?'

The Spanish girl looked at her, amused. 'Many people ask for that. But I'm not allowed to give it to tourists.'

Milla nodded, disappointed. Leandro seemed to be very popular with women. She imagined he'd exploited that a good few times. Poor Diana. How could she be so stupid as to imagine that he was interested in her?

Then she heard his lovely, dark voice behind her and turned around. 'Hello, back in my café again?' It felt to Milla that his dark eyes saw straight through her.

The young waitress grinned at her slyly and went to serve a young couple.

For a moment, Milla forgot what she was going to say. Then she drew in a deep, steadying breath. 'I'm here on business.' In her mind, she added, *Don't get your hopes up, mate.*

'On business? Do you want to sell me your shop after all?'

Milla hesitated. 'Let's say I can imagine it under certain conditions.'

'Which are?'

'Spend a day with me on the beach.'

He looked at her nonplussed, then smiled. Milla bit her lip. Had she really said that? Quickly, she added, 'I mean, of course . . . we could combine business with a nice time. I've not seen a lot of the island, and I'm sure you know a few lovely spots.'

Leandro was still smiling. 'Of course. My favourite haunts.' His darkly penetrating gaze hadn't left her face.

Milla stared back for as long as she could, then she blinked.

Leandro stopped the waitress who was just passing. 'Franca, I'll be off and won't be back before tonight, I think.'

Tonight, Milla thought, her heart beating faster. If he was planning to spend so much time with her, it had to mean something. Or not?

It probably only meant that he was keen on her shop. That was all.

Nervously, she followed him out onto the street. Leandro pointed to his scooter, parked at the corner. A scooter like Johann's, all those years ago . . .

'I always carry a second helmet. The beach I'd like to show you isn't really accessible by car.'

'Okay,' Milla replied, trying to sound cool. In reality, though, she was a little scared. Her mother had told her time and again how dangerous scooters were. 'Don't tempt fate, Milla,' she had said.

Should I really do this? she wondered. Of course she must. How else could she work out her feelings? She put on the helmet with difficulty – it was tight and squashed her curls. Clearly, Diana had a smaller head than her.

Leandro looked at her through the visor of his own helmet. 'Alright? Does the helmet fit?'

'Perfectly,' Milla lied, even though it felt like her head was being squeezed in a vice.

Leandro smiled, mounted and turned around to Milla, who tried not to show her fear. She climbed on behind him but wasn't sure what to do with her hands. Should she put her arms around him? He was so close to her now, his scent all around her.

'Put your arms around me, Milla.' His voice was suddenly very gentle. And he had called her by her name. Had he sensed her confusion?

'If I have to,' she said, doing as he suggested. But she doubted he heard it as he had already started the scooter and shot off, and soon they were driving through Palma's old town. Despite her initial fear, Milla found the feel of the wind in her face as the streets sped past liberating.

'Where are we going?' she called, but the engine noise was too loud. It didn't really matter, anyway.

Leandro was a confident driver. They passed the Gothic cathedral La Seu at some point, and she recognised the Parc de la Mar, and then they were on the road leading out of the city.

Milla closed her eyes and, clinging on to Leandro tightly, enjoyed the feeling of the wind enveloping her body as if in a tender embrace.

When she opened her eyes again, they were following a bigger road. Leandro drove fast, but Milla liked it; she felt safe with him. They carried on for about an hour until they reached Portocolom, where Leandro stopped at a petrol station by a roundabout, turned around and asked Milla whether she was alright.

'You're only asking me now?' She nodded smilingly.

Leandro grinned back and drove off again until they reached a mansion, Son Forteza. At the iron gates to the drive he stopped and gestured to her to get off. Milla lowered her arms and climbed down stiffly, feeling as if she had been sitting on a horse for ten hours. She took off her helmet. *I probably look dreadful*, she thought and quickly gave her curls a shake.

'You wanted to see a very special place, and that's what I'm going to show you.'

'Where are we going?'

'To the Cala Varques. It's a small bay, only seventy metres long, but magical.' He looked at her as if he had described her.

When Leandro took the helmet from her their fingers touched. Milla felt his warm, soft skin and a tingling in her stomach. What was going on? Why did she feel like this?

Leandro clipped the helmets on to the scooter, opened the iron gates a little and slipped through. 'Come on.' His dark eyes were challenging.

'Is it allowed?'

He shrugged, looking amused, and she followed him through a pine forest. They were silent as they walked but Milla felt at ease with him; no words were necessary.

At last they reached the fine white sand of the Cala Varques. The beautiful little bay was surrounded by lush green trees and shrubs. There was no bar and only a few tourists were walking by the water, while others were sitting under a tree looking out to sea. They could have driven to the main house in her car, Milla thought. Had he wanted the close embrace on his scooter?

'Do you like it?'

'Very much!' Milla exclaimed. The sun was amazingly warm for February and Leandro took off his shirt and walked towards the water. Soon he took off his trainers too and threw them on to the sand. *He certainly knows how to impress a woman*, Milla thought, suddenly feeling intimidated by him. Pushing down her nerves, she followed him, her eyes fixed to his tanned, muscular back. She thought of her own white skin, which never got enough sun in wintertime Berlin. But Paul had always said he liked her pale skin. Paul! Oh, God, Paul! What was she doing here?

'Are you coming, Milla?' Leandro rolled up his jeans and walked into the surf, looking towards the horizon, at the glittering waves.

'Yes.' She followed him as if under his spell, and stood beside him, shading her eyes from the sun.

'I love this island,' he said quietly. 'I was born here, my family is from here, it's my home.'

'You're a lucky man. Until a few days ago I didn't even know that my family was from here. My mother always claimed we were from Andalusia. For some reason she didn't want me to know the truth. That we have Jewish ancestry.'

'Why not?'

'She wanted to protect me.'

He looked at her with his beautiful dark eyes. 'I've never experienced any problems.'

Milla looked at him. 'You too . . . ?' Why hadn't it occurred to her? But what difference did it make? Nowadays it didn't matter any more. Or did it?

With a smile he waded back to the beach, spread his shirt on the sand for her and lay down next to it.

What a gentleman! Milla smiled, took her denim jacket off and sat down.

'About fifteen years ago,' Leandro started, 'there was a poll on the island, and some locals actually said that they would never marry a *xueta*. Some even said they didn't want to be friends with a *xueta*. Fifteen years ago!'

'Really?'

'Yes, but as I said, I've never experienced anything like that. My family was harassed, but that was a long time ago.'

He looked over at her, and Milla couldn't help getting lost in his dark gaze. *Please don't*, she caught herself thinking, *please don't take my hand. Please do.* 'I would always honour your grandmother's shop,' she heard him say. 'If you sell it to me.'

What? Was he being serious? Had he only had her shop in mind all the time? Was that all? Milla felt like a fool. He wanted her shop, but he wouldn't get it!

'Ah, you would honour it, would you?' Her voice was cracking. 'But Grandmother wanted me to keep the shop, for whatever reason.'

'Maybe sentimentality? She was a woman quite preoccupied with her past.'

Milla took a deep breath and decided that, now things were clear between them, she should at least sound him out. 'How well did you know her?'

Leandro hesitated and dug his feet into the sand. 'Quite well,' was his short answer.

Milla was alerted. Why this brief response? 'Do you happen to know why she didn't contact me earlier? Has she ever mentioned my mother?'

Leandro nodded and seemed to think about his answer. 'She once told me with tears in her eyes that she was missing her daughter very much. And her granddaughter. That was probably six months before her death.'

Milla swallowed hard and imagined a lonely old woman who would have liked to get to know her granddaughter. She was flooded by a feeling of compassion and yearning. Why had her grandmother not tried to find her earlier? Or had she tried, and Sarah had prevented a reunion?

The sea sparkled, a seagull above them shrieked. 'Did she say anything else? Every detail could be important.'

Milla held her breath, but Leandro regretfully shook his head. 'I only know that, as she got older, she was very sorry about her relationship with her daughter. That's all. Ah, yes, once she said that it was all her fault.'

'Her fault?' Abbigail had used the same words in her letter. What had she meant? Confused, Milla looked out to sea. 'Can we go now?' she asked abruptly.

Leandro looked at her, surprised. 'I wanted to show you a few more of my favourite spots on the island.'

'What for?' She felt a stab in her heart.

'What for?' His smile charmed her again. 'Because you asked me to.' He caught her glance, and his dark eyes sparkled. Was he flirting with her now? Milla felt as though she were on a roller-coaster. He always seemed to look at her so passionately – or did he simply look at every woman like that?

Milla turned away from him and looked out to sea again. A couple was walking hand in hand along the water. They looked at each other lovingly and then kissed.

'I'd rather go,' Milla breathed. She was shocked at the strength of her longing for Leandro. What did this mean for her and Paul? How could she have forgotten him so easily? The man she had wanted to marry until a few days ago? Confused and unsettled, Milla got to her feet.

Leandro got up too, but instead of picking up his things, he took off his jeans, exposing his tight underwear. Overwhelmed, Milla stared at his well-shaped legs, but before she could say a word, Leandro ran into the water, which was probably cold at this time of the year.

'You're crazy!' she called after him.

He turned around, laughing, and called, 'Yes! Sometimes one has to do crazy things.' Then he headed into the waves and disappeared in the surf.

Against her will, Milla was impressed, and stared at the point in the water where he had disappeared. After a few seconds he emerged again. Spluttering and laughing, he waved her in. *No way!* Milla thought. But then she remembered the young Abbigail who was so much more courageous than her, and without further ado she stripped off her yellow top, unbuttoned her jeans, and ran into the lapping waves in her underwear. Oh, God, it was cold! Her heart nearly stopped, but the water felt wonderfully energising. How long since she had last felt this carefree? She felt as if a weight had lifted from her shoulders. Leandro was watching her admiringly and Milla laughed, dipping under the water before emerging again, spluttering.

Leandro swam towards her. 'Oh, how I love the sea,' he whispered.

'Me too.'

Milla closed her eyes and let herself be carried by the waves.

'You know, you look quite a bit like your grandmother.'

She opened her eyes, laughing. 'Is that a compliment or do I need to use more anti-wrinkle cream?'

His smile emphasised his white, even teeth. 'No, that's not necessary. You probably look like Señora Fuster did in her twenties.'

'Ha! How would you know?' The two smiled at each other. Suddenly, Milla felt cold. What was she doing? If Paul could see her now! Shocked by this thought, she turned around and swam back to the beach. Leandro let her go. She could see from the corner of her eye that he was looking at her admiringly as she walked back to her clothes in her wet underwear. Feeling exposed, she quickly pulled on her top, then tried the jeans, but they clung awkwardly to her wet skin.

Leandro came over, grinning at her awkward attempts to get dressed. Milla examined him covertly from beneath her lashes. The guy was very good-looking – tanned, muscular, slim. Paul, with all his fitness training, looked more athletic, but Milla liked Leandro's slender, graceful figure.

'Can you please drive me back to Palma? I'm cold, and my mother is waiting for me.' She had to get away from here as quickly as possible.

They walked back to the scooter in silence, and Milla thought again of what Bescha Baum had told her about Abbi's day on the beach with Johann. Some people say that history repeats itself, but was that also true for love stories? Abbi, just like Milla, had tried to deny her feelings, to suppress her racing heart; the passion. But there was a big difference. Abbigail in the fifties didn't have a choice. She wasn't allowed to follow her great love. But Milla could. Bescha's voice had cracked with emotion when she told Milla of Abbi's desperate sadness.

Chapter Eight

Mallorca 1956

Abbi was standing in her shop, polishing the tiled counter, her mind on the wonderful day at the beach with Johann, their passionate kiss. Remembering it, her cheeks flushed.

Suddenly, she spotted Pomade on the other side of the street. He seemed to be waiting for something or somebody. Abbi froze. Several times Pomade's fingers went through his greasy hair; he chewed gum and blew a bubble. His ear was covered by a bandage.

Frantically, Abby contemplated what to do. She felt safe inside her shop because there was a constant stream of customers, but what if he wasn't put off by that? The memory of the dark alleyway flashed through her mind – his face contorted with pain when she had nearly torn off his ear. She wished Johann would come, but he was still at work, and they weren't meeting again until tomorrow.

A plump German tourist in a tight pencil skirt was examining the oven gloves with the embroidered 'Palma de Mallorca' and 'Sun Island' logos.

'Can I help you?' Abbi asked in her by now passable German. At the same time she sent a quick glance out to Pomade, who was greeting two of his mates.

'Oh, thank you. How lovely! I need a present for my auntie. This is very fine embroidery.'

'Yes, I had it done locally.'

'Very nice. But a bit expensive.'

'Do you think so? It's handmade.'

'Yes, yes, but no. My husband, he's not for spending money.' She turned to leave.

'No!' Abbi exclaimed in panic. 'Please don't go!'

The corpulent woman looked at her, astonished. 'What? Why not?'

'Because . . . I might have something a bit cheaper for you.'

Desperately, Abbi looked around for something less expensive, which was difficult because the oven gloves were among the lower-priced items.

'Ah, I have these painted shells.'

'Shells?' The woman frowned. 'You can find them on the beach and paint them yourself.'

She turned around to go, and Abbi froze. Pomade was standing in front of the shop window now, staring at her, his expression full of hatred.

'But not shells like these. I mean, they're special . . .' Abbi stammered anxiously. 'If you hold these . . . I mean, when you hold them to your ear you hear the sea . . .' Abbi stared, transfixed, at Pomade's bandaged ear.

The woman laughed slightly mockingly. 'Yes, yes, my husband keeps saying that. But I'm not buying anything.'

The doorbell rang as she left. Pomade grinned at her. He waited until the woman had left the shop, nodded towards his minions and walked towards the door. Abbi took her chance, ran out after the woman and called, 'Sorry! Can I ask you something?' He wouldn't attack her in broad daylight in the middle of the street.

Pomade stopped, looking frustrated. The woman turned around. 'What? Yes.'

Abbi was in a panic. 'Where in Germany do you come from?'

The woman gave her an astonished look. 'From Hanover. Why?'

'Er . . . I'm learning German and was wondering whether you were speaking with a dialect?'

'No. In Hanover people speak High German.'

'Ah . . .' From the corner of her eye Abbi saw that Pomade, who was closing in on her, had stopped to light a cigarette.

'Well, have a nice day,' the woman said, and walked on.

Abbi's heart sank. She felt paralysed and her whole body was shaking. 'Just a moment, please,' she called in sheer desperation. 'I'm going the same way as you.' Without locking her shop, she ran after the woman.

The German lady was getting more and more irritated with Abbi now, suspecting she was going to con her in some way, and hurried on, holding on to her handbag with both hands. Abbi followed her at the same speed. Meanwhile, Pomade and his friends followed behind, their heels clicking loudly on the cobblestones.

What can I do? Abbi's thoughts were racing, but her brain seemed to be in lockdown. Then her body failed her, and she stumbled and fell. The woman stopped for a moment, but when she saw the nice young men helping Abbi up, she hurried on.

Pomade grabbed Abbi by the arm and squinted at her. His grip on her arm was painful. Involuntarily, she stared at the bandage.

'Eh, you little Jewish whore. Do you really think you can rip off my ear and get away with it?'

'No . . . I mean, it was self-defence.'

'I'll tell you what self-defence is.'

'If you hurt me, I'll call the police.'

Some passers-by were watching the scene and Pomade realised that this was the wrong time and place for his revenge.

'I've got plenty of time, you little whore. But I tell you one thing: stop behaving like a prostitute. You're an insult to all Mallorquin women.'

'And you to all Mallorquin men.'

His mates laughed. Pomade didn't like it.

'You belong in the house, in the kitchen, like all other women. But you would rather cheat people out of their money and whore around with a German!'

Some American tourists stopped but they didn't understand Spanish and thought it was a family dispute. Abbi looked at them helplessly, but the tourists didn't seem keen on getting involved. They walked on, studying their map, and left Abbi behind with her attackers.

'Let me go!' Abbi hissed, nearly beside herself with fear.

But Pomade didn't loosen his grip. 'You just wait!' he growled. 'And one more thing: if you don't toe the line soon, your parents will have to pay for it as well.'

Then he let her go.

Abbi stared at him, aghast. 'My parents? Leave my parents out of this!'

Pomade grinned, sucked hard on his cigarette and blew the smoke into Abbi's face. 'Oh no. They must learn to control their daughter. They haven't brought you up right. To rip off people's ears! You don't do things like that. But what can you expect from *xuetes*, such primitive people!' Then he spat in her face.

Abbi winced and began to tremble, barely managing to stay upright.

'Do you understand? Think of your poor parents, Jewish hussy. If you don't toe the line soon, they will suffer for it.'

'Leave my parents out of it,' Abbi pleaded, but her voice was failing her. 'They're honourable people, unlike you. They've never done anything wrong.'

'Do they know that you're fucking that German?'

Abbi bit her tongue and decided she was better off keeping silent now. Her tendency to answer back had caused too many problems before. She hadn't slept with Johann. But even if she had . . . this guy was behaving as if he was jealous, she suddenly realised.

Pomade came another step towards her and she smelled his awful breath again. 'You either finish with this German, or your parents will pay for it.'

After another hard stare that even Abbi recognised as jealous, he turned around, waved his mates over and strode down the street as though he were a cowboy in a Western, leaving Abbi feeling as if she were about to faint. She was shattered. Her parents, her wonderful parents! They had suffered so much already! No, he mustn't hurt them, but how could she prevent it?

In a trance, Abbi went back to the shop she'd abandoned and saw that somebody had exploited the situation. A few cups were missing, the till was open, and all the cash gone.

Abbi sank onto a chair behind the counter, covered her face with her hands and started to cry. She had to finish with Johann, rip him out of her heart. That was the only way to save herself and her beloved parents.

'Abbi, darling, is that you?' Esther called from the kitchen when Abbi came home at midday.

'Yes, Mother. What's for lunch?' Abbi was still shaking but trying hard to control it. Something smelt delicious.

'Go and wash your hands, my child,' Esther called. 'It's nearly ready.'

'Okay,' Abby whispered, and went to the bathroom. She stared at her face in the mirror. She loved Johann so much, but could one ever compare the love for a man with the love for your parents? How could this bastard ask this of her? Which feeling was more important? She loved her parents above everything. But she loved Johann too! Just as he loved her.

Men come and go, Eli had once said. If that was the case, Abbi had to finish with him; hurt him, destroy him. Just as she would be destroying herself. She knew for certain that she would never again open her heart to a man, never again love like this. Her eyes in the mirror looked sunken and sad. If only she had followed tradition and found a man within her own community, she would never have got into this conflict. Her left eyelid twitched; she looked pale, her lips thin.

'Abbi, where are you? Papa is at the table. The pie is getting cold.'

Forcing herself to wipe all expression from her face, Abbi took a deep breath.

'Abbi?' This time it was the stern, deep voice of her father that called out to her. She had always been a Daddy's girl and admired her tall, intelligent father. Rachel's death had changed everything, and the love between Noah and his now only daughter had deepened. It was a wonderful bond between the two of them which Pomade seemed determined to destroy. It mustn't happen. Abbi clenched her fists for a moment, then loosened them. With a forced smile she went to the kitchen and praised her mother's pie. She thought about her cookbook, and how from now on she always wanted to be a good daughter.

'You're looking pale, child. Is everything okay?' Noah looked at her searchingly.

Abbi smiled briefly. 'No, father. I . . . had a very bad dream last night and was just thinking about it.'

'What was it about?' her mother asked anxiously.

'Oh . . . let's not talk about it or I might dream it again tonight.' Abbi noticed her parents exchange a worried glance. She poked the food on her plate, but without any appetite.

'Is something wrong, Abbi?' her mother asked. That she had to lie to her angel of a mother hurt Abbi deeply. 'Nothing, Mum . . . I've argued with Eli. She's never on time, you know.' Her parents knew that Abbi didn't like this trait in her friend and that the two girls sometimes argued about it.

Silently, they continued eating, until her father cleared his throat. 'I had a letter this morning at my office.' He hesitated. 'Someone called me a greedy *xueta* who cheats everybody.'

Abbi was shocked. Had Pomade started his revenge campaign? 'Who was the letter from?' she whispered.

Esther too looked at her husband worriedly and wrung her small hands until they went pale. Noah shrugged. 'People who would never say their names. People who sow hatred without a reason. Because they are afraid – of the future, of life.'

Abbi heard the bitterness in her father's voice and understood it. It hurt to be treated as an outsider time and again without ever doing anything to deserve it. It hurt.

Her father was a kind and good man. He had represented people who didn't have a penny; helped them to get justice without payment. Where did it come from, this deep-seated hatred of their kind? Abbi knew their history over the centuries and knew that any kind of fanaticism and narrow-mindedness was utterly alien to her family.

'Abbigail?' Her father interrupted her thoughts. 'Are you not meeting up with Eli so often any more? After your argument?' He looked at her searchingly. Of course he had guessed that all these apparent meetings with Eli were really a cover-up for meeting a man.

Abbi hesitated, then looked at him openly. 'No, Father. I'll be at home more often from now on.'

Her parents exchanged a relieved look and continued their meal. Abbi's mouth was as dry as powder at the thought that she would now lose Johann, the love of her life. That she had to say goodbye to him for ever. Her hands began to tremble. Quickly, she put them on her knees, out of sight. But she had to do it. She didn't have a choice.

Chapter Nine

Mallorca 2016

'Paul! What are you doing here?' Milla exclaimed, and stared at her fiancé, who was sitting in a worn armchair in the lobby of her hostel. As usual, he was looking at his iPhone. Smiling, he adjusted his black baseball cap.

'Surprise, *chica*!' Then he looked at her questioningly. 'Why is your hair wet?'

'I've been swimming. In the sea.'

'In February?'

'Lots of things are possible on Mallorca,' she quickly retorted, her guilt nearly choking her.

A minute ago she had been riding with Leandro on his scooter. A minute ago she'd had her arms wrapped tightly around his body. Fortunately, Paul hadn't seen how they had said goodbye to each other outside. Or had he?

Paul smiled at her expectantly. Milla knew she should be overjoyed and run towards her good-looking fiancé and kiss him. But after her time with Leandro that felt wrong and false. 'Well, you don't seem to be very happy to see me,' Paul commented drily. She saw how disappointed he was and felt sorry for him.

'Of course I'm glad to see you.' But Milla didn't feel very happy. She only felt pity for him. Was that the right response when your beloved surprises you with a visit? Would Abbi have greeted Johann in this way if they hadn't seen each other for a few days? Milla hoped that her heart was playing tricks on her. She loved Paul, didn't she?

Suddenly, she felt uncertain, and the old jealousy came to the fore. Why had Paul come here? Was he cheating on her with Corinne? Did he want to confess something?

Paul stepped towards her, his arms outstretched. Milla hesitated for another second, but then he was holding her in his strong arms and she leaned on his broad shoulder, which had so often given her strength. He smelt lovely, and she dug her nose into the nape of his neck, as she always did.

'Where have you been all this time?' Paul whispered longingly. 'I arrived earlier this morning and had planned to kiss you awake. Normally, you never get up that early.'

'Yes, but since I've come here . . . everything is different.'

'What's different?'

She gently stepped back from his embrace. 'Well . . . everything. I mean . . . why have you come?' Had Corinne dumped him? Another silly, jealous thought. She pushed it away. 'You could have told me. I could have picked you up at the airport.'

'But it wouldn't have been a surprise.'

'You know I don't like surprises.'

'Ah . . .' He'd obviously forgotten.

'The meeting with the client was postponed, and I was keen to see Mallorca and you. Come on, let's go out into the sunshine, to a nice little café. It's really warm here for February.'

Milla nodded and reluctantly followed him. Should she tell him of her jealous thoughts?

Once they had their ice creams, Milla gathered all her new-found courage. They were sitting in the Ca'n Joan de s'Aigo, a *chocolatería* in Palma's old quarter that had been there for more than three hundred years. As usual, it was crowded with tourists, all enjoying the sunshine and the delicious almond ice cream – a speciality of the café.

'Paul, I have to ask you something.' It had just come out, even though she had planned to ask him quite casually and not so bluntly.

'What is it?' He smiled at her.

'Are you having an affair with Corinne? If you are, I want to know.'

'*What?*' He looked stunned. 'Of course not. What makes you think that?'

'Well . . . because . . .' God, she felt like a fool. But then again . . . why not ask him directly? He had been behaving strangely recently. And that text message . . .

'I happened to read a text message on your mobile. Not on purpose. Your phone was lying there, and I thought it was mine . . .'

He frowned. 'You read my texts? Milla, I don't like that at all.'

'I know.' She swallowed the last lump of her ice cream, which made her throat hurt. 'I don't like it either. But you were always away, at strange times . . .'

Paul looked at her as if he couldn't believe what she was saying. Then he understood. 'Ah, that.'

'*Ah, that.* Is that all you have to say?' Milla folded her arms.

'Milla.' Paul leaned over and put his hands on her knees; his warm fingers calmed her. 'Well, it looks like I'll have to tell you then.'

She was right! Milla was shocked, and her heart sank. He was cheating on her, and now it was coming out.

'Yes, I've met up with Corinne a few times. You're right.' A tourist at the next table laughed shrilly, as if mocking Milla for her naivety. But the woman was laughing at her friend, who joined in. 'But only to . . .' Paul continued: 'because I had planned a surprise for you.'

'Another surprise?' Milla said quietly.

Paul smiled and nodded. 'But I'm sure you won't mind. It's for our wedding.'

'I'm not as naive as I was a few days ago!' Milla exclaimed. She didn't believe him. Or should she?

Paul looked peeved. 'Okay, if you don't trust me, which I find really hard to take, I'll tell you.' He took a deep breath and, after watching a pigeon picking up some crumbs for a moment, said, 'I'm learning to play the guitar. Corinne is teaching me.'

'Guitar?'

'You told me once that you really like men who play the guitar.'

Milla's face flushed a deep red. She felt utterly foolish. 'Yes . . . I did say that.' Should she believe him?

He looked at her thoughtfully. 'And you? Can I trust you?'

'What do you mean?'

'Where have you been all day?'

Milla hesitated. 'On the beach.'

'And who with? Your mother is in her hotel. I sent her a text message asking where you were.'

Milla swallowed and found it difficult to answer. 'Alone.'

'Alone? You?'

Paul knew her very well. She normally hated going out alone – sitting in a restaurant or a bar on her own. It always made her feel like the most lonely, deserted person on the planet; as if nobody liked her. Total nonsense, she knew, but that's how she felt. Feverishly, she looked for an excuse.

'Well, Mum didn't want to come, and, being on such a wonderful island, I didn't want to spend the whole afternoon doing more research on my family. I feel as though I'm a bit stuck with it.' She distracted Paul by telling him the latest developments – about the visit to the posh old people's home and the former Nazi officer Franz-Xaver Schuller, who in his old age found himself living under the same roof as the Jewish woman Bescha Baum . . . And how, apparently, her grandmother had had a hand in it: courageous, rebellious Abbigail. In the fifties, she must have a been a real force to be reckoned with.

But she didn't mention a word about Leandro.

Paul listened to her with fascination and asked her lots of questions. When she had finished, he took her hand and, fiddling with her engagement ring, he said, 'There's really no need to be jealous, Milla, okay? Is everything between us alright again?'

Milla nodded with a sigh, even though nothing was alright. But the story about the wedding surprise was typical of Paul. She stared at the silver ring she herself had made with so much love. How happy she'd been when Paul proposed last December. It had come as a big surprise and was quite unconventional. They had been on a winter walk at the Lietzensee. In high spirits, they had thrown snowballs at each other and messed around. Laughingly, Milla had finally thrown herself into the snow. Paul had dropped down next to her, looked at her and, out of the blue, asked, 'Milla, what do you think, shall we get married?'

It had sounded like a crazy idea, another game that Paul had just invented, but Milla had been longing to have her own family, a sense of belonging and stability, and immediately and happily said yes.

'Really?' he'd said uncertainly.

'Yesyesyes.' Pulling her woolly hat over her ears, she saw herself in a white wedding dress. That same evening, when she met up with Tine, she had told her the news.

Tine had hugged her friend exuberantly and, fuelled by a few glasses of Aperol Spritz and lots of chocolate, the friends had started a guest list and discussed possible venues. It was a lovely evening; everything had felt light-hearted and carefree. Later, though, Paul told her he thought their plans were too elaborate and he just wanted a party. Milla had given in, like so often in their relationship.

And now? Was Milla abandoning her plan to have a family with Paul because of a romantic Mallorquin man who was actually in a relationship? Although she felt that Leandro's heart wasn't in it; if that weren't the case, he wouldn't have looked at her like that. It wasn't the usual clumsy German flattery but the very special southern one: passionate and extremely seductive. But then again, he wanted her shop, so perhaps he was just using his charm – of which he had plenty – to make sure he got it.

Her grandmother had led her to him. Or had fate determined it? Milla sighed. What had her grandmother done to her? How different her life felt since she'd received Abbi's letter. How much more exciting. Milla suddenly realised that her life in Berlin with Paul was very predictable. Berlin – the sexy, cool city – had a lot to offer, and their life there was good. But at some point their evenings had become repetitive. Sooner or later, all day-to-day life becomes repetitive, Milla told herself. It would be the same with Leandro, in the sunshine, on this dream island.

'Hey, darling, what are you thinking? You're very quiet.'

'Me?' Milla felt caught out and looked at Paul. 'I'm just wondering why on earth Grandmother has left me her shop.' She tried to distract him.

'Perhaps she wanted to leave her only granddaughter a bit of money. When you sell, you'll have a lot of dosh. Do you want to know what I've been thinking?'

'No, what is it?'

'We could buy a loft in the city centre. That would be cool.'

Milla was speechless.

'Well, it would be your loft. I could pay you rent.' Paul smiled. 'Imagine, we could have roof terrace parties.'

A loft in the centre? Was Paul thinking about children at all? Should they grow up in the middle of the polluted city centre? Were they actually dreaming the same dream? Milla swallowed; the mere thought made her choke. 'The shop isn't worth that much money. And you know how much properties in the centre cost. Crazy amounts. Apart from that, I still haven't decided whether to sell or not.'

Paul frowned, but seemed to decide not to press the issue any further. He ordered two colas without asking Milla, as usual – in the past, she had always accepted it. But now something inside her balked. She wanted to make her own decisions.

'Sorry,' she called after the waiter in Spanish. 'I won't have a cola; I'll have a *café solo*.' The waiter nodded and went inside.

Paul looked at her with surprise, took her hand and squeezed it quite firmly. For a while they sat silently in the spring sunshine. Then Milla received a text message from her mother. *Where are you? Need to talk to you. In my hotel.*

Milla was suddenly on the alert. Did her mother want to tell her something about her family's secret after all? She gestured to the waiter who was bringing the *café solo* and the cola that she wanted to pay straight away. After she had settled the bill, she drank her coffee, rose to her feet and looked at Paul impatiently.

Paul quickly finished his cola and got up as well. 'Hey, chill! Why would she tell you something important right now, when she's kept schtum all these years?'

'Maybe the sun has melted away all her coldness?' Milla tried to joke. 'I haven't got a clue.'

Hand in hand, they walked through the picturesque streets of old Palma towards her mother's hotel.

Sarah was sitting in the lobby having a lemonade with mint leaves when they arrived.

'There you are.' She frowned, then looked at Paul. 'Paul, nice to see you.'

'I'm very happy to see you too, dear mother-in-law,' Paul joked easily. He knew how to handle Milla's aloof mother, who even smiled a little.

'What's the matter, Mum?' Milla asked. They sat down, but Sarah didn't seem inclined to talk in front of Paul.

'Shall I leave you two lovelies alone? I find it a bit cool in here anyway,' he suggested, sensing the mood.

'Would that be alright?' Milla smiled at him gratefully.

'Of course, babe.' He kissed her on the forehead and went outside.

Milla looked at her mother expectantly. Sarah looked as though she was bursting with news.

'Milla, Johann is still alive!'

'What?'

'He returned from Germany a few weeks ago. To his *finca* in the west of the island.'

Milla stared at her mother, who seemed just as excited as she suddenly was.

'Johann!' Milla mumbled, quite overwhelmed. Her thoughts were all over the place, but she tried to stay calm. Johann would be able to tell them about the love affair between him and Abbigail and how it had ended. Maybe they would finally solve her grandmother's secret. 'How did you find out?' Milla asked.

'Sheer coincidence. Or fate – call it what you like. I met Eli at the bakers at the Plaza de España. I just heard the sales lady calling her by her name, her *xueta* name, Pomar. Eli Pomar. Then I looked at her more closely and saw it. A birthmark on her neck. You might not have noticed it, but I knew it even when I was a little girl. I didn't like it and thought she was a witch. But I recognised the young, beautiful Eli: the nose, the mouth . . . not everything had changed.'

'We have to see him. Did Eli tell you where his *finca* is?' Milla asked eagerly.

'No. She had written it down on a piece of paper at home and also gave me her number. She'd wondered why you never rung her. Then she realised that she might not have given you the right number.' Sarah dug out a piece of paper with a phone number written in a spidery hand and showed it to her daughter. Milla compared it with the number Eli had given her, and, yes, two figures were the wrong way round. So that was why she hadn't been able to get through to the woman.

Milla took out her mobile and dialled the new number. It rang several times and she was just giving up hope of an answer when there was a click and Eli's croaky voice came over the line. 'Hola?'

'Hola! It's Milla Stendal, Abbigail's granddaughter. I haven't been able to contact you because the number was wrong. My mother has just told me that you've met.'

'Yes, that's right.

'Tell me, Eli, could you please give me the address of Johann's *finca*?' Milla held her breath.

'Wait.' There was a rustling sound at the other end. 'It's Finca El Molino near Santa Maria. I haven't got the exact address. His name is Johann König. But you can ask around. I myself have no contact with him.' Eli sounded strangely cool.

'Thank you very much, Eli. I'm so grateful to you. Ah, another thing. Why didn't you tell me straight away that Johann was still alive?'

Eli hesitated. 'Because I only heard it after we'd met, from a woman in the Jewish community, when I mentioned Abbigail. Not that I've been doing this a lot,' she added quietly.

Milla wondered for a moment whether to ask why Eli and Abbigail had been out of touch for such a long time, what had happened – and many more questions. But she decided to address that face to face with Eli, not on the phone.

'I have to stop, my soup is boiling over,' Eli said.

'Okay. Well, thank you very much! We must meet again while I'm here. How about tomorrow? I have so many questions. When would you have time?' But Eli didn't answer; she had ended the call.

Paul came back into the lobby, looking questioningly at Milla. 'I just wanted to say . . . do you need more time? I'm very hungry, and if this is taking longer . . . I'll go for dinner on my own.'

Smiling and excited, Milla got up. 'Guess what! The love of Grandmother's life, Johann, is alive! He's returned to the island. I would love to go and see him. Will you come with us?'

'Okay, in that case I'll just get a burger. That man must be well over ninety?'

Milla smiled happily, until she realised that her mother was wringing her hands and looking agitated.

'Mum, are you coming?'

'Why should I?' There she was again, her cool, detached mother.

Milla was surprised. 'Because he loved Grandmother and can give us an explanation that might help us?'

'Please go without me. I . . . can't.'

Milla tried to hide her disappointment. Her mother's response felt like a real setback and once again she felt as though Sarah wasn't on her side.

'I'll come with you,' Paul said. She smiled at him gratefully, suddenly glad he was here. Taking his hand, they left the hotel.

Once outside, he put his arm around her shoulder and pressed her close to him. 'Never mind,' he said consolingly.

At that moment Leandro, holding some shopping bags, came around the corner towards them. He froze and looked at Milla as if she had betrayed him. His dark eyes seemed even darker now, or was it caused by the shadows cast by the houses around them as the sun sank lower in the sky?

Paul had noticed Leandro's glance and looked at Milla questioningly. 'Do you know the guy? Why is he looking at you like that?'

'Er . . . he's the owner of the shop next to Grandmother's. He's the one who made the offer the solicitor mentioned.'

'Ah. But why is he looking at you so strangely?'

'How should I know?' Milla evaded. 'Maybe because I'm still not sure whether I want to sell or not.' Her heart was beating faster. Those eyes! The passionate look. Leandro clearly had deeper feelings for her, and it looked as if he had only realised this the moment he saw her in Paul's arms.

'Ah, I see. You're finding it difficult to decide again,' Paul joked, and pressed her closer to him. 'Does he speak German?' he whispered in her ear, and then adjusted his baseball cap as if to prepare for a duel.

'Yes, lots of people here do.'

Paul squared his shoulders and, his arm around Milla, walked towards Leandro, who seemed rooted to the spot. '*Hola*, I'm Milla's fiancé,' he introduced himself, closely watching Leandro's face.

At the word *fiancé* Leandro seemed to wince slightly. But he controlled himself quickly and beamed at Paul. '*Hola*, and I'm Leandro.' Then he looked at Milla. 'Milla, can we meet up for a glass of wine later?'

Milla's stomach tightened. Her face fell, and she looked at Paul, alarmed. Leandro kept on smiling. 'That's the way we discuss the sale of a property on Mallorca.'

Milla breathed a sigh of relief. The bastard had done it on purpose. 'Maybe,' she replied. 'We have a few things to do. If we're not back too late, I'll call you.'

'Have you got his number?' Paul asked immediately.

'No,' Milla said with a forced neutral voice. 'But he can give it to me now.'

Smilingly, Leandro gave her a card, looking straight into her eyes and touching her hand as if accidentally. Then he turned and walked off.

Milla's heart was jumping wildly after the touch, and she could only hope that Paul hadn't noticed. 'Let's go. I can't wait to see this Johann and hear what he might have to tell us.'

With Paul in the passenger seat, the two of them drove inland in the little hire car; the atmosphere between them felt tense. According to the satnav, the journey to Santa Maria would take about twenty-five minutes and, as she drove, Milla, lost in thought, hummed along to 'Can't Remember to Forget You' by Shakira and Rihanna, which was playing on the radio. What did Johann still remember of the time with Abbigail? Often elderly people recall the old times especially clearly. She hoped that would be the case with him.

Palm trees, flowering shrubs, barren rock formations and light pink almond blossoms flashed past outside. 'The island is very beautiful at this time of the year,' Paul commented admiringly. For him, this trip inland was nothing more than a holiday excursion. But for Milla it meant so much more.

'Not only at the time of the almond blossom,' she replied, realising that she had fallen hopelessly in love with this island, the home of her family. 'There are quite a few beautiful beaches, and I'm determined to discover many more of them.'

Paul smiled at her and stroked her neck. 'Do you know what? We can come here for our honeymoon.' Being short of funds, they hadn't booked anything yet.

Milla froze slightly and only nodded. Paul looked at her sideways and kept on massaging her neck. 'You're quite tense, you know.'

'That's not surprising. I'm soon going to meet my grandmother's true love. Who knows what he'll have to tell us about their lives?'

Silently, they drove on for a while, then Milla turned off towards the picturesque little town of Santa Maria, situated on a plain at the foot of the Tramuntana mountains – Milla had Googled it.

Suddenly, she felt sick. 'Can we buy some water here? And ask the way to his *finca*?'

'Okay, sweetie.'

They entered the town and saw numerous colourful signs advertising leather goods and free drinks in the *bodegas*.

'Shall we stop for a while in one of the *bodegas*?' asked Paul.

'You want a break when we're nearly there?' Milla didn't understand him. How could he suggest something like that?

Paul simply shrugged, let the window down and hung his arm out.

Milla parked the car next to a small grocery store and went in to get mineral water. At the till, she asked the young Mallorquin woman in Spanish, 'Could you please tell me the way to the Finca El Molino somewhere around here?'

'No. But ask in the restaurant Can Calet. They know every place around here.' With a smile, she pointed the place out to Milla.

'Okay. Thank you.' She went back into the sunshine and to Paul. 'Any luck?'

'Nothing. We're to ask in the restaurant over there.' She opened the bottle with a hiss and took a few gulps. Her knees were trembling. Why was she so nervous about the imminent meeting with this old man? Would he know why Abbigail had been so distant to her own daughter? Milla was sure that he would. Her stomach was telling her.

They found the restaurant and Milla went in and nervously asked for directions. The older waitress did indeed know the *finca* and its owner, who had only recently come back to Mallorca. 'He probably wants to die here,' she added, and called him a bitter old fool. Milla asked why but didn't get an answer.

Confused, Milla steered the car over a track higher up into the mountains. Paul sensed her nervousness and stroked her arm. Almond trees in full blossom were stretching into the distance. How beautiful it looked: all imaginable shades of white and pink. It wasn't surprising that every year the almond blossom brought thousands of tourists flocking to the island. It looked like paradise.

Finally, they saw an old wooden sign with the words *El Molino*.

'Found it!' Paul exclaimed, looking encouragingly at Milla, whose stomach was clenched with nerves. They got out and walked hand in hand towards the building. The door opened suddenly, and a very old, white-haired man came out holding a stick. He didn't seem to see his visitors but to hear them. He lifted his head. 'Who's there?' he asked grumpily in Spanish.

'*Guten Tag*. I'm Milla Stendal,' Milla answered nervously. What could she say next? The man seemed nearly blind.

'And who else?'

'This is Paul. Paul Bergmann.'

'I'm Milla's fiancé,' Paul added.

'Are you tourists?' He didn't seem to like tourists.

Milla hesitated for a moment and then answered: 'No, not really. My family – well, my mother's family is from the island, and I . . . I've come to do a bit of research about it.'

The old man frowned. Milla could tell that Johann had once been an attractive man. His hair was white now, his eyes watery but still dark blue. Wrinkles marked his fine, weathered features.

Milla glanced nervously at Paul, then continued. 'The almond trees around here are most beautiful. And the scent . . .' she began carefully.

The old man nodded and looked a bit friendlier. 'I've missed the scent of the almond blossom so much.' Then he smiled bitterly. 'There are hardly any almond trees in Germany.'

Milla wasn't sure what to say next, so she continued along the same theme. 'Why are there so many almond trees on Mallorca?'

Now the old man smiled and seemed more at ease. 'Oh, there's a lovely old story. Would you like to hear it?'

'Yes, please.'

Clinging to his stick, he began. 'An Arab prince is supposed to have planted them. He wanted to please his favourite wife in the harem because the princess came from Granada, and she missed the snow in her hometown. She only became happy again when the white almond blossoms were falling from the new trees like snowflakes.'

Milla and Paul were enchanted. Milla took in a deep breath of the sweet scent.

'But that's not the reason you came here, I'm guessing?' The old man broke the silence.

'No.' Milla swallowed and then took courage. 'You are Johann König?'

The old man looked startled. 'How do you know?'

Milla looked helplessly at Paul, and he intervened, first clearing his throat. 'Milla learned only a few days ago that her family on her mother's side is from Mallorca. She received a letter from her grandmother, Abbigail Fuster.'

Milla saw that the man winced at the sound of the name, as if someone had hit him.

Paul whispered to Milla, 'Maybe he doesn't know she's died?'

Milla nodded and stayed silent.

'Abbi?' Johann whispered. He swayed slightly and clung more tightly to the handle of his stick. 'I never heard from her again. Only that she married the other one.' Again, he swayed.

Milla rushed towards him and, holding his arm, spotted a bench on the nearby terrace. 'Shall we sit down?'

He was trembling slightly. Milla led him to the seat and helped him to sit down. It was true then, what her mother had said. Her grandfather was someone else.

'How is she?' he finally managed to say. 'Was she happy with that man? I've never dared to ask after her. Please don't get me wrong, I don't bear her a grudge. But I'd like to see her again so much.'

Paul and Milla exchanged a horrified glance. He didn't know. But he understood their silence. 'Is she in heaven? I've waited too long. Is she still alive?'

'I'm afraid not. She died last week. I'm so sorry.'

He turned his face towards the blue sky, even though he probably couldn't see very much. Milla and Paul followed his gaze. A single, soft white cloud hovered peacefully right above them. Milla stilled for a moment, unaccountably moved by the sight of it.

'Leave me alone, please.' Johann's voice cracked, revealing his pain. 'Please go.'

Paul nodded to Milla, who got up.

'Can we come another time?' Milla dared to ask. 'I won't be here for much longer and would love to ask you some . . .'

But Johann was wiping a tear from his eyes and shooed them away with a gesture. He didn't answer her request and instead shouted loudly, 'Go away! Go away, I said!'

Deeply troubled, Milla walked back to the car, Paul following closely behind. She turned around one more time and then got in.

'Well, sweetie?' asked Paul.

Sadly, Milla shook her head. 'No, we haven't come a single step closer.'

'Let's give him some space for now and come back and see him tomorrow. He's only just heard that the love of his life has died.'

Paul was right, and it was good to have him by her side. How silly of her to have doubted that even for one moment. Or was it? Her thoughts involuntarily drifted to Leandro. Should she go for a glass of wine with him later? It was only early evening now, so she had time, but if she met him, wouldn't she open a Pandora's box? Or had she done that already today at the beach? Milla sighed and started the car, the tyres screeching as she reversed out of the drive and put her foot down hard on the accelerator.

Surprisingly, it was Paul who made up her mind for her. As they drove back to Palma, he said, 'Now you've got time to meet up with this Leandro for a glass of wine to discuss the sale of the shop after all.'

'What? No.'

'Why not? You haven't got much time, Milla. It's clear the guy is keen on you, but I don't have to worry about that, do I?'

'No.' The answer had come a bit too quickly. How had Paul noticed that Leandro was keen on her?

'Milla, it's a best-case scenario if that guy buys your shop. He seems a nice, easy-going type.'

'That's only superficial,' Milla couldn't help saying. 'Apart from that . . . I don't want to sell the shop.'

'Milla, we live in Berlin! What are you thinking?'

Milla exhaled. Maybe Paul was only thinking about the loft. 'Grandmother didn't want me to sell the shop. I have to respect that . . .'

'You have to do what is best for *you*. And that's why you are going to meet him for a drink later.'

'And you think that's in my best interests?'

'Yes, exactly.'

Hope he's not wrong here, Milla thought. *But, well . . . if he insisted . . .*

Because there was only a single bed in Milla's room and her hostel was fully booked, Paul was staying in a hostel a few streets away. So, after dropping him off, Milla went back to her own room and called Leandro, who suggested they meet at a small wine and tapas bar called Cucu, not far from the Plaza Major on the steps towards the Rambla.

She changed quickly, choosing a red dress – the last item she had thrown into her suitcase – freshened up her make-up and combed her frizzy curls. When she was finished, she stared at herself in the bathroom mirror. What was she doing? Milla's stomach was tight. What if tonight she really fell for Leandro? The mere thought shocked her. Paul had come to Mallorca because he'd sensed that she was not a hundred per cent committed to their relationship any more. She believed his story with Corinne and the guitar lessons. It sounded absurd, but typical of Paul. Only he could have an idea like that, and she loved him for it. She tried not to think of the wedding in a few weeks' time because she had to find out first which of the two men was the right one for her – just as her grandmother had advised in her letter.

Milla applied red lipstick and took one last look in the mirror. The red dress made her look seductive. But maybe too seductive?

She shook her head, setting her dark curls bouncing. Two men were interested in her; she had never experienced anything like this before. For once, she should simply enjoy life!

'Thank you, Grandmother,' Milla whispered with a smile, 'you have turned me into a confident and desirable woman!'

◆　◆　◆

She spotted Leandro straight away among the hordes of tourists. He was leaning on his Vespa in front of the Cucu bar, hands in his pockets and his dark hair tousled. His expression when he saw her seemed full of regret. But why? Was something bothering him? Or was she mistaken?

Milla stepped towards him in her high-heeled red sandals, wishing she had worn her flats instead.

'*Hola!*' she greeted him, her voice cracking slightly.

'*Hola*. You look . . . ravishing.' He spoke quietly – almost a whisper.

'Thank you.' She nearly added *You too*. His hair, framing his face, was slightly wet from the shower and his black shirt was open at the neck, showing the top of his smooth, tanned torso. His scent was intoxicating. Milla cleared her throat and tried to concentrate. 'So this is Cucu?'

Leandro's eyes caressed her body as he answered. 'It's one of the few bars where I don't know the owner.'

Milla's mood sank as they walked into the bar. He didn't want to be seen with her. What was that about? If he was hoping for a secret affair, he'd be disappointed!

It was a modern place, but cosy. On the counter was a row of large white plates with various delicious-looking tapas. Milla sat down on the bench with her back to the wall, Leandro opposite. His eyes never left her. 'They have Spanish and Italian tapas here, some with spicy *puttanone* paste, or *sobrasada*.'

'Sounds great.'

'Until the waiter comes, we can talk about Grandmother's shop,' she suggested coolly. 'Because that's what you're after, isn't it?'

'That's not what I wanted to talk to you about.'

'What is it then?'

Leandro looked at her searchingly. 'Diana is a wonderful woman. She's intelligent, beautiful, witty . . .'

'Why are you telling me this?' Milla interrupted him, hurt.

But Leandro continued regardless. 'But still, I will split up with her.'

Milla looked at him, speechless. Was he joking? Why did he want to split up with Diana?

The waiter appeared then and asked, 'Can I get you any drinks?'

'A shot of something. Anything.'

The man looked at Leandro questioningly, as if he had to give permission.

'*Cerveza* for me, please.' The waiter nodded and went away. 'The tapas are self-service,' Leandro said to Milla, as if they had just been talking about the weather.

Milla stared at him, still stunned. She bit her lower lip and cleared her throat. 'Why?' she asked. 'I mean, why do you want to separate from this amazing woman?' She had an inkling now and hoped it would be true, but she found it hard to believe. Diana was definitely better looking and certainly more amusing, funnier, cleverer . . . Or so she imagined.

Leandro looked at her intensely. 'It is . . . because I know you now, Milla. That's the only reason. You.'

Milla's heart skipped a beat, and it felt as though her blood stopped flowing.

Leandro's dark eyes were sparkling as he said, 'I know you're together with Paul and that you want to get married. But I also know now that I cannot marry Diana. It wouldn't be fair. And there's nothing worse than standing in front of the altar with a bad feeling in your chest.'

A bad feeling – Milla knew it too well. What was this man doing to her and Paul? Wasn't she in the same position? Didn't she have the same fear of being in church and not being able to say 'I will' from the bottom of her heart? Of making such a mistake? The mistake of her life?'

Leandro watched her closely, clearly noticing the goose bumps on her naked arms, all the tiny hairs standing up. Abruptly, he rose and went to the counter, returning a short time later with two plates of tapas.

Milla's stomach was one big knot. The prawn, tomato and mozzarella kebabs looked delicious. But she couldn't take a single bite. Leandro took a prawn and ate it. Chewing, he looked at her.

'You can't do it. You can't simply walk off.'

'I have to.'

'But you mustn't. Poor Diana.'

'I know. I haven't planned it, believe me . . . I can't help it.'

'Of course you can help it!' countered Milla angrily. She didn't want to be responsible for another woman's unhappiness. There was hardly anything worse than being dumped by your boyfriend. But then, her inner voice said, *It would be worse to be with someone who didn't love you one hundred per cent.*

The waiter appeared with the shot Milla had ordered. She had no idea what it was but took the glass, threw the drink back in one go and handed the glass back to the surprised waiter. Once again, he looked at Leandro questioningly. Leandro nodded, and the man disappeared.

The alcohol set Milla's throat on fire; her head was humming. *Why?* she asked herself again. *She's prettier than me, certainly more educated, funnier* . . . But she knew the answer: Leandro had fallen in love with her, Milla. For whatever reason.

And had she fallen in love with him? Suddenly, she felt as if a weight had descended onto her shoulders. Did Leandro expect her to split up with Paul? No. *Under no circumstances*, a rebellious voice inside her protested. It wasn't that easy. She and Paul, they were special; had always been special. With Paul, things were easy – at least, they had been so far. He wanted children with her.

And Leandro? She hardly knew him. And he didn't know her. How could he change his whole life because of a strong feeling? Were all Mallorquins like that? Passionate and impetuous? Germans were not like that. Milla wasn't like that. Or was she? She was, after all, half Mallorquin, and it felt as if these two halves of her soul were struggling against each other. Milla sighed.

Leandro smiled at her apologetically, as if he had guessed her thoughts. 'You don't have to say anything now.'

'I won't.'

'I just wanted you to know.'

'Okay.' Milla took one of the kebabs, pulled off a piece of mozzarella and ate it. Then she took a prawn. And a tomato. She cleared the plate. But she couldn't put off saying something for much longer. They had to talk. Small talk wasn't her thing, but she couldn't talk to him about her feelings. She could, though, ask him about Johann. 'Did my grandmother ever mention a man called Johann? Johann König?'

Leandro smiled. 'Of course. She often talked about Johann.'

'Really?' She was annoyed that she hadn't asked Leandro earlier. 'What did she say?'

Leandro waited a bit, making her more impatient. 'You're like her. Intelligent and beautiful.'

'Don't detract. This is important to me.'

He understood and gave in. 'She told me that he was the love of her life. That she always felt inexplicably close to him.' Leandro's expression was intense and set the butterflies fluttering in Milla's stomach, as if the vibration of his voice was resounding inside her. 'When she talked about him, her features softened, her voice became tender.'

Chapter Ten

Mallorca 1956

Abbi's heart ached whenever she thought about Johann, which seemed to be all the time. And this morning she had woken up with a headache, because today was the day she had to do it. She had to rip Johann's heart out – and her own as well.

During the day she compared every man who came into her shop with Johann. At one point she was serving a German tourist from Bavaria and was having some difficulty understanding his dialect. She tried hard to remain friendly, even though, as far as she could make out, he was complaining about the food on the island. No schnitzel anywhere on Mallorca!

'But surely you have come here to try the Spanish cuisine?' she asked diplomatically.

The Bavarian man gave her an irritated look and mumbled that he had come here for a holiday. And holidays meant good food. Schnitzel and dumplings.

Abbi couldn't help shaking her head – this man was so different from Johann – but she refrained from making a sarcastic comment, as she normally would.

The man continued to complain. 'Do you know any Bavarian restaurants at all?'

'Beg your pardon?'

'A Bavarian restaurant. In Palma?'

'In Palma?' she repeated, aghast. She couldn't hold back any more. All her anger about the injustices of life, Pomade, the feeling of having been backed into a corner, erupted. 'Why do you travel at all if you don't want to experience new things? Why don't you just stay in Bavaria?'

The man looked at her indignantly, mumbled something and left. The doorbell clattered.

At last she was alone. Abbi put her hands to her head and tugged at her hair. She couldn't do it. She loved Johann too much. But her fear of Pomade and his minions attacking her beloved parents was growing with each minute. She knew that Pomade was capable of anything.

Maybe she had made it worse by injuring his ear? Someone like him wouldn't let that go unpunished. Abbi was surprised that nothing had happened so far. She felt as though she were sitting on a time bomb that was ticking louder every minute.

She looked at the clock: it was nearly closing time. She would meet Johann, as usual, by the fountain. Her heart, her whole body was yearning for him, for his kisses. The seconds and minutes crawled by.

Johann had suggested they go to the beach again. Abbi assumed he didn't want to wait any longer. They had been meeting in secret for weeks now but still hadn't made love. Johann had given her time – time she had needed after Pomade's attack.

Eli had teased her about the fact that she was still a virgin, even though she now had a boyfriend. That was typical of her, but Abbi had brushed it aside. She needed time, and Johann had given it to her. Which was exactly what made him so special to her.

But today, she thought, should be the day. She knew he had planned a romantic picnic with her on the beach at their special place. Abbi had heard a lot about the 'first time' but couldn't really imagine it. Making love was not acceptable before you were married, that much she knew. Eli didn't care about that rule, though. She wanted to enjoy life, and somehow, she had managed to keep her parents in the dark. In the end, she would have to marry one of those men, but so far she had avoided it. Abbi's previous boyfriends either hadn't wanted to wait or had been totally unsuitable anyway, so she'd never had to make the decision. Only Johann had turned her into a liar who betrayed her own parents.

Finally, the clock showed seven. Abbi looked in the mirror next to the coat hooks, put on a white cardigan over her red dress with the full skirt and the petticoat and gave her unruly hair a quick brush. She looked pale. Quickly, she put on some bright red lipstick, but it made her look even paler and, unhappy with her looks and very nervous, she locked the door and stepped outside. From the right, a large, looming figure approached. Startled, Abbi cried out. But it wasn't Pomade; it was her father in his black coat. He greeted her with a worried and searching look. 'Abbi, what are you frightened of?'

'Oh, Father, nothing . . . I was just lost in thought.'

'And what are you preoccupied with all the time? Do you really think I wouldn't notice?' He scrutinised her. Some neighbours were passing and stared at them curiously.

'Nothing, Father, I'm just tired.'

'And why are you tired?' She felt that he wouldn't let her off the hook. 'Abbigail?' He now looked at her even more seriously. 'I know that you won't bring shame on us.'

Abbi was hurt and lowered her gaze. Did he know something? Did he sense it? Of course he did. He was an intelligent man. Abbi had admired him for that since she was a little girl.

'You know that your mother has suffered enough, that she has a weak heart, and after what happened to Rachel . . .'

'Yes, Father!' Abbi interrupted him. Her hard tone surprised her, and she apologised quietly. 'I'm sorry, but I'm Abbigail. And I'm alive. And don't worry, Father, I won't bring shame on the family. I love you far too much for that.'

Noah looked at his daughter with relief and love. Abbi had to try hard not to cry, because there was no going back now. Abbigail and Johann. Johann and Abbigail – from tomorrow, that would be the past.

'My child, tell me where you are going so done up?' He made a dismissive gesture towards her red dress and red lips.

Abbi swallowed and wiped some of the lipstick off, desperately looking for an excuse. 'Father . . . you don't have to worry. I have to do something. And I promise that everything will be alright.' Noah gave her a sceptical look, and she quickly changed the subject. 'Did you know I'm planning to publish a cookbook of mother's recipes with almonds? And the ones from Grandmother and Great-grandmother . . .'

'A cookbook?' She had managed to distract Noah; or maybe it was just because he didn't want to hear the truth.

'Yes. You know a few publishers, don't you?'

'Yes, I do.'

'I wanted to ask you to show it to them. But only when I've finished it.' She tried to smile at him.

Noah, looking tired now, stroked her hair as if she was a little girl and nodded. 'I'll ask around. It would make your mother very proud of you.'

Abbi smiled and confirmed. 'Yes, I think so too.'

'Come home before dark. Will you promise me?'

'Promise.'

With one last intense look, Noah turned and walked away. Abbi looked after him, worried. How much he had aged in the last few months! She had hardly noticed it until now. And her mother's heart? Had it deteriorated? Abbi felt a pang of conscience; over the last few weeks her thoughts had revolved entirely around Johann and herself and she had completely ignored how her parents worried, but that would change now. It had to!

When she arrived at the fountain and saw Johann – her Johann – she forgot all her good intentions immediately. He smiled at her, his blue eyes warm and full of love and his blond hair shining in the evening sun, and she knew she couldn't hurt this man.

'Abbi, at last!' He pulled her into his arms and twirled her around. 'I have the most wonderful news.'

'What is it?' she replied, but she had barely got the words out when his lips were on hers and he was kissing her so tenderly and passionately that all she could do was close her eyes and enjoy it. Then he let her go and looked deep into her eyes. 'Later. Come on, we'll go to our beach. I've brought some nice things for our picnic.'

'Some nice things? Again enough to feed a whole army?' she teased him.

They went to his scooter and Abbi put her arms around his muscular torso and closed her eyes. She loved being so close to him, but this would be the last journey she would take with him. No, that would be the journey back from the beach. But then everything would be over. He would drop her at home, and she would never see him again. Never again smell him, feel him, kiss him.

She had forgotten her scarf so the wind tousled her hair, but she didn't care. She just wanted to imprint the feeling of her body tightly pressed against his back onto her memory, so she would never forget.

Unusually for this time of day, their beach was busy. A group of German tourists was celebrating something. They had food, were drinking cava, and one of them had a guitar. The young men were wearing skinny jeans, and one of them sported a black leather jacket, while the girls wore petticoats, like Abbi. The one in the black leather jacket played some rock 'n' roll music and imitated Elvis Presley's hip movements while the group danced.

Johann and Abbi listened for a while, hand in hand. Abbi liked the music, and Johann told her the song was 'Heartbreak Hotel' by Elvis Presley. Abbi looked at Johann and knew she could never, ever let him go. Never.

'Let's go to a different beach, where we can be more alone,' Johann whispered to her when the song ended. But Abbi was suddenly gripped by a fear that she might give in once they were alone and shook her head vehemently. In a deserted bay, she would simply melt in his arms like butter in the sun. Maybe she *should* make love with him so she could at least be close to him once – and he would be her first. But she doubted she would be tough enough to end the relationship after that. So she preferred to stay near the tourists so she could tell him it was over. But it seemed impossible now.

'No, let's go over there, to the rocks, where we can hear the music.'

The expression on Johann's face told her that he had had other plans, but he was a sensitive man and didn't try to dissuade her. Together, they went over to the rocks, spread out the blanket, and unpacked the food. Like last time, there was a variety of Mallorquin delicacies: figs in brandy; sun-dried tomatoes in olive oil; *salchichón torrens*, a Mallorquin hard sausage; goat's cheese with herbs; and *ensaïmades*, a Spanish pastry.

'You're crazy.' Abbi smiled sadly.

'What's the matter?'

'Nothing.'

'Please tell me.'

Shaken, she looked into his beautiful blue eyes, took his face between her hands and kissed him on the lips, tenderly at first, then more and more passionately. It would have to be their last kiss, and it turned into a kiss of desperation.

Johann seemed to sense it and leaned back after a few minutes, breathing heavily. He stared at her suspiciously and then shook his head imploringly. 'Abbi, you can't do this! Why? You're a modern woman!'

'I have to!' she cried out.

A few of the tourists looked over curiously, but then let them be and carried on dancing. The one in the black leather jacket started another Elvis song, imitating the deep baritone, '*I want you, I need you, I love you!*' and Abbi began to cry. Tears rolled down her cheeks like little dew drops, unstoppable, one after the other.

'But . . .'

'No but. We can't be together. Ever.' Angrily, she wiped away her tears.

'I know that,' he said quietly.

She looked at him, astonished. 'You know it?'

'Of course. I've heard about the hostilities against the *xuetes*. But Abbi, it's the twentieth century. We live in a modern society.'

'I know. But it's different here. Society doesn't tolerate us. My parents would pay for it.'

'Abbi, I love you.' He took her hand, but Abbi withdrew it. She remained quiet now, wringing her hands, staring out to the sea, where the sun had begun to sink. The small waves seemed to foam up and get wilder.

'Abbi. Let's go to Germany.'

'Are you mad?'

'Sorry. What about mainland Spain?

'No.' It was hard to remain firm. 'I won't leave my parents.'

Johann clawed his hands through his blond hair. 'Abbi, we have a unique love. You're very special. I'll never meet another woman like you. Do you want to destroy my life, and yours too?'

'Yes, to save my parents' lives.' Abruptly, she got up.

Johann got up as well, grabbed her hand and looked her in the eyes. 'Abbi, do you love me?'

She hesitated but had to say it. '. . . Obviously, not enough.'

Johann winced as if she'd hit him and staggered backwards.

The guitarist sang words of love, of romance, of hope.

'Can you take me home now? I promised my father I'd be back early.' Having said what she needed to say, Abbi's strength had deserted her and she felt as limp as a ragdoll.

The song's lyrics played mockingly in the background. Maybe people were more enlightened in Germany, but she lived on Mallorca. This was her world. She was afraid of Pomade, of his revenge, and fearful for her parents.

'Please,' she whispered. Then she knelt and packed all the lovely food into Johann's bag. Neither of them had eaten a morsel.

Johann seemed at a complete loss. Abbi folded the blanket, took the bag and looked at him challengingly. Finally, Johann seemed to sense that she meant it, that today he would be unable to change her mind. He knew how stubborn she could be.

His shoulders sagged as he relented. 'Okay, I'll take you home. Tomorrow is another day.'

She nodded silently but was already fearful of tomorrow, of her own weakness. The thought of the loneliness to come overwhelmed her and suddenly she burst out, 'I want to be with you properly. Just once.'

Johann stared at her and understood. 'Come with me.' He took her hand and led her to the scooter. Together they drove to a beautiful, lonely cove. There was an early moon in the sky and it was cool now, but they didn't care.

Without a word, they stood close together and looked into each other's eyes in desperation. Then they kissed, tenderly at first, then more and more passionately. They ripped off each other's

clothes and made love full of emotion, passion and deep anguish.
And it was uniquely wonderful.

◆ ◆ ◆

The ride back into Palma seemed endless. Feeling frozen and lifeless, Abbi clung to Johann's body and breathed in his scent, trying
to store the memory in her brain fore ver. But she knew it was
impossible.

He dropped her, as usual, at the corner so her parents or neighbours wouldn't see them together and looked at her, his eyes full
of misery. Abbi hesitated, wanting to kiss him one more time. It
felt like a magnetic pull, but this time she managed to hold back.
'*Adiós.*'

Now he sounded hurt. 'Is that all you can say?'

'Yes,' she whispered, turned around and left her life behind.

Chapter Eleven

'Oh, no!' Milla exclaimed involuntarily, deeply moved. 'And what happened afterwards? Did they ever meet again?' She looked at Leandro; his eyes sparkled in the light of the candle on their table, and she suddenly realised that this could happen to her with this man too. That she couldn't remain firm. She had to go.

'I'm sorry, I don't know,' he said quietly.

Feeling overwhelmed, Milla abruptly got up. 'I . . . have to go.'

'Please stay!' Leandro took her hand, but Milla withdrew it.

'I'm sorry, it is . . . late, and my grandmother's story has deeply troubled me. And . . . Paul is waiting for me in the hostel,' she lied.

'I understand.' Leandro pushed his hands through his hair, his expression sad. Then he got up too and waved to the waiter to settle the bill.

'This is on me.' Milla turned around.

'Definitely not.'

'Yes, please.'

'No! Maybe it's a custom in Germany to let women pay the bill, but not on Mallorca.' His voice sounded passionate and determined.

Milla put away her purse. 'Okay, then. Thank you.'

Leandro settled the bill and led her outside. His hand just about touched her lower back. Milla had to admit she liked this subtle, chivalrous gesture. German men had a lot to learn and it felt good to be treated like a desirable woman. For Paul, she was more like a mate to hang out and do things with. And she liked that too. But the way Leandro treated her was new to her. Maybe it was just the novelty that made his touch feel so enticing, but she knew she wanted to find out more.

As she drove through the town with Leandro, she tried to concentrate on what she had just heard. Her grandmother had tried to finish the relationship with the love of her life. Had she succeeded? Johann would be able to tell her how the story ended. She planned to go and see him again at his *finca* the next day.

Paul was indeed waiting in her room when Milla returned to her hostel, tired and confused. She was startled when she saw him lying on her narrow bed.

He greeted her with a smile. 'Aren't you happy to see me?'

'Oh, yes.' Milla took off her high heels. Her feet were hurting. Did he regret having sent her into Leandro's arms?

'So, what happened?'

'Well, it was okay. I'll tell you tomorrow. You won't believe how tired I am.'

'Just briefly, then. Have you settled on a price?'

Milla turned around and looked at him, taken aback. For a moment she didn't know what he was talking about. He was like a stranger to her.

'The sale of the shop?'

Now Milla understood and shrugged. 'Quite honestly . . . not really.'

Paul scrutinised her. Did he sense she was still thinking of Leandro? 'Milla, I thought you were settling that today, so tomorrow we could explore the island a bit more.'

'Paul . . . I'm sorry. I can't talk about that now. We'd planned to go and see Johann again, hadn't we? And I haven't made much progress with Mum either. She had opened up a bit, but now the shutters are down again, and I really want to know why. Do you understand? I mean, time's running out, and I can hardly keep up with everything, and you want to go on an excursion with me?'

He looked at her, hurt, but pulled himself together and made an inviting gesture to share the narrow bed with him. Milla hesitated, because she felt as if she had just cheated on him. At least, her heart had.

Embarrassed, she shook her head. 'Please don't be cross with me. I just want to go to bed and sleep. I'm so tired.' She rubbed her painful feet. Why did women walk in these things?

'You know what, Milla? Just let the past be the past.'

'What? You can't mean that. After everything I've learned about my family? I can't.'

'And why not?'

'Because . . . I need to know . . . why I'm the way I am. It hurts me that my mum and I have such a bad relationship. You know that. My chronic gastritis – it's all because of that.'

'Because of her?'

'Yes. She's always distant and cool with me; without love. And I find all that hard, and I'm sure that's why my stomach gets so bad.' Did Paul ever understand anything?

Paul sat up and looked at her sadly. 'You can be like that too.'

Startled, she turned around to him. 'Loveless? Me?'

He nodded and took a deep breath. 'The main thing is that you don't treat our children like she treated you.' He looked at her expectantly to see how she would react to this.

Milla swallowed and nodded. 'Exactly . . . I don't want that to happen. And that's why I have to find out why she's like that.'

'I understand.'

At last! She smiled at him apologetically and went to the bathroom, closed the door, undressed and got in the shower. The hot water calmed her.

Her thoughts were swirling around like leaves in an autumn storm. Did she really still want children with Paul? She thought of Leandro, who wanted to split up with Diana because of her. Would he really do it? She thought of her upcoming wedding and all the things still to be organised. Of her grandmother, who had lived in a time when a woman of Jewish descent on Mallorca was not allowed to marry whomever she loved, even in the middle of the twentieth century. She herself had the choice. But she couldn't decide. It was a crazy world.

When she came out of the bathroom, a towel wrapped around her naked body, Paul had gone.

The bar, Cristal, had been around since the thirties, as Milla learned when she Googled the place. It must have seen many guests come and go. Nazi officers had their coffee here, presumably many *xuetes* too, as well as tourists and locals. While Milla was waiting for her mother in the morning sun, she chatted with the manager who had taken over the place in 1955. Maybe her grandmother had been a customer here, sipping her *café solo*? Milla didn't hold out much hope that the manager might remember Abbi, but one never knew. Mallorca was an island, and in those days everyone knew everyone. So while she waited for her mother to join her for breakfast she asked him. But much to Milla's disappointment, he couldn't recall Abbigail.

Lost in thought, Milla sipped her coffee and stared absently out of the window. She soon spotted her mother in the distance. Sarah looked elegant, as always, wearing a colourful dress with a flowery pattern, red lipstick, sandals. But she seemed rushed and flustered.

'Where is Paul?' she asked, out of breath.

'Good morning, Mum. He's coming later. He sleeps in the hostel nearby, remember.'

Sarah lifted an eyebrow. 'Have you two had a row?'

'No,' Milla replied quickly. 'There was no room at my place.' Or had they indeed had a row? Yes, somehow, but not really. You couldn't have a proper argument with Paul because he was always willing to compromise.

Sarah sat down. 'A cappuccino, please,' she said to the waiter. 'Without cocoa!'

'Si, Señora.'

'And now, don't keep me in suspense. How was it with this Johann? Did he tell you anything?'

'Not much, unfortunately. He hadn't heard that Grandmother had died. When he decided to return to the island, he must have thought she was still alive. After we told him she'd died, he nearly collapsed.'

'Oh, my God. What happened then?'

'Then he sent us away. Pretty harshly.'

'Pretty harshly?' Sarah repeated, then stayed silent for a while. 'And you let him just send you away? Without any further questions?'

'Yes. Because I sensed it was the wrong moment. I think deep down Johann is a very nice man, but he just needed some time. Also, he's blind.'

'Blind?'

'Nearly blind, it seems. Which is very sad, because around his *finca* are so many almond trees, and with the white and pink blossoms the place was a dream. I'll go and see him again. I wonder whether he returned to Mallorca to see Grandmother one more time before he died. Maybe he wanted to die closer to her. That says it all, doesn't it? That he has loved her all his life.'

'Oh, yes, darling. True. Very tragic.' How long had it been since Sarah had called her darling? The word filled Milla with warmth.

'How terrible, after all these years, to hear that the love of your life has died.' Sarah was obviously overcome by a wave of empathy.

Her mother's words gave Milla hope. At last, her heart is truly opening up, she thought. But then her mother's next words startled her.

'Milla, you'll have to sort out your chaotic feelings before it's too late. Meet up with this Leandro as soon as possible. You have to find out what is happening between the two of you.'

Milla was shocked her mother seemed to know so much about what she was thinking. Had she always been like this, or was it this trip that had made her pay more attention to Milla's feelings? Whatever it was, she was grateful for the motherly advice – the first ever.

'But how, Mum? I mean, how do I find out just by meeting him?'

'You'll know, I'm sure.' She put her hand on Milla's and stroked it gently. How rarely she had done that!

The waiter brought the cappuccino.

'Thank you.' Sarah withdrew her hand and said pensively, 'It's strange that this Johann hadn't looked for my mother years earlier.'

'Yes, I've asked myself that too. And you have no idea why?'

'No. If I did, I'd tell you. Johann must have known there was this other man in Abbigail's life – my father, Baruch. That's probably the reason he never dared approach her again.'

Milla agreed. 'Johann seemed like a very decent man.'

Her mother had never talked much about her father and always responded very curtly whenever Milla asked about the grandfather she'd never met. Milla only knew that he had been a distant figure but had always treated Sarah fairly and often reproached Abbigail for not treating her more kindly. So as far as Milla could tell, her grandfather was unlikely to be the reason that Abbigail had changed so dramatically from the happy, open young woman to a cool and distant mother. Maybe . . . A thought suddenly occurred to her. Maybe Baruch was still alive and not dead, as Sarah had told her years ago?

Choosing her words carefully, Milla asked the question, conscious that she didn't want to damage the fragile bond she'd built with her mother.

Sarah shook her head, tears in her eyes. 'I'm sorry, darling. He really is dead. I know that might be hard for you to believe after the lie I told you about my mother, but it's the truth. I'm really, really sorry, Milla. I know how important the family is to you. For everybody. For me too. But by the time I left my mother was dead to me. It was all those little everyday hurts inflicted by a loveless and hard mother. Nothing major happened, but it was an accumulation – all the hurtful barbs and indifference had wounded me deeply over the years – and some of those wounds are still bleeding. Can you understand that?'

'I think I can understand it, Mum. More and more.' The two women smiled at each other.

'Don't you remember when we received the death notification card for my father? For a long time it was on our fridge in the kitchen, held there by the apple magnet.'

Milla remembered a card with a black border, and as a little girl she had imagined that her grandfather was trapped inside it. She never dared to unfold the card in case Grandfather fell out. At some point Sarah had thrown the card in the bin. 'It looks a bit faded now,' she had explained. Milla remembered how heartless she had found this gesture.

'Mum, before we go up to Johann's again, tell me more about Baruch.'

Sarah sighed. 'There's not much to tell. He was a *xueta*. That's why Abbigail married him. But she never loved him like she loved Johann. He wasn't important to her.' She took a deep breath. 'And for him, his work was more important than me. Like in so many other families.'

Milla felt sorry for her mother. What a childhood! Both parents incapable of loving their child.

At that moment Paul turned up in his baseball cap and sunglasses. He was rubbing his face and looked as though he hadn't slept very well.

'Good morning.' He kissed Milla briefly on the lips, smelling of toothpaste. He shook hands with Sarah as usual, and then sat down. 'One thing I know now. I'm too old for those hostel beds.'

'Was it that bad?'

'My back! A totally worn-out mattress. But never mind.' Then he turned serious. 'Milla, when are we off? I won't do the beach today; I'd rather come with you to see Johann.'

Milla winced and looked at her mother for help. How was she to sort out her feelings for Leandro when Paul was with them all day? 'That's very sweet of you, but it's not necessary,' she said carefully.

'I know I don't have to, but I'd like to. For you. When are we off?'

Sarah helped Milla out. 'Paul, Milla and I wanted to go to the beach later. Is it okay if we have a few hours just to ourselves?'

'What? Yes, of course. And you can go to Johann later in the afternoon. How about that?'

Milla nodded and gave her mother a grateful glance.

Sarah finished her cappuccino and got up. 'I'll get ready in the hotel; you have a nice breakfast. Will you pick me up, Milla?'

'Okay. See you later.'

Paul sat down next to her now, adjusted his baseball cap, then looked at her pleadingly and said, 'I've been thinking about our conversation, and I just wanted you to know that there is nothing going on with Corinne; never will be. Believe me. Not even if she was the only woman on the planet,' he joked. 'I only took guitar lessons with her to surprise you at our wedding. We get on okay, yes. But that's all. Am I not allowed to go for a coffee with another woman? Will that be a problem?'

'No, it's not that.' Milla knew that only a few days ago this had been a problem for her, but not now. Her problem was Leandro, and it was occupying all her thoughts.

'Or is it about this guy?' Paul asked.

Was he reading her mind? 'What guy?' She tried to buy some time.

'Well, this Leonard you went out with last night.'

'Leandro,' she corrected him.

'Well, Leandro. You are so different, Milla. On the phone, you already sounded strange. That's really why I flew out. And now I've sent you straight into his arms, haven't I? Has he conquered you with his Mallorquin allure?'

'You know very well that I'm completely immune to that,' Milla answered, upset. She watched a couple of pigeons picking up crumbs between the tables. Pigeons apparently mate for life. How do they manage to do that?

'Milla, hello?'

'Maybe . . . I'm a bit more preoccupied with myself?'

Paul smiled and pressed her hands. 'That would be a good thing.' He exhaled. 'I get the feeling that all the things you've dug up about your grandmother have triggered a lot in you.'

'Yes, you're right. She was a very brave woman and wanted to live her dreams. And I haven't even thought about what my dreams might be. We never think about that in day-to-day life. And we don't pursue them either.'

'That's changed now. You're totally right.' Paul looked at her lovingly. 'Please stay with me. Will you promise me?'

Milla stared at this good-looking man she was about to marry. For now, at least.

She hesitated. Then she heard the beep of a text message arriving, saw Leandro's name and grabbed her mobile so Paul wouldn't see. She clicked it on.

'What's happening now?' Paul sounded a bit peeved. 'Your mum?'

'Yes . . . sorry.' She read the message. Leandro was asking whether she had time to visit Palma's Jewish quarter with him – now. It was fate, for sure. She quickly texted her mother that she was meeting Leandro and would be in touch and suggested a meeting point to Leandro.

'Milla?'

Oh, my God. Paul! 'Sorry, it was my mum. She's ready and wants to go. Would it be okay for you to have breakfast on your own?' What on earth was she doing?

'Okay, I'm easy. The sun is shining, and this café seems quite cool.'

'Exactly. And you're cool too.' She smiled and kissed him briefly on the cheek, her heart beating fast. Yes, the sun was shining.

Leandro was walking so close to Milla she could breathe in the scent of his aftershave. Time and again he looked at her longingly.

'The old Jewish quarter in Palma is now practically invisible, but during the last few years they have put up signs with the old

Jewish street names and places. They have been inscribed on glazed tiles, according to tradition, and with old techniques.'

'How lovely! I never noticed them before.'

'When on holiday, you should always walk around with your eyes wide open.'

Milla laughed. 'Yes, that's true.' More quietly, she added, 'Particularly when this is more than a holiday destination for me.' They smiled at each other.

Leandro showed her various tiles with the place names and then took her to the Calle Monseñor Palmer, where, only a short distance from the port, a small Jewish community had been established in 1971, the first in Palma since 1435.

Milla tried to concentrate on what Leandro was telling her, not daring to ask about Diana. She looked around and wondered whether she might find out more about her grandmother here, even though Abbigail had never practised her faith, as Leandro had told her. But there had to be witnesses from that time; after all, a woman from here had told Eli that Johann was alive and had returned. Maybe the head of the Jewish community knew more?

'Are many of the *xuetes* now members of the community?' she asked.

'No. There are about thirty thousand *xuetes* on the island, but the community has only about a hundred members. Most of them have moved here from Turkey, Eastern Europe, Latin America, Morocco. Many *xuetes* don't want to return to the Jewish faith. Others are not interested, and still others have got used to Catholicism. But for those who would like to return, a rabbinical court has confirmed that it's possible. The *xuetes* have been officially recognised as Jews.'

Milla was very interested in what Leandro was telling her. It was her history; it concerned her family and herself. Leandro led her to a wrought-iron gate with two Stars of David in the Calle

Monseñor Palmer. He rang the bell, and the wooden door behind it was opened by an older man wearing a kippa. He ushered them in with a welcoming smile.

The rooms of the synagogue were filled with a warm light. Leandro explained that Milla had some questions, and the man with the kippa asked them to wait.

While they were waiting, Milla stared around in awe. Leandro stood so close to her that she could feel his breath. From the corner of her eye, she could tell he was looking at her searchingly.

'Milla, what's going on with you? Right now, here? Isn't it . . . mystical?'

She couldn't look at him; her hands were trembling. She pretended not to have understood him. 'I'm not a religious person. I don't feel anything.'

Somewhat disappointed, he turned as a man in his forties with a friendly face came towards them. This must be the head of the community. Milla explained what she wanted, but he shook his head regretfully.

'I'm sorry, but I'm not allowed to give out the names and phone numbers of our members. You do understand? I don't want to interrupt your prayers any longer.'

'Of course.' Frustrated, Milla thanked him for his time. What had she expected? Maybe Eli could give her the name of the woman who had told her that Johann was alive? Maybe that woman knew more about what had happened in the past? She had to follow every little clue, however tiny. Time was running out.

Milla took out her mobile and tried to ring Eli, but the old lady didn't answer. She was annoyed with herself. She should have arranged another meeting with her during the last phone call, but then Eli had ended it very quickly.

'Come on, let's go,' she said to Leandro.

They left the synagogue and Leandro showed her the so-called 'invisible' Jewish quarter – the Calle Major and Calle Menor in the old city.

The medieval buildings didn't exist any more, only the original course of the streets. There had been an old synagogue at the site of the Montesión church, and some of the stonework was still visible from the Calle Vent. The central street, Calle Menor, boasted numerous stores, and in the Calle Argenteria it was mostly jewellery shops, which, according to Leandro, were owned by *xuetes* to this day.

Leandro's charm and easy ways brought it all to life for Milla, and she felt as though she were back in the olden days. Leandro was so well educated and curious, and she couldn't help comparing him with Paul. Paul was interested in politics and history, but these days didn't read much more than the headlines on his phone apps. But he was well informed about sport, knew who had scored how many goals, which managers had been sacked, the league tables. That was his thing. Milla wasn't that keen. What Leandro had just told her, however, was not only fascinating, it moved her. She asked more and more questions and learned that in the seventeenth century the *xuetes* had been subjected to bloody persecution. Many of them had been executed, three burned alive.

Milla was shocked. 'Burned alive? How cruel people can be!'

Leandro nodded. 'And all under the pretext of some God's will.'

It was getting hotter, and the old city was bathed in beautiful sunlight. Had all those terrible things really happened on this lovely island?

'For more than a hundred years they exhibited the hair shirts of those poor souls in public to deter others. That's the reason the names of the fifteen executed people are still known. Fuster is one of them, Pico – my name – another. And only the descendants of

175

these executed people are called *xuetes*. None of the other forcibly converted Jews bear that name.'

'I see.' Milla was listening, wide-eyed.

'And those fifteen families were outlawed.'

Milla was aghast. 'Then I'm . . . also outlawed?'

'We both are.' He looked her straight in the eyes.

Milla turned away and whispered, 'Sometimes it's good not to have a faith.'

'Are you saying that you don't believe in anything?'

'No. Please don't try to convert me now.'

'Of course not. Come here.' He led her through a small alley-way. 'Over here there used to be a school,' he continued. 'Children of the *xuetes* have only been allowed public schooling since the end of the nineteenth century.'

'Unbelievable.'

'Exactly. But it brings it home how lucky we are to be alive today, whether on Mallorca or in Germany. How grateful we should be. We should be conscious of that every day.'

'You're so right.' Milla smiled at him and could no longer deny the spark between them.

Then his mobile rang. It was Diana, and Milla was brought back to earth with a thump. What was she doing? Leandro and Diana belonged together, and she and Paul did too. She understood from their talk that he hadn't split up with her yet.

'Of course. I'll call as soon as I can.' He tried to end the call. Milla noticed the tension in his face, his desperate glance at her, and felt an incredible longing for him. He put the phone away and looked at her, embarrassed and silent.

'I have to pick up my mother,' she said quietly. 'We're going to the beach, and maybe I can manage to meet up with Eli. I have a feeling she's avoiding me.'

'Maybe.' His hands went through his dark, glossy hair. 'I'll meet up with Diana later. I'm even more sure than last night.'

'Please don't do it,' she begged. 'Please.'

'I have to, Milla. I can't help it.'

She thanked him briefly but genuinely for the walk, kissed him on both cheeks, breathed in his scent then turned and rushed away.

◆ ◆ ◆

She arrived at her mother's hotel earlier than expected. Sarah was sitting in the shade of a palm tree in the garden, reading a book and fanning herself with a colourful advertising leaflet. 'Mum, are you alright?'

'Oh, this heat. I'm not used to it any more.' Sarah's breathing was fast and laboured and her right hand was resting on her stomach. 'I'm feeling sick.'

'Sick? Have you eaten?'

'Yes, some fruit and a piece of toast.'

'Has something upset your tummy?'

'Maybe. I've been sick once.'

'Oh, no!' Milla looked at her mother with worry, but also a bit sceptically. Maybe she didn't want to see Johann. Was she pretending? But why?

'There's a strange kind of pressure in my chest.'

Milla sighed. 'Mum, if you don't want to come and see Johann, just say it.'

'No, darling, it's not that. How about we take things easy and go to a nice beach for a couple of hours?' She tried to joke. 'Johann and Eli aren't likely to disappear in the next two hours.'

Milla had to laugh. 'Okay.'

'Paul came around a while ago.'

'Did he?'

'I'm to tell you that he's gone to the beach, and he left his mobile with me, in case it gets stolen when he goes swimming. His hostel doesn't have a safe.'

'Okay. Maybe we should meet up with him. Which beach has he gone to?' Milla asked, feeling guilty.

But her mother looked at her ruefully. 'Er . . . I must admit I've forgotten. It wasn't a beach I knew.'

Fate again, Milla thought. After the walk with Leandro she needed time to come to her senses.

'Then let's leave Paul's phone at reception and go. I'm sure you must remember a nice beach from your childhood.'

'Oh, yes. Cala Bendinat.' Milla was pleased that her mother, whose breathing was still laboured, had suggested they have a bit of downtime.

Cala Bendinat, a small beach outside Palma, was fringed with pine trees and rocks. Sarah had often played here as a child, collecting shells and other treasures in a little basket.

Picturing her mother as a small child made Milla feel unaccountably emotional. She looked around her, drinking in the view. The sky was bright blue and the sun warmed the air – it really was the most amazing weather for February – and as she looked out at the calm sea she felt herself relaxing. She should have a break more often, she thought, even when there was a lot going on. But when she looked at her mother, she started to feel anxious – her breathing had worsened since they'd arrived.

'Sit down over there, on that wooden box.' Milla pointed over to a wooden crate.

'Okay. I don't know . . . what this may be.'

Milla led her mother over, alarmed at her wheezing, and helped her sit, stroking back the hair from her face.

'Mum, you're soaking wet!'

'Well, I'm sixty, after all – an old woman,' Sarah replied, trying to joke, but Milla realised now that her mother was really unwell. The worry held her stomach in a firm grip.

A wiry Spanish man came jogging towards them, pointed to Sarah and asked in broken German whether he should call a doctor.

'No way!' Sarah protested.

Milla smiled at the man and shook her head then gave her mother some water from her bottle. 'You have to drink more, Mum. Are you in pain?'

'Only in my chest.'

Milla was alarmed. '*Only!* You're joking! We need to get you to a doctor!'

Sarah stubbornly shook her head. 'I'm on holiday. I don't want to be sitting in some crowded waiting room.'

'How can you be so obstinate? It's your health that's at stake. Mum, I don't understand you.'

Sadly, Sarah looked at her daughter. 'I know. I don't understand myself very often. But . . . I don't want to see a doctor . . . and I don't want to see Johann either.'

Milla was disappointed. So that was the reason. 'You could have just told me. You don't have to pretend to be ill.'

'I'm not pretending. I'm not feeling very well, and maybe it's simply that . . . that I want to leave the past behind. I'm sure I'll be better soon. I don't want you to find out any more about why my mother didn't like me. It has been very hurtful, do you understand? Sometimes you just have to accept things, no matter how hard they are.'

Milla swallowed. 'But . . . the point is . . . maybe your mother didn't mean to be cold and it was circumstances or an event we don't know about that made her like that. Or there were other reasons why she couldn't love you as she should have. Her own child, Mum. It's about me, too. You have never found out from her, and

I'm not blaming you, but I just want to know why this has been happening in our family for two generations now.'

Sarah looked at her daughter, deeply shaken. Had Milla said too much? Had she hurt her mother? Suddenly Sarah grabbed at her heart, her face contorted with pain, and moaned.

Alarmed and overcome with guilt, Milla stepped towards her and held her arm. 'Mum? I'm sorry.' But her mother didn't seem to hear her as she bent forward, groaning with pain. 'Oh, God, Mum, what's the matter?' Milla looked around for help, feeling lost and very alone.

A young local man came walking by and, noticing the two women, he explained he was a medical student and asked what Sarah's symptoms were. Milla told him quickly.

He looked alarmed and said that it might be a heart attack. Women's symptoms were sometimes slightly different to men's.

Her heart racing with shock, Milla sat down next to Sarah and put her arm around her tenderly. 'Please, can you call an ambulance? I don't know the number here,' she asked the young man with a trembling voice.

'Of course.' The young man took out his mobile and rang the emergency services.

Sarah didn't say a word. She was visibly in pain, could hardly breathe and seemed close to panic.

Milla tried to support her but felt herself infinitely alone and lost. Luckily, the beach wasn't too far away from Palma. *Please, God, if you exist, don't let her . . .* she couldn't finish the thought.

'Mum, be strong. I'm so sorry. Please forgive me. I never wanted this!' But her mother didn't say anything. What had Milla done with her harsh words?

◆ ◆ ◆

The journey in the ambulance seemed endless and Milla didn't even notice the beautiful landscape as it raced by. Initially, she had tried to hold back her tears, but now she let them run freely down her cheeks.

As soon as they arrived, a group of doctors and nurses had surrounded her mother and taken her off to be examined. Their urgency terrified Milla and she wrung her hands as she waited nervously in the corridor by the emergency department. Her mother mustn't die! She had suffered too many losses in her life. She reproached herself for what she had said about her mother's coldness, regretting bitterly that she had thrown all those accusations at her. What mother can take that? Milla knew she would feel guilty for the rest of her life if her mum didn't recover.

This journey into the past had been her chance to get closer to her mother and to understand her better, and Sarah had opened up a bit already. But Milla had pushed her too far. With a few thoughtless words she had destroyed everything.

A short, sturdy nurse approached her and explained to Milla in Spanish that she couldn't see her mother for the time being, but she refused to answer any further questions. Milla tried to remain composed, but her tears were unstoppable. She took out her mobile. She couldn't reach Paul, as his phone was at the hotel, but Tine would pick up – her best friend was always there for her.

While the phone was ringing Milla gripped it so hard that her knuckles went white. She thought of her grandmother and wondered what secret in her past had made her into the harsh, unloving mother she became. If she could finally solve the mystery, maybe her mother would feel better. Had she overlooked any clues in the information they had gathered so far? Some trace that would lead them further? Milla went over everything she had found out in the last few days in her mind.

Chapter Twelve

Mallorca 1956

In the days after the separation from Johann, Abbi was inconsolable. Every night, she cried bitter tears, but quietly, so her parents wouldn't hear her.

In the shop she served her customers without a smile, quite different from her normal, cheerful way; and at dinner she reacted tetchily when her parents asked her what the matter was.

'Let her be,' Esther whispered to her husband. 'She needs us.' She suspected she knew what was upsetting her daughter so much.

Since Abbi had finished with Johann, she hadn't seen him, nor had he been in contact. This made her in turn deeply sad and angry. It not only hurt her heart, but her pride. Why wasn't he fighting for her? Not a single word from him. Did she mean so little to him after all? Had she deceived herself about him? Had she been gullible to believe his declarations of love?

Eli often visited her in the shop because Abbi was rapidly losing weight. She tried to comfort her with delicious sweets, like *piñónes*, little pastries with pine kernels, and other delicacies. But Abbi refused them all.

'Why doesn't he fight for me?' was all Abbi wanted to know, but Eli didn't know the answer and instead ate a *piñóne* herself, with visible enjoyment.

'Maybe Germans are like that. They simply lack temperament, have no passion. Maybe they cannot love as intensely as Mallorquins,' Eli stated, oblivious of the hurt she was causing.

'What rubbish!' Abbi hissed at her friend.

'Okay, okay . . .'

The doorbell rang, and Pomade came in, startling them both.

'Well, my lovelies?' Turning to Eli, he continued, 'You get lost now, as quickly as you can.'

'I won't,' Eli countered angrily.

She looked to Abbi for help, but her friend only nodded. What could Pomade do to her now, since she had lost the man she had given her heart to?

Eli hesitated for a moment and then left the shop, staying outside to watch out for Abbi.

'What more do you want?' Abbi whispered, staring at the floor. She felt numb and empty.

'I just wanted to make sure that it's over between the two of you,' he snorted.

'Can't you see that? Just look at me,' she ground out, and Pomade nodded. 'And from now on leave my parents in peace,' she continued angrily.

Pomade pulled himself together and stepped threateningly towards her. 'I will, if you toe the line.' Then he looked at her grimly one more time, turned around and left.

As soon as he was out of sight, and before the doorbell had stopped ringing, Eli whizzed into the shop again. 'What did he want?'

'Me.'

'What?'

'I think he's taken a shine to me. I've suspected that all along.'

'Oh, my God!' Eli exclaimed. 'Then you'll never get rid of him.'

Abbi looked at her in despair. 'I can't bear it any more. Eli, I can't go on. Please help me.'

Eli nodded, looking thoughtful.

◆　◆　◆

On the following Sunday Eli secretly took her brother's Vespa and invited Abbi for a little trip to cheer her up. Abbi wiped away a tear that the wind had squeezed onto her cheek and forced herself to smile. 'Eli, where are you taking me?' she asked her friend over her shoulder, holding on tight to Eli's back.

'You'll see. You're always so nosy!'

'That's the way I am.'

Maybe it was a good idea to escape from her grief for Johann when every street, every stone, in Palma reminded her of him, and to get away from the constant fear of Pomade. Good to leave the city behind. 'All okay at the back?' Eli asked, and put her foot down further. Abbi nodded and shouted in Eli's ear, 'Yes. Is this the road to Santa Maria?'

'Not a bad guess.' Eli briefly turned around and smiled at her.

'Why are we going there? I thought we were going to a beach.'

'Ah, always the beach. I wanted to show you something different today.'

'Let me guess, you have met two nice men and want to pair me off with one of them. With your second choice, of course.'

'Of course,' Eli giggled. 'The best-looking one is for me, naturally.'

Abbi gave her friend a little slap, and Eli squeaked. 'Don't, or we might end up in a ditch.'

'I'm amazed we're still upright, the way you're driving.'

Eli gave her a push with her elbow but then concentrated on the road ahead.

The warm wind caressed Abbi's face and she closed her eyes. Images of her and Johann riding on his Vespa came into her mind and she tried to remember his scent, but realised, sadly, that she already couldn't quite recall it.

Eli went into Santa Maria del Camí and stopped in the plaza. The busy Sunday market was underway, with sellers offering fresh fruit and vegetables, leather goods, clothes and meat.

'This is by far the best market in the area,' Eli said with a smile.

'Yes. But why are you taking me to a market?'

Eli grinned. 'Why not? Maybe you can find some nice things for your shop that you can sell on.'

'Okay.' Abbi wasn't in the mood for shopping, but to please Eli, who had been such a good friend over the last week, she smiled back at her.

Women with full shopping bags started to hurry home to get dinner ready in time for their husbands and children, as was expected of them.

And me? Abbi thought sadly. *No husband, no children, and nearly thirty years old, when every decent woman has been married for years.*

Then she saw his blond hair between the heaps of lemons and buckets of olives. He was looking at her with his warm blue eyes. Her stomach tightened. Johann. What was he doing here? She looked at Eli and realised: they had plotted this together.

Angrily, she turned to face Eli, her best friend, who had betrayed her. 'What are you doing, Eli? What were you thinking?'

Eli tried to calm her. 'Abbi, if we stop believing in love, what sense does our life have?'

'None. For me, life doesn't have any sense any more. And even less now, when I can't even trust my best friend.'

'Abbi,' Eli whispered, annoyed. 'I didn't betray you. I only want you to be happy. Believe me, you'll be unhappy if you give him up because of your ageing parents.'

Abbi stubbornly shook her head. 'No man in this world, no love in this world is worth more than the love of my parents.'

Johann stepped closer and murmured, 'Abbi,' in his deep, warm voice. From behind his back he drew a branch covered with pink and white almond blossom and held it out to her. 'Please, Abbi, just listen to me. And smell this!'

He held the branch right under her nose, and though Abbi meant to refuse, the sweet, irresistible scent of the almond blossoms made her dizzy.

As Abbi didn't say a word, Johann felt encouraged and took another step forward, so the scent of the almond blossoms mingled with his. 'Abbi, I just wanted to give you some time. And I was busy, so I asked Eli to bring you here, because I know how much you love almond trees. On the beach, on our last evening, I told you I had some good news. Do you remember? I've saved a bit of money and borrowed the rest from my father, so I could buy a little *finca* and restore it all by myself. Your parents will realise that I have something to offer, even though it's not a lot. As I cannot carry on working on this island as a geologist, we can always live off the almond plantation. Your parents can't object to that kind of decent work. I know you feel the same as I do.' Abbi was becoming confused by his speech. 'Your parents love you beyond everything, and that's why I'm sure they want to see you happy. Because you deserve it. Because you are an unusually brave and unique woman.'

'They want me to marry a *xueta*,' Abbi interrupted him quietly, and repeated it like a mantra. She could feel herself weakening. Weak from this mixture of scents, weak at the prospect of how life could be, here in this wonderful hilly landscape, to live in a little cottage with him, surrounded by almond trees. How wonderful life could be! If there hadn't been a war, if what had happened in the past hadn't divided the people and created so much hatred. If religion was no longer important.

Abbi realised her hands were trembling. To steady herself, she ripped the branch with the almond blossoms from his hand and stared at the flowers. How pure they were, so beautiful! It wasn't their fault that life was so unfair. Her parents weren't to blame either. They simply stuck to the rules of society in order to survive. Like generations before them. They knew what was best for Abbi, their only, beloved daughter.

'You will like the *finca*,' Johann continued nervously. 'Please come with me and at least have a look at it.'

Eli, who had stepped aside, came forward again and nodded at Abbi encouragingly. 'He's described it to me, and it sounds wonderful.'

Abbi looked at her friend with deep disappointment. 'Why have you plotted against me? I trusted you!'

Eli helplessly raised her arms and, in her usual light-hearted way, said to Johann, 'Well, I'll leave you to it. I spotted a few sailors over there.' Then she winked and walked towards a group of cheerful-looking men.

Time seemed to stand still as Abbi and Johann stared at each other wordlessly, a world of emotion in their eyes. Finally, Johann imploringly held his hand out to her.

Abbi bit her lip and hesitated, as her head and her heart battled for supremacy. Her heart won and she put her small hand in his, and he led her along to his Vespa.

Sitting behind him, she tried not to touch him. Without a word, they drove through the town and up the mountains through the blossoming almond trees.

He parked where the road forked and they got off. Abbi's heart was pounding so hard that she feared Johann could hear it. But the birdsong and the light breeze seemed to drown it out. Several times Johann, more hopeful now, looked at her sideways. He couldn't seem to believe his luck, and Abbi tried unsuccessfully to repress a little smile. He had bought a *finca* for the two of them! Could he have declared his love for her in a more beautiful and convincing way?

After a short walk they could see the small stone house, their new home. It was waiting for them, surrounded by olive, almond and palm trees and the picturesque Mediterranean landscape. For at least a few minutes Abbi could see herself living here as if in a dream. She tried to forget all the obstacles in her life and just concentrated on the moment.

'There it is,' Johann pointed out, watching her reaction.

Overwhelmed by the beauty of it all, Abbi smiled with delight. 'How wonderful!' She laughed and threw herself into his arms, giggling. Relieved, he joined in her laughter, embracing her tightly and twirling her around once.

'You have no idea how happy you make me!' he said, keeping his arm around her.

At those words Abbi froze, realising she had lost control of her feelings and suppressed all thought of the obstacles in her way. Nobody could take this moment away from them. She would always remember this, for the rest of her life.

'Come on, have a look inside.'

Abbi hesitated, but her curiosity won out. Johann took her hand again and led her inside, where it was pleasantly cool. Abi looked around in excitement. There was an old stove, a brown cupboard, a table and four wooden chairs. A door led into the bedroom, another one into a bathroom. On the table was a bowl with almonds and a bunch of purple wildflowers.

'Oh, my God!' Abbi exclaimed with wide eyes. 'And you've done all this by yourself?'

He grinned. 'Does that surprise you?'

'No, not now.' She smiled and Johann grasped her hips and pulled her closer, his lips lowering to hers as if drawn by a magnet, but Abbi withdrew. 'No, please don't.'

Chapter Thirteen

Mallorca 2016

Surrounded by red and yellow flowers, Milla sat on a white bench in the hospital park and, trying to hold back her tears, she told Tine about Abbigail and Johann, of their love, their heartache, in the hope that Tine might have some ideas as to what she should do next.

Although Tine had no fresh ideas, just hearing her voice comforted Milla, and she realised how much she had missed her. Tine wondered why Milla's grandmother had been so disappointed by Eli. 'She only meant well,' she commented.

'Of course. But Abbi's unhappiness must have got worse, after Eli secretly arranged the meeting with Johann. She went too far. Grandmother didn't want to see him any more, to avoid more heartache. Well, I understand Abbi.'

'I don't. Some people need to be pushed to be happy. Like you. Don't even think of cancelling the wedding with Paul just because some holiday romance has gone to your head. Even though you haven't mentioned him much. But that says it all. I am your bridesmaid, after all, remember? My dress was unbelievably expensive.'

Milla had to laugh, even though that was the last thing on her mind right now. 'No, no, I'm not cancelling the wedding,' she replied quietly, aware she sounded uncertain but hoping her friend wouldn't notice. But they knew each other too well for Tine not to pick up on her tone.

'Hey, sweetie, if you're really unsure, then let's talk about it when you're back, okay? Even if it takes all night. But don't mess up now. Be kind to Paul. He's not a bad guy, and you know how many nasty men there are around.'

'You're right.' Milla exhaled. 'But Mum is more important now. That she'll be okay again.'

'Exactly.'

'She will be, won't she?' Milla was overcome by anxiety.

'Of course. Modern medicine is marvellous.'

'But they didn't let me see her.'

'Doesn't mean anything, sweetie.' Tine, who was normally a chronic hypochondriac, seemed to be controlling herself very well.

'I shouldn't have told her so bluntly how unloved I felt. I feel so guilty!'

'Well, it had to come out one day, and you said that things were getting so much better between you. It's okay to tell the truth occasionally.'

'Do you think so?'

'Yes. Otherwise there's no real closeness, only fakery. Sweetie, to talk about what bothers you is always better than bottling it up. Her heart had been damaged before, the doctors said. That can't be your fault.'

Milla sighed, somewhat comforted. 'You're right. She wasn't well before I said these things to her.'

'Okay then. Love you. Your mum will be okay again. Are you all on your own at the hospital?'

'Yes, for a while. Paul is on the beach and left his mobile behind.'

'Oh, no! Shall I come, sweetie? I would have to find somebody to mind the shop . . . and a cheap flight . . .'

Milla was overwhelmed by this offer and smiled. 'You really are one in a million. But Paul will be back soon.'

'See? In an emergency, it's always nice to have someone you can rely on.'

'Yes. Love you too. I'll keep you posted.'

'You'd better. *Ciao*, sweetie, and give my love to your mum when she comes round.'

'Okay. Kiss-kiss.'

Milla ended the call, smiling to herself. How good it was to have a friend who was always there for you and would be with you like a shot if needed.

She dialled her mother's hotel and left a message for Paul, which he would get when he picked up his mobile.

Suddenly Milla felt very lonely, like a fledgling left behind in the nest. Despite the warm sunshine, the worry about her mother made her shudder. Maybe she should call Leandro. He was the only other person she knew here. She hesitated for a moment and then tried his number with shaking fingers. He didn't answer so she left a message. Then she got up and, knees wobbling, went back to the intensive care unit where her mother had been transferred. This time, she was let in.

Sarah was asleep and looked very pale. The nurse told Milla that her condition was unchanged. Milla needed to be patient.

Quietly, Milla sat down on a cold chair by the bedside. She looked at her mother, shaken, and wished she could pray. She wasn't religious, but now she rather envied people who had faith and could turn to a God for comfort.

'Please, Mum, I love you so much. I need you. Please pull through,' she whispered, unsure whether Sarah would hear her.

After a short time the nurse sent Milla back to the park to wait. 'She needs rest now. I'll call you when she wakes up. Promise.'

Back in the park, Milla slumped down again on the white bench and checked her mobile to see whether Paul had sent a message. But he still seemed to be on the beach. Didn't he sense that she needed him? Looking up, she saw Leandro rushing towards her, his expression worried.

'Milla, I'm so sorry I couldn't come sooner. I've only just got your message. How is your mother?'

Out of breath, he sat down next to her under the tree with its white blossoms, and Milla immediately felt comforted. Her heart was pounding, and all her worries came out in a rush. 'The doctors said that she was conscious for a brief time but sunk back into a deep sleep afterwards. We can only wait and see how things develop. It wasn't a heart attack, but a severe attack of angina pectoris, which is nearly as bad. They've asked me whether I knew that mum has a bad heart, and the worst thing is, I didn't.'

Milla's voice was cracking. How much was there she didn't know? What else would be uncovered? She remembered Sarah telling her about Abbi's mother, her great-grandmother Esther, who had also had a weak heart. Was it a family illness? Did all the Fuster women have a weak heart? Did she maybe suffer from it too?

Her heart was confused, that much she knew, because since Leandro had sat down beside her it had started to beat too fast. She shouldn't have called him, she admonished herself. What if Paul rang now?

'If it wasn't a heart attack, you shouldn't worry too much,' Leandro said gently. 'Will the doctors put in a stent?'

'Yes, exactly. How do you know these things?'

'I know a little. My auntie has one – well, actually, three.'

'The doctor also said that the next three days will be critical. And she hasn't woken up yet.' Milla was trembling now. Leandro

192

stroked her arm tenderly, causing goose bumps to rise on her arms. She continued quietly, so that he could barely hear her. 'I don't even know how serious her heart condition is. She never told me anything. Never.' She looked anxiously at Leandro. 'And who knows whether she'll ever be able to tell me things again.'

'Shhh.' He put his arm around her shoulders. 'Of course she will. There are very good doctors at this hospital; she'll recover, and you'll have plenty of time together.'

Milla exhaled, somewhat calmer. With the possibility that her mother's heart might stop beating at any moment, she now realised how much she loved her, more than she had ever thought. No matter what her faults were, you only had one mother, and losing her would be unbearable. Did it always need a crisis or an illness to make you realise how much someone meant to you?

Milla wondered nervously how important the investigations about her grandmother were now. As far as she could see, they were more important than ever, as she could hopefully convince her mother that Abbi's coldness and distance to Sarah hadn't been her fault. And if she ever discovered anything too hurtful – well, Milla didn't have to tell her.

Milla discussed all this with Leandro, and he nodded in agreement, offering to help with further investigations.

His calm acceptance and willingness to help relaxed her. It was wonderful to feel she had his strength on her side. *I won't give up*, she thought. Definitely not. She needed to know why her grandmother hadn't been able to love her daughter. Maybe there was a plausible explanation that could help to reconcile Sarah with her late mother's memory.

Leandro looked at her intently and carefully took her hand. Milla let him, holding her breath. Leandro's hand felt warm and reassuring. They sat in silence for a while as Milla considered what to do next. She wanted to see Eli again, but she wasn't sure if the old woman would answer the phone.

Milla's thoughts were interrupted when, from the corner of her eye, she spotted a woman behind the shrubs who looked very much like Diana, staring at them with big, sad eyes. Realising she was still holding hands with Leandro, Milla pulled away and looked anxiously at the man next to her.

'It's Diana . . . over there . . . look!'

Startled, Leandro looked over to where Milla was pointing, but Diana had disappeared. Leandro suddenly seemed nervous.

'Have you . . . have you told her what you wanted to say?'

He hesitated. 'Yes, a while ago. Before you rang.'

Oh, no, Milla thought. The poor woman. She had probably followed him. Milla instinctively moved away from Leandro. 'I told you not to do it,' she said quietly.

'And I said that I can't help it,' he replied gently. 'Milla, I don't want to put you under pressure.'

'But that's what you're doing!' she burst out desperately. Leandro looked at her, speechless.

Just then a young nurse hurried towards them. 'Señora Stendal?'

'Yes?' Milla jumped up and tried to read the nurse's face.

'Your mother . . . will you please come?'

'Is she getting worse?' Milla held her breath, but the nurse didn't answer. With Leandro close behind her, Milla followed the nurse along the path between the pink flowering shrubs, palm trees and lush vegetation. It could only have been a couple of minutes, but the walk felt endless to Milla.

'Why can't you tell me anything?'

'The doctor will talk to you,' the young nurse replied evasively. Milla looked at Leandro helplessly.

'We're nearly there.' He tried to calm her.

At last they reached the main building. At the entrance were several patients in their dressing gowns, smoking. 'Señor Bayarri, you shouldn't smoke. Remember your heart,' the nurse said in passing. The man nodded and took another drag on his cigarette.

In the foyer they had to wait for the lift, which seemed to be stuck on the fifth floor. Milla's mind was racing while they waited, her nerves stretched taut. Finally, the lift doors opened. She remembered suddenly how, as a child, she had been knocked over by a cyclist. The man hadn't even stopped, leaving her lying on the pavement in tears as blood flowed from her knees. Afterwards, her mother had been so loving and tender, buying pink plasters and singing to her. There had been warm moments between mother and daughter, after all, just not very often.

She remembered other scenes from her childhood. The times she had been in bed at night, hoping her mother would come and cuddle her, like she had seen with Julia and her mum when she had stayed over. But there was hardly ever more than a goodnight kiss that barely touched her cheek for Milla.

How she longed now to take her mother in her arms and to forgive her all this, to tell her how much she loved her anyway. To tell her that now she knew a bit about her family history, she understood that Sarah couldn't help herself.

At last, they got to the intensive care unit. A young Mallorquin doctor asked them into his office.

'Shall I come in?' Leandro asked considerately.

Milla shook her head, trying to be brave.

She followed the doctor and stiffly sat down on the grey plastic chair.

'Señora Stendal, I'm off to do the rounds soon, so I'll come to the point quickly. Is your mother always this stubborn?'

Surprised and deeply relieved, Milla laughed. 'Stubborn? Does that mean she's alive?'

'Of course. Has nobody told you?'

'No. The young nurse looked quite worried.'

'I'm sorry. She's a trainee. Yes, your mother is alive and being quite awkward.'

Milla smiled at him happily. 'Sounds like her. What's it about?'

'Quite simply, she urgently needs a bypass of an artery that cannot be stented. Otherwise, the risk of a heart attack is quite high. It would mean an operation, but your mother is refusing to give her consent.'

'What? But why?'

'Because she wants to have the operation in Berlin.'

'Okay. And you don't agree?'

He shook his head. 'It's a risk.'

'Why is she against it?'

'You'll have to ask her yourself.'

Milla nodded. 'Will do. Can I see her?'

'Yes, but not for long. She needs rest.'

'Okay.'

'The nurse will show you to her room. Wait here.' He got up, shook her hand and went out.

Milla was left alone in the cool white room, her body vibrating from the news. On the one hand. she felt great relief; on the other, the fear remained. Sarah was still at risk, the doctor had said. Why had her mother decided against an operation? Maybe she didn't want to live any more? Milla shuddered.

Leandro looked around the doorframe. 'How is she?'

'She's refusing to have a bypass operation!' Milla exclaimed. 'But she's alive.'

He beamed at her. How could he mirror her own feelings so well? Leandro was such an empathic person. Like Paul, she suddenly thought. Who could be here any minute, once he'd received the message at Mum's hotel.

'Leandro, thank you so much for coming, but I want to be alone with her now.'

'Of course. I'll wait downstairs in the park for you.'

'No, no – I mean, that's lovely of you, but I'll be alright now.'

He looked at her for a second, then nodded his understanding. He put his arms around her and for a moment Milla leaned on his shoulder. Oh, the scent of this man! Then he let her go, gave her an encouraging smile and left.

A nurse took Milla to her mother's room, where Sarah was lying with her eyes closed.

'Mum?' Milla said, alarmed at her mother's pallor.

'She's gone to sleep again,' the nurse said in Spanish, and smiled at her encouragingly. 'Sit with her. She should have slept enough now.'

Milla did as she was told. After a short time Sarah opened her eyes, looked around, confused for a moment, then recognised Milla and smiled. It was an honest, warm smile. 'Milla, sweetheart, you're here. How lovely!'

Milla beamed at her mother. 'Of course I'm here.'

'If you hadn't been there on the beach . . . you saved my life.'

'Oh, Mum . . .' Milla searched for the right words. 'Why have you never told me you have a weak heart? I wouldn't have let you come with me on this trip.'

'That would have been a shame, don't you think?'

Milla smiled again. 'It really would have.'

'Milla, I'm so, so sorry that I've been such a—' Sarah stopped. 'A what?'

Sarah hesitated, then took a deep breath. 'Such a bad mother.' Then quickly, as if she didn't want to be interrupted, she continued. 'I can't bring back the years. But you can. Be different to your own children, that's what I wanted to tell you. At least try.'

'Mum!' Milla contradicted gently. 'You haven't been . . . I mean, you aren't a bad mother, but rather . . .'

'Please, let it be now.'

'No! You couldn't help it, because your own mother didn't exactly shower you with love. You've done everything you could for me. You've raised me on your own without financial help. Without the help of grandparents . . .'

Sarah nodded sadly. 'I don't want to talk about them again, okay?'

'Of course . . .' Milla hesitated before carrying on. 'But we have to talk about something else which is very important. Why won't you have the operation here, as soon as possible? Bypass operations are routine almost everywhere now.'

Sarah exhaled and looked out of the window. Milla followed her gaze. Up here on the fifth floor, all you could see was the deep blue sky and a few white clouds.

Sarah avoided giving her a direct answer. 'I'm seeing . . . a specialist in Berlin, darling. I trust him. I want to find out whether it's really necessary. Don't worry, Milla, life is never without risks.'

'That makes sense.' Milla exhaled. Her mother looked tired. 'Okay. Shall I stay here, or would you rather be on your own now?'

'Please go out into the sunshine, enjoy Palma, Mallorquin food, your Paul, or this other man if you like. Enjoy life. Do it for me. You know, in a situation like this, one becomes aware of how fragile life is. It could have been a proper heart attack. Then it might all have been over.'

'Please, Mum, don't say things like that. You must pull through and get well again. For me. Will you promise me?'

Sarah nodded and smiled. 'If you promise to enjoy life, every minute of it.'

'That's not always easy, but I'll try.'

Shaken, Milla walked through Palma, absorbing the sights and sounds of this wonderful city; the scent of life. Could it really only be lunchtime? So much had happened in a few short hours. How quickly life could change. Until only a few days ago she didn't own a souvenir shop in Palma and had been happy with Paul – jealous, yes, but on the whole content with her life. But was she really? Suddenly, she stopped walking as a thought hit her like a giant wave crashing over a small ship on the endless ocean: she was like her grandmother in her younger years. She seemed to have the same longing for new experiences, for something grander in this world.

Milla exhaled deeply. She was facing the Palacio Real de La Almudaina, the royal palace opposite the cathedral La Seu, and looked at her smartphone for some background information. She was determined not to go through life ignorant any more but to absorb everything interesting in her surroundings. 'The Palacio is the seat of the captaincy of the island and one of the residencies of the Spanish king,' she read. What a large, impressive building it was! How much history had it seen? 'It was once the seat of the Arabic rulers and after the Christians won it back it became the residence of the Mallorquin royal house.'

Milla stopped, held her face towards the sun with her eyes closed, feeling alive and strong. Even though she was worried about her mother, she realised that she had to be strong for her now, and this made her feel powerful. At some point, the roles of parents and children changed, but it was much too early for that. Sarah was only sixty years old and hopefully had many years ahead of her.

Milla decided to be optimistic. Wasn't she close to the bakery where her mum said she had met Eli? She looked around and, just as she remembered it was at the Plaza de España, she was shocked to see Diana coming towards her, eyes red from crying. She was wearing an elegant light beige suit, emphasising her elegant fig-ure. Even in her grief she looked ravishing. Milla imagined for a second what she herself would look like if the love of her life had just dumped her: her eyes would be swollen from crying, her hair a mess, she'd be wearing jogging bottoms. But this woman managed to remain composed, even in this situation.

'Sorry, Milla, can we talk for a moment?' Diana implored her quietly. 'It's urgent.'

'Of course.' They agreed to go to one of the street cafés, ordered a *café solo* each, and Diana began to talk immediately. 'You probably know that Leandro has ended our relationship?'

Milla hesitated but confirmed it. 'Yes, and I've told him that I don't like it at all.'

Relieved, Diana nodded, then hesitantly went on. 'Until a few days ago we were going to be married.' She stirred her coffee. 'Which means, until two days ago, he was very much in love with me.' Desperately, she continued. 'This love, it cannot have evaporated so quickly, can it? Just because he's met you?'

Milla swallowed. 'You're right.' But she reflected that she was going through the same thing with Paul now. What did Diana want from her?

'I really like you, Milla. That's why we're talking now. I'm sorry to say this, but I'm sure that Leandro will forget you just as quickly. Like all the others. After a few weeks, maybe months, he'll dump you.' *What did Diana mean?* 'Only, I'm so stupid that I always take him back.' Diana looked at Milla meaningfully. 'The sad fact is I'm dependent on him. Even though he chases after anything in a skirt. And then, once he's got his prey, he returns to me. I just want to warn you. It's for your own sake.'

'Hang on . . .' Milla replied flatly. 'Are you saying that he's cheated on you more than once?'

Diana nodded and covered her face with her hands. 'The things we suffer for love. Some women tolerate being beaten; others stay with alcoholics. Maybe this time I will stay away from him for good. Though . . . maybe I appear tough, but I'm not sure I can.'

Diana put some money for the coffee on the table and got up. 'Please don't tell him that we talked. He would deny everything, of course. But for your own peace of mind, keep away from him. *Adiós.*' Diana turned and walked gracefully down the street.

Milla stared after her, confused. Should she believe Diana? Or was it the desperate attempt of a hurt woman to destroy the lives of others around her? Milla took a few deep breaths and tried to pull herself together. She paid the bill, put on her sunglasses and walked away in the opposite direction, her heart beating faster.

She told herself there were more important things to do than think of Leandro. Or Paul. Like getting her mother well as soon as possible. That's what counted, not the men in her life.

'Do you know a lady called Eli Pomar?' The bakery in the Plaza de España smelled deliciously of fresh bread and cakes. Milla looked at the salesperson behind the counter expectantly, but the woman's face didn't give anything away. 'Why are you looking for her?'

She must know her. She knew her! Milla was so excited she nearly choked.

'I'm the granddaughter of her best friend in her younger days. I just want to find out something about my grandmother.'

'What's your grandmother's name?'

'Abbigail Fuster. She recently died. Did you know her?'

'No.' The woman's face softened a bit. 'But I know Eli Pomar.'

'Oh, really?' Milla beamed at her. 'Could you please tell me where Eli lives?'

'Of course. Just around the corner from here.'

Milla thanked her effusively and hurried out, walking swiftly towards the address she had been given. Once there, she looked up to the small flat with a balcony on the first floor of a house near the Plaza de España. The balcony was an abundance of red and pink hanging geraniums; behind them were some tea towels on a washing line.

Nobody answered when Milla rang the bell. *Great*, she thought. *What now?* She looked up again and saw a curtain moving. *She's at home and won't open for me.* Milla was incredulous. What secret was Eli keeping from her? Why was she avoiding her? She pressed the doorbell a bit harder, and after a few minutes Eli must have realised that Milla wasn't going away. Leaning on her walking stick, she opened the door with a forced smile.

'Come in. I didn't hear you straight away, because my hearing isn't very good, you know.'

You only hear what you want to hear, Milla thought, but tried not to show how annoyed she was.

Eli's flat was small, dark and airless. Milla looked around. Everything appeared tidy and looked after, not exactly modern, but with style. A few antique pieces, an old brown leather sofa. 'Heirlooms from my family,' Eli explained when she noticed Milla's glance. 'I couldn't just throw them out, even though I thought . . .' She stopped.

'What?' Milla wanted to know.

'Well, I wasn't too fond of my parents . . . unlike Abbi,' she added. 'But somehow one is always close to one's parents, even though we don't like to admit it.'

'Yes, maybe. And sometimes you only realise it when it's too late. My mother nearly had a heart attack!' Milla couldn't help exclaiming. 'It was a serious attack of angina pectoris.'

Eli looked at her in shock. '*Dios mío!* But she's alive?'

'Yes, but still in hospital and refusing to have the necessary operation.' Milla took Eli's arm. 'Please, please, tell me everything you remember from the old days. I must find out why my grandmother was so cold towards my mother. Maybe there's an explanation that would help my mother to understand. Maybe she would fight harder for her life. Somehow, I have the feeling she's given up.'

Eli's face remained expressionless. 'Has she told you about Baruch?'

'Baruch, my grandfather?'

'Yes.'

'Not much at all. Only that it was a marriage of convenience, but that can't be the reason why a mother doesn't love her child.'

'You're probably right. Marriages of convenience were quite common then.'

'Please tell me about my grandfather. Maybe then things will make sense.'

Eli nodded. 'Would you like a cup of ginger tea?'

'Yes, please.'

Eli hobbled to the kitchen, turned around once and said, 'You remind me very much of Abbi.'

'How do you mean?

'She would always do anything for her parents.'

Chapter Fourteen

Mallorca 1956

Abbi watched two German tourists sifting through the gifts on display. Time and again, she glanced out onto the street, as was her habit now. Secretly, she was hoping to see Johann, but she was also afraid of spotting Pomade. What would he do next? Abbi tried in vain to dispel her anxious thoughts.

She longed for Johann, for their *finca*, where they had spent such a brief and wonderful time. She would remember those few precious minutes until her dying day.

'What kind of a plate is this?' one of the tourists asked in broken Spanish, holding up a piece of ceramic that Abbi's aunt had painted.

'It's a fruit bowl,' she answered in Spanish.

'The paintwork is quite primitive,' the man said to his friend in German, not knowing that Abbi could understand him.

'Not everyone has a sense for art,' she remarked sarcastically in German. What she'd endure from the tourists had its limits. The young man in his suit and hat looked at her in surprise and then whispered to his friend, 'The women at home are never that rude. Come on, let's go.'

The other one nodded and said on leaving, 'If mine answered back like that, she'd regret it.'

Abbi took a few deep breaths. Not all Germans were like them, that much she knew. Her Johann was different. Many others were different. Her thoughts went back to the day at the *finca* – their *finca* – which Johann had bought for her. How beautiful it was! And how much she loved the scent of the almond blossoms. A tear rolled down her cheek.

She sighed and made herself a cup of coffee for comfort. It was small consolation for the loss of her love. Again, she had put a dagger into Johann's heart, had told him again that their love had no future. How desperately he had looked at her, but he'd also sensed that she would remain firm, that she really meant it.

Eli had waited for her in the village. 'Why did you bring me here?' Abbi had snapped at her when she found her.

Eli was annoyed. 'I'm asking myself the same question. I can't stand your constant whining about Johann any more. I've had enough of it. Enough of our friendship.'

Lost for words, Abbi looked at her friend. Eli had always been the more light-hearted of the two in every respect, and now her ally, the only person she thought would understand her, was breaking off their friendship! How could she? Eli had always been her best friend, and that she suddenly didn't want their friendship any more came as a shock.

Muted and hurt, Abbi had mounted the Vespa behind Eli. She just wanted to get away from Santa Maria, but she hardly held on to her former friend on the journey home. What would it matter if she had an accident now?

When Abbi got home her mother was in the kitchen kneading dough, her arms covered in flour. She looked up, smiling. 'Well, how are you today, my darling?'

'Okay,' Abbi answered curtly and, to change the subject, added, 'What are you baking today, Mother?'

'Almond bread. Your father loves it so much.'

Almond bread . . . In her mind's eye, Abbi saw the blossoming almond trees around Santa Maria again.

'Me too,' she said quietly. Another recipe for her cookbook.

'There's some news,' Esther said, but not very cheerfully.

'Has something happened?'

'Well, you could say so. Your father wants to talk to you.'

'Tell me, Mother, what is it?'

But Esther shook her head. 'We always only want the best for you, my child. You have to believe us.'

Abbi wondered frantically what it could be. Did they want to send her away? *Please, no!*

'The almond bread will be ready in three quarters of an hour, then I'll make coffee. You will have to be patient until then.'

But patience wasn't one of Abbi's virtues. With a sigh she went to her room, lay down on the bed and stared at the ceiling. Had her father found out about her forbidden love? Had Pomade threatened her parents?

Time crawled past. Finally, the aroma of freshly brewed coffee and almond bread wafted through the flat, and Noah emerged from his study. When Abbi came out of her bedroom she saw that the coffee table was beautifully set, and there was even a little vase with a yellow flower. What her parents were going to tell her was probably important, Abbi thought with a shudder.

The atmosphere was tense as they sat down at the table, not looking at each other. Esther served her husband first, then Abbi and herself. When they each had a slice of the delicious-smelling almond bread on their small gold-rimmed plates, Noah cleared his throat and looked at Abbi uneasily. 'Abbi, we have to talk to you.'

'Yes, Father. What is it?' Abbi tried to sound calm.

206

'You're nearly thirty years old and still haven't found a husband,' Noah started, haltingly and with a heavy heart.

I do have a man, Abbi was tempted to cry out, but she controlled herself, bit her lower lip and waited.

'The son of a client of mine, from a *xueta* family, is really nice. I've met him myself.'

No, no, please no! Abbi cried silently, but managed to suppress her despair and let her father go on. 'He has a sense of humour, good looks, I think. He's quite well off, too. He's a publisher.'

Abbi's broken heart couldn't have sunk any deeper. She looked at her mother for help, but Esther was staring at her plate, where the warm almond bread was still slightly steaming.

'Abbi, you'll have to admit that we've given you a lot of time and freedom.'

'Yes, you're right, Father.'

'But we want to see you well looked after. And the choice of men of the right age, of Jewish descent and still unmarried is getting smaller and smaller. It's tiny enough already.'

'I know,' Abbi said flatly. 'Why is *he* not married yet? If he's so entertaining, educated and well off?' Again, that was her loose tongue, and her father reacted with irritation.

'I could ask you the same,' he replied sternly.

'Noah, please,' her mother intervened quietly. 'Darling, Father would never find a man for you who wouldn't be good to you.'

'How do you know? That he'll be good to me?' Abbi shouted in desperation. 'I don't need anybody looking for a husband for me!' With those words she got up, ran to her room and threw herself on her bed in tears, beating the mattress with her fists.

In the following days Noah mentioned the man again and again. Abbi should at least consent to a meeting with Baruch Bonnin. But Abbi didn't feel up to it. She knew she couldn't love this Baruch, couldn't love any man other than Johann.

Johann came to her shop a few more times, looking forlorn and sad, but every time she sent him away. She was amazed that she could be so steadfast and cool with him, but her fear of Pomade, who frequently turned up in front of her shop window, was too strong.

Each day was a struggle for Abbi. To occupy herself at night, she would work until late, writing down the almond recipes for her cookbook. Finally, she agreed to meet Baruch Bonnin at least once. 'He could be your publisher,' coaxed Noah, but Abbi wasn't interested. She would find a publisher anyway. She agreed to this one meeting, but only to do her father a favour and to demonstrate her goodwill as an obedient daughter. When, afterwards, she said that she didn't like him at all, her parents would leave her alone. At least, that was her plan.

Baruch Bonnin wasn't bad looking. He was tall, nearly as slim as her father, had dark, short hair and wore round glasses. From the conversation, it was obvious that he was an avid reader, something Abbi liked very much. He had small, swift eyes and a large nose, which gave his face a certain manliness. The conversation in Café Bosch at the end of Passeig del Born was stilted. Abbi didn't make an effort, and Baruch seemed to be nervous and of a quiet temperament anyway. He seemed the type who wouldn't hurt a fly.

Abbi hadn't done herself up for the date but had come straight from the shop after a long, hot day. But despite this, Baruch didn't seem put off by her stubborn and aloof attitude. He kneaded his fingers while talking about his work in the publishing house and asked about her plans for the cookbook Noah had told him about. After nearly an hour, which was the expected amount of time, Abbi excused herself politely and said goodbye.

The poor man. He had obviously liked her, whereas Abbi's flame of love had been extinguished for ever. She thought of Johann and how much she liked his warmth and sensitivity.

After the date her mother caught hold of her in the dark corridor. 'Well, Abbi, did you like him?'

'Not at all, Mother. He seems like a good man, but not my type. He's . . . boring.'

Esther sighed and stroked Abbi's hair. 'I guess he was very nervous,' she said, before hurrying off to continue with her evening chores.

At dinner her father enquired about Baruch. 'Don't you find him open-minded? Exactly what you've always wanted?'

'No, Father,' Abbi replied firmly. 'And even if he is, I don't love him and will never fall in love with him.'

'How do you know? Love is unpredictable. It can grow.'

'And what if it doesn't?'

'Abbi.' Now Noah sounded sterner. 'I've told you once before, you will not bring shame on our family. I've discussed everything with Baruch's father. Baruch is delighted. He'll see to it that you are treated like a queen. I'm sure he's the best thing that can happen to you at your age.'

Stunned and angry, Abbi stared at her parents. 'You can't do that to me. Mother, please say something. You've been in love with Father, haven't you?'

'Sure, darling. Very much so. And we love you. We only want what is best for you.'

Noah nodded decisively. 'There will be a wedding. As it should be.'

Abbi jumped up, alarmed. 'Even if Baruch was the last man on this planet, I'll never, ever marry him.'

◆ ◆ ◆

Over the next few days, her parents mentioned Baruch a lot, but Abbi stubbornly avoided the topic. How long would she be able to stand this? Baruch kept sending her flowers and chocolates, but Abbi gave the presents away to others.

A few days later she was doing her daily round of the market to buy some fruit for her afternoon break when suddenly her stomach tightened. Surely not! She blinked as though trying to clear the image from her mind, but when she opened her eyes they were still there: Johann and another woman walking closely together only two hundred metres away from her. It had only been a short time since their separation! Abbi kept staring at the couple, too stunned to move. The woman laughed and, joining in, Johann put his arm around her shoulder.

He must be doing this on purpose to make her jealous. Johann knew that she came here often. Abbi's thoughts went crazy. Or was he already in a new relationship? She needed to find out for certain. Quickly, she hid behind a market stall. Abbi had always been a suspicious person and became jealous easily. She knew she ought to try to curb these feelings because they would only torture her in the long run, but it was easier said than done. She started to follow the couple inconspicuously as they walked ahead of her, laughing and joking. Abbi forced herself to wait at every corner and to walk quietly on her high heels without clicking. How could he laugh like that, so carefree, while she was eaten up by her longing for him?

With mounting anger, she watched them. The woman was wearing a blue petticoat dress and black high heels. She was tastefully done up, and her dark hair was, like Abbi's, short and back-combed. Abbi's mood was getting darker and darker. Had he simply turned to the next Mallorquin woman he'd come across, but this time made sure she wasn't of Jewish descent?

She was fed up of being permanently excluded because of her religion. Her stomach hurt; her joints were aching. Please God she wasn't becoming ill now! Her father had once explained to her that years of intermarriage had caused a rare genetic illness within the *xueta* community called Familial Mediterranean fever – *fiebre mediterránea familiar en Mallorca* – and Abbi had been prone to this throughout her life.

Her forehead was soon covered in sweat, but still she followed Johann and this woman. They sat down in a street café at the Plaza Mayor – of all places, where everyone could see them! Abbi was more and more certain that Johann had deliberately set out to hurt her, because he knew she went shopping in the market every day.

Just as Abbi had decided to go back to her shop Johann suddenly leaned over and kissed the other woman! Abbi couldn't see whether he kissed her on the lips or the cheek, but her world collapsed. Her head felt like it was exploding. And if one of their *xueta* neighbours hadn't come across her at that moment and taken her by the arm and brought her home, Abbi probably would have broken down on the Plaza Mayor and howled.

Now she was bedridden with aching joints and being looked after by her mother. Esther put cold compresses on her hot forehead, mumbling, 'My darling, everything will be alright soon.'

'Nothing will be alright, Mother,' Abbi whispered. Even if what she had seen was a set-up, Johann had hurt her more deeply than anyone ever had before. That he could be like that, so mean and cold! Didn't he understand anything? That for her this wasn't a game? That it meant something to be a *xueta*, that it was a heritage, a burden, a fate? That it was impossible to ignore this ancient heritage? At least, if you were a woman. Even if you were a courageous, rebellious woman. Because even this rebellious woman lived in terror of the devil Pomade. And even if he didn't exist, if he vanished into thin air, no one would accept her relationship with Johann. She would be met with hostility and discrimination and be harassed for the rest of her life. Could she do that to Johann, to her parents or herself? Had Johann ever really thought about it?

Abbi tossed and turned as these thoughts tumbled over and over in her feverish mind.

She dreamt of Pomade, of Johann, of her father. It was a wild and terrible nightmare. She and her parents were on trial and were condemned to death, just as their ancestors had been. After the verdict they painted a picture of them on a hair shirt, a *sanbenito*, and wrote their names on it. It was publicly exhibited in the abbey of Santo Domingo to forever remind everybody of them, the condemned ones. It was the same fate that many of their ancestors had suffered. Afterwards, Esther, Noah and Abbi, in their white *sanbenitos*, were led through a jeering crowd. Right in the middle of it she saw Pomade and his minions, grinning at them.

'No, no!' she shouted, and woke up covered in sweat. But the nightmare wasn't over. In the evening, when, despite a high temperature, she had dragged herself to the shop, Pomade suddenly turned up outside the window and stared at her gloweringly. It would never end, never.

When Abbi came home later, pale as a sheet, her mother was making tea. 'What's the matter, Abbi?' She asked, offering her daughter a cup.

'Mother,' Abbi croaked, staring at the floor.

'Yes, darling?'

'Mother, could you please tell Father something from me?'

'Of course. What is it, sweetheart?'

'To tell Baruch Bonnin . . . that I will marry him.'

Chapter Fifteen

Mallorca 2016

Milla left the hospital, quiet and lost in thought. She had visited her mother again and, according to the doctors, her condition had, fortunately, stabilised.

Milla was pondering what Eli had told her about her grandparents' marriage of convenience. What might the young Abbi have felt when she walked down the aisle with him? Milla had carefully mentioned at her mother's bedside what Eli had told her about Baruch, but Sarah hadn't wanted to talk about him.

'Don't be cross with me, darling, you know enough now. After this crisis I don't want to talk about the past any more, and from now on I'm determined to only live in the here and now,' she had said in a tired voice. 'It wasn't a particularly good marriage, my mother once told me, but he never treated her really badly. I wasn't a love child, but that applies to many children. It can't be the reason Abbi couldn't accept me.'

Milla let it be, kissed her mother on the forehead and promised to come back soon. It was late afternoon when Milla left the hospital and, as usual, a group of smokers was standing by the hospital entrance. How could they be so careless with their lives?

'Milla!' It was Paul's familiar voice, and she looked up to see him rushing towards her. 'Oh, my poor love, and I wasn't with you! How is she?'

Milla told him what had happened. 'She needs rest and has just sent me away. You know how stubborn she can be. She told me to enjoy my life and the island and not to think about the past any more.'

'Maybe she's right. Does it mean she's getting better?'

'Well, there might be complications at any time. She's in urgent need of a bypass but has decided to have it done in Germany.'

Paul hugged her, but Milla didn't feel as reassured in his strong arms as she used to. Did it mean she didn't love him any more? Gently, she freed herself. 'Let's walk a bit. I don't want to talk about it now.'

'Okay.' He sounded puzzled.

Silently, they walked through the hospital grounds. The colourful flowers were a bizarre contrast to all the suffering inside the building.

Suddenly, Paul stopped and, taking her hand, looked at her uncertainly. 'Milla, I know this isn't the right moment, but I have to ask you something. Are you still looking forward to our wedding?'

She could see the doubt in his eyes. 'Of course,' she replied quickly, her heart pounding. Her reply seemed to satisfy Paul, and his grip softened as they walked on.

Milla's mind, however, was in turmoil as she tried to work out how she felt. Diana's words about Leandro and his tendency to cheat were on her mind, but she realised she didn't want to stay with Paul just because Leandro was no longer an option. She needed to be certain that he was the right choice, no matter what.

Spontaneously, Paul kissed her ear and whispered, 'I just want to tell you that I will always be there for you. I mean, if something should happen to your mother . . . I mean, you've got *me* now; I'm your family. Okay?'

'My mother will be okay,' Milla answered huskily.

'I know. I didn't mean it like that.'

'Then don't say things like that. Come on, let's go to the old town.'

'And where to?'

'Don't know.' Milla felt lost.

'I know. Let's go to your grandmother's shop.'

'No, please.' They would bump into Leandro, and she didn't want to be seen with Paul. But he seemed determined.

'Please, let's, because I haven't seen it properly. Your new cool fifties shop.' Smiling, he took her hand again and held it so tightly that Milla, exhausted, gave in, and they kept on through the grounds, along the yellow flowerbeds, yellow as the Mallorquin sunshine.

Leandro wasn't standing outside his shop and Milla quickly tugged Paul across the road, hoping Leandro wouldn't see them, but it was too late because, as she glanced anxiously through the café window, she saw he had spotted her, and their eyes met. Milla flushed. Had he really cheated on Diana so often? How could a woman like Diana tolerate that? She certainly wouldn't. She glowered at him.

Leandro looked confused at her expression and hurried outside. '*Hola*, Milla,' he said gently. 'I've tried several times to ring you. How are you? How's your mother?'

Paul's face darkened, and he adjusted his baseball cap and straightened his shoulders. He had tried to contact her? Milla checked her mobile, which had been on silent. Indeed, ten missed calls from Leandro.

'My mother said she's indestructible.'

'What do the doctors say?'

'Nothing new. That mum should have the bypass operation as soon as possible.'

'You look worried, but there's no need.'

'How do you know?' Paul intervened, sounding irritated.

'I can feel it.'

Milla smiled at him gratefully.

Paul cleared his throat. 'I'm here for you, darling, you know.'

'I know. Thank you.' Then she quietly added to Leandro, 'She doesn't want me to be with her. Do you think that's odd?'

'No, it's not,' Leandro reassured her. 'Mine is the same. Whenever she's ill, she chases everyone away. I think it's a good sign. She loves you and doesn't want you to see her as a sick, complaining mum.'

Milla smiled. 'Do you think so?'

Leandro nodded, his expression gentle and full of love. Milla felt hypnotised. She just couldn't resist the way he locked eyes with her. Was she already as dependent as Diana? Would she allow him to do anything he wanted? Paul cleared his throat again and possessively put his arm around Milla's shoulders. He sounded sharp when he asked Leandro whether his shop was doing well.

'Yes, fantastic. Our almond cake is very popular.'

'You seem to be a in a prime location here in the old town.'

'Yes,' Leandro replied, but his eyes never left Milla's as he said meaningfully, 'It's perfect for me.'

Annoyed with Paul, Milla carefully disentangled herself from his arm, then went to the padlock at the door to her grandmother's shop, hoping to open it and get inside quickly. But it was jammed.

'Shall I help you?' asked Leandro.

'I'll help you,' Paul interjected quickly, and pushed himself forward.

'Hey, please stop, you two. I can do it on my own!' Milla exclaimed.

The two men looked at her in surprise. Milla hadn't known she could be so assertive.

At that moment a pretty Spanish woman in a short white skirt which emphasised her tanned legs tottered past on her high heels. Her face broke into a wide smile when she recognised Leandro.

'Leandro, *amor mío! Como estas?*'

Milla listened jealously to the Spanish conversation while she was fumbling with the padlock. It seemed the other woman was one of his exes and Milla felt it like a stab in her heart, because it meant that Diana might have been right.

I must forget him, this Mallorquin heartbreaker. Grandmother probably would have warned me off him. But then, she led me to him, didn't she? Milla sighed, angry with herself. What on earth had she been thinking? Leandro had told her the *xuetes* were said to be cursed and, judging by the events of the last few days and what she'd found out about her grandmother, it seemed he was right.

Finally, the padlock opened, and Milla stumbled into her shop – her grandmother's haven, and hers too now.

Paul followed her. 'What does he have that I don't?' he asked, trying to make a joke of it. 'Every woman seems to be after him.'

'I don't know,' Milla replied.

'Come on, tell me, you're a woman.' Milla felt sorry for him again.

'Er . . . Eli said recently that he's very romantic. Maybe it's that?'

Paul nodded, seemingly pondering her words. Outside, they could hear the Spanish woman's laughter and Milla felt a sharp pain in her stomach.

◆　◆　◆

'Where are you taking me?'

'I'm not telling you,' Paul replied, his tone both nervous and excited. It was well into the evening, and after the seemingly endless day all Milla had wanted to do was eat and go to bed. Instead, Paul had urged her to shower and change into a dress, and now he had wrapped one of Milla's colourful silk scarves around her eyes and was leading her over the soft sand. The air had grown chilly, the moon was high in the sky, and all Milla could hear was the voices of a few German tourists.

As she walked across the sand, Milla thought of her mother. According to the nurse, there hadn't been any further complications. Tomorrow morning, Milla was planning to go to her early and bring her some fresh fruit. The Mallorquin oranges were delicious and juicy and hopefully would make her feel better.

She let her mind drift and thought again of her grandmother, of her wedding, to which she hadn't invited Eli, her former best friend. It was understandable, because Abbi had felt so betrayed by Eli. But Eli had found out where the ceremony was taking place and had watched it from afar, hidden behind a tree. She had described Abbi's sad, resigned face so vividly that Milla's heart was still aching from it. Eli had confirmed that Baruch was no longer alive. How much Milla would have liked to meet him, because he might have been able to tell her important facts. Now Johann was the only person left who might be able to help her. But because of her mother's illness, the second visit to Johann's *finca* had been postponed, and she was uncertain now whether they would be able to go. Apart from that, Johann might not know anything about the time after Abbi's wedding. But even so, she wanted to see him again while she was here.

'Careful, something's in the way.' She heard Paul's voice and felt his strong hand pulling at something, but it was too late. Milla stumbled and knocked her big toe.

'Ow! That hurt.' What was Paul planning? Had he forgotten that she didn't like surprises? She was only playing along to humour him.

'You hate being led, don't you? It was the same when we took dancing lessons,' he teased her.

'What was it?'

'Oh, only a box for life belts.'

'Tell me where you're taking me!'

'You'll see in a minute.'

'Where are we?'

'On a very pretty little beach.'

'I'm hungry.'

'Wait, I've got something for you.' His voice sounded excited and full of anticipation, but also a little nervous.

Milla sighed. Couldn't he see she was exhausted?

'We're here now. Please wait one more minute.'

Milla felt him move away from her and heard something rustling and a lighter being clicked several times. She wondered what he was doing, and then it dawned on her.

'Can I take the scarf off now?'

'I'll help you.' Gently, he took the silk scarf from her eyes. Milla blinked as she saw the tealights and red petals Paul had laid out in the shape of a huge heart on the sand. He stepped inside it and looked at her with an uncertain smile. A few tourists on the beach smiled and took photos of the burning heart with their smartphones. Milla swallowed, feeling overwhelmed and uneasy.

'Milla, look, I'm a romantic too. I've got more to offer than you might think.' He was fighting for her.

'I know that.' Oh, my God, what had she said earlier? But this wasn't the kind of romance she meant. At least, not since she had met Leandro. Leandro didn't need rose petals and candles, like in some kitsch movie. It was what he said and how he said it: he expressed his view of life and love with passion, yearning and deep feeling. Suddenly, Milla saw exactly why she liked him so much. On the other hand, she also liked Paul's casual, easy-going way, but deep inside she was longing for the passion and unconditional love her grandmother had craved when she was young. And even if Leandro wasn't the right man for her, she wanted a man like him.

Milla guessed what Paul was planning and felt alternately hot and cold. But she didn't say a word.

Paul smiled, taking her silence to mean that she was too overwhelmed to speak. 'Milla, why wait any longer? I want to ask you here and now, on Mallorca, this beautiful island: do you want to be my wife? Now?'

Milla stared at him, and the world stopped turning. She heard Paul talking and the waves rushing to the shore, but she felt unable to move. 'I'm sure we can sort out the paperwork and get married here. Milla, remember what your mother said, that we should live in the here and now, so let's just do it!'

Wide-eyed, Milla looked around at the group of tourists that had boldly gathered around them to snap photos with their mobiles.

They all smiled in anticipation, as if this was the most normal thing in the world. As if every woman simply had to say yes when she was being proposed to amidst candles and rose petals. Rebellious feelings began to stir inside her. Yes, she wanted to live in the here and now, but she wanted a choice, unlike her grandmother, who couldn't follow her heart when choosing a bridegroom. She wouldn't have that choice taken away from her or be put under pressure.

'Paul.' She started quietly, because her throat was dry. 'I really don't feel up to that right now. Because of my mum, because of everything I found out about my family. I . . . I'm afraid I can't do that just now.'

Paul looked at her, stunned with disappointment. The tourists moved away, looking embarrassed. One of them even booed.

Paul gave them an annoyed frown and then turned to Milla, looking hurt. 'What do you mean? Not now, or not at all? You don't want to marry me?'

'I . . . don't know anything any more. Please don't be cross with me, it's just the wrong timing.'

'Okay, if you say so.'

'I'm so sorry. You've made such an effort.' The little tea-lights flickered in the breeze. Milla shuddered, feeling unwell, and stared into the darkening sky. What was it that her grandmother had written to her? She should follow her heart and only marry a man who was right for her. And if she didn't know one hundred per cent who that was, she wouldn't marry anybody.

But she felt terribly sorry for Paul. A few tourists were still looking at them, whispering. Paul knelt to blow out the candles and pick up the tea-lights and the petals. Milla knelt next to him. 'Please, Paul, I'm so sorry. Please give me a bit of time. You're great, just as you are . . .'

Paul tried to smile. 'Don't worry. I can deal with it. At least if it was only the wrong timing.'

Relieved, Milla smiled at him, took his hand and gently kissed it. 'I'd like to be on my own now. Would that be okay?'

'Of course. But do you want to be all by yourself here on the beach, in the dark?'

'Just for a little while. And I won't be completely alone. There are still a few tourists around.'

'But we came together in the car. We have to leave together.'

'What . . . well, you take it. There's a bus stop over there. I'll take the bus.'

'A bus?'

'Yes, I'm sure there will be one. Otherwise, I'll call a taxi. It's not that far to Palma.'

'I don't know . . . you were so hungry earlier.'

'At the moment I couldn't eat anyway. I won't starve.'

'Okay. But I need a steak now or something. We'll meet tomorrow morning and have breakfast together somewhere, okay?'

'That would be nice. I hope the bed in the hostel doesn't do your back in again.'

'Well, it doesn't matter now.'

'Will you pick me up for breakfast tomorrow? Then we'll see Mum in the hospital and drive to Johann afterwards. Okay?'

'Alright, Milla. You're an incredible woman, you know. At least for me. And in the last few days here you've turned out to be even more extraordinary than before.'

'Is that possible?' she joked, and gave him a little nudge. He returned the nudge with a smile, but it didn't reach his eyes.

'No, not really. See you tomorrow morning. I'll leave my jacket with you; it's turned quite cool now.'

'Thank you, that's very kind of you, but I don't need it, really. See you tomorrow morning.'

They kissed each other gently on the lips. Then Paul carefully put the rose petals and tea-lights in a bag and walked towards their hire car. Milla looked after him dejectedly. She felt awful, but also somewhat relieved. With a sigh, she sat down on the cool sand and looked out to sea. What on earth had she done? Was it possible to ever forget such a rejection? Would Paul ever forgive her?

Suddenly, Milla longed to be with her mother. She got her mobile out and tried to ring her but got no reply. She tried the ward, and a nurse promised to check on Sarah. A short time later she returned to say that Señora Stendal was sound asleep and not to worry.

That was easily said. Milla felt that her relationship with her mother had improved significantly, and that the heart problem might

222

have something to do with it. Her mother seemed as stubborn as ever but had been much gentler and more empathic in the last few days. Milla had postponed her flights immediately after her mother had gone into hospital. The airline had charged her a fortune, but it couldn't be helped. Tine understood the problem and had said she would shut the atelier while she was in hospital for her operation. Milla was sorry not to be with her friend, who was so frightened about the procedure. Under normal circumstances, she would have been by her side. She just hoped Tine would be able to conceive after the operation, as that was her biggest dream. And Milla's? Did she want children? And if so, with whom? She was in her thirties already, and if she really should decide against Paul, she might not fall in love again quickly and easily. Not head over heels, as she had with Leandro, the heartbreaker. Milla sighed. What if what Diana had said wasn't true? She pulled up her knees and put her arms around them to stay warm.

She thought of her grandmother, who had to let go of her one and only love. She thought of her mother, who had lost her husband, Milla's father, so early. Maybe it was the fate of the Fuster women to find their true love but not to keep it?

Her mobile beeped. Leandro had sent a text message. *Where are you? I need to see you.*

But I don't need to see you, she wrote back, and sent her answer without hesitation.

He replied immediately. *What's the matter? You've changed.*

Nothing, Milla wrote. Then she leaned back and stared at the moon. *Ha, nothing*, she thought. Never in her whole life had she been faced with as many problems as she had been in the last few days.

No reply from Leandro. After a few minutes he wrote, *What did Diana tell you?*

How did he know they had talked? Milla wondered. She was about to reply *That you are a cheat*, but instead she wrote, *Everything*.

That sounded dramatic, and she liked it.

His response was immediate. *Diana is lying. She's hurt. I've got to tell you something important about your grandmother.*

The bastard! He knew exactly how to get to her. Milla was annoyed and told him with a resigned sigh where she was. Then she added, *Bring some drinks.*

Less than half an hour later he was standing before her wearing a black leather jacket and dark blue jeans. He seemed nervous. He pulled a bottle of red wine and a corkscrew from his shoulder bag, spread out a blanket, then sat down without a word. He smelled as if he had just had a shower.

'Milla, what has Diana told you?' he asked quietly.

'It doesn't matter. Tell me what you've found out about my grandmother. That was just an excuse, wasn't it?'

He looked at her, bent over to her ear and breathed, 'That you are becoming more and more like your grandmother. That's what I wanted to tell you.' Then he smiled passionately. 'You're getting much more confident, more courageous . . .'

'Rubbish!' she interrupted him angrily. Angry that she had been taken in again by him, angry that she knew this and had still wanted to see him.

He opened the bottle, took two glasses from his bag and poured the wine.

'Honestly, you've become more courageous, quite a rebel. Otherwise, you would be sitting here with Paul drinking wine.' He gave her a glass and looked at her meaningfully.

She felt caught out, looked at him sideways and took a large gulp from the glass. The Mallorquin wine tasted fruity and rich. Leandro was right. Only a few days ago, she wouldn't have had the courage to say no without knowing what the future would bring. She would have needed the security, the stability, the sense of belonging and routine. She now felt a little bit better than a young fledgling who had been left in the nest. Now she was beginning to realise that it wasn't that difficult to learn how to fly.

It was getting cold, and the last few tourists had left the cove. Soon they were by themselves. Milla wrapped her arms around herself as if for protection, even though she knew it wouldn't help.

'You're cold. You know, there's a hut belonging to a friend of mine over there. He runs the bar here during the summer months and then lives there. I know where the key is.'

It sounded enticing; adventurous. Milla felt the wine going to her head. 'I don't know . . .'

'Whatever Diana told you, it isn't true. She's hurt, and I'm very, very sorry about that . . . but she doesn't have the right to spread lies about me.'

'Then it's her word against yours.' Milla took another sip of wine. She had never needed much alcohol to feel tipsy.

'That's right. But why don't you listen to your gut feelings, your heart?' Again he looked into her eyes, and she could feel his longing, his love and the closeness throughout her body.

Sometimes you have to try things out first to know whether they're right for you, she thought. *Damn, those eyes! If he kisses me now, I'm done.*

His lips were coming closer, as if he had read her thoughts. Milla couldn't resist his magic; she closed her eyes, and then felt his lips on hers. At first, he kissed her gently, but gradually the passion grew. Milla relented. Life was to be enjoyed, in the moment, in the here and now. Above them, the stars were glittering, and she felt the sand beneath her, sensed his lust and his tenderness, his unconditional love.

Milla hesitated one more moment, but then decided to enjoy the moment and just be happy – everything that her grandmother hadn't been allowed to do all those years ago. 'Let's go to this hut . . .'

◆ ◆ ◆

Very early the next morning Milla woke up naked and shivering on a simple hard bed. The sun shone through the slats between the wooden boards of the hut and bathed the room in a warm, glowing light. What had she done? Her clothes were all over the wooden floor. A naked Leandro was lying next to her, a tartan blanket thrown over him. Shocked and suddenly dead sober, she rubbed her eyes and looked around. Leandro's friend kept stacks of cola and beer cans in the corner for his summer bar, and their empty wine glasses were on the table.

Leandro's tanned body looked beautiful, peaceful and relaxed. Milla forced herself to look away, but her eyes kept going back to him. Quickly, she grabbed her slip, her bra, her dress – everything that Leandro had taken off her last night so expertly – and got dressed. Had she been out of her mind? Had the wine taken hold of her senses? She had never been good with alcohol, but that it made her so passionate and yielding was new to her. What would she tell Paul, who she was going to meet for breakfast? What if she was pregnant now, despite being on the Pill? Oh, God. Had they used a condom? For the life of her, Milla couldn't remember. The passion and the alcohol had robbed her of all her senses.

And all that with this Mallorquin heartbreaker! Desperate and bewildered, Milla pushed her fingers through her tousled hair. She had never been so irresponsible. What had this island done to her? Quickly, she looked for her red sandals, and found them under the bed. And all this had happened on the beach where, only hours before, Paul had romantically proposed to her with candles and rose petals.

But the night had been beautiful, so close and passionate, with more lust and love than she had experienced for a long time – if ever.

Milla was just trying to sneak out when Leandro woke up. He blinked, looked at her dreamily and smiled. 'Good morning,' he whispered. 'I hope you were warm enough last night.' He sat up.

'I was a little cold.'

'Come here, I'll warm you up.'

'No.'

'Milla, you're so beautiful. Do you know that? I don't think you believe me.'

'Do you say that to every woman the morning after?' She turned away, unable to contain her anger, mostly at herself, any longer.

'No, not to everyone. What do you mean? You're very special to me.'

He got up, as naked as the day he was born, and came over to her, looking at her intently. 'You're the woman I've been looking for all my life. The one I intend to spend the next fifty years with.'

'Only the next fifty years?' Milla couldn't help asking.

Briefly, he smiled, causing her breath to catch, but then he was serious again. 'Please, Milla, I know it's not easy, because you don't want to hurt Paul. But would it be fair when you don't really love him?'

'How do you know?' But her words sounded hollow after all that had happened last night. She heard a seagull cawing.

'Milla, please don't rubbish something that not every person can experience. Something that your grandmother was never allowed to experience.'

'Stop it! Leave my grandmother out of this!'

'I'm sorry. Please, I only want you to . . . give us a chance. Give me a chance.'

His hand reached out to hers and she shook it off. 'Let me be. I need to get back to Paul, to my mother in the hospital. Paul will be worrying about me.'

Leandro let her go. 'I thought he slept in a different hostel.'

'Yes, but he was going to pick me up for breakfast and then we were going to the hospital together.'

With trembling hands, she pulled her mobile from her hand-bag. Hopefully, there had been no complications with her mother last night. There were no messages from the hospital, and it was only seven o'clock, so she relaxed a bit. Paul probably hadn't missed her yet.

'Can you please drive me to my mother?' She had to leave.

Her hands were shaking when she sat down on the Vespa behind him and slung her arms around him, the thought of what they had done the night before making her cheeks burn.

'Mum, how are you today?' Milla was worried when she saw her mother lying between the white sheets, her eyes closed, looking pale and small. She had sent Paul a message that she was going to see her mother on her own first and would meet him for brunch later.

Sarah opened her eyes and blinked. When she saw Milla she smiled. 'Okay, darling. How often do I have to tell you, you won't get rid of me that easily?'

'I very much hope so!'

Sarah gave her a loving smile, something that Milla realised she wasn't sure she'd ever seen before. 'Everybody should go through a near-death experience,' Sarah continued. 'I haven't seen any angels or a white tunnel, nor did I meet a horned devil, but I realised that I'm very attached to you and to my dreary little life.'

Milla breathed a sigh of relief. 'Mum, your life doesn't have to be dreary. That's all up to you.'

'Very true, my darling.'

'You've simply hidden in your flat and behind the cheese coun-ter for too long. Am I right?' she teased.

'Well, what kind of tone is that?' Sarah smiled.

Milla returned the smile. Suddenly, she felt light-hearted and carefree. 'Sorry, but that's how it's been, hasn't it?'

Sarah seemed to ponder this, shaking her head. 'Doesn't everybody hide behind something? Or simply stay on the sofa? Because it's so nice and cosy?'

'Yes, but you miss out on the rest of life.'

'Milla, you look radiant. What happened last night?'

Milla felt caught out and lowered her eyes.

'Milla?'

With a sigh, she looked at her mother again. 'Well . . .' she started, then stopped. She had never talked to her mother about intimate things.

'Well what?' Her mother sat up awkwardly and looked at her expectantly.

'Mum, are you allowed to sit up? What with all the tubes and things?'

'Of course. I must get moving again. Well, what happened? I'm listening.'

Milla felt agitated, and like a little girl wanting to be comforted. Where to start? 'Well, it's . . . Paul proposed to me again.'

'Again? Why? Because he felt bad for cheating on you?'

'What? No, no! He had only taken guitar lessons with a colleague. As a surprise for our wedding.'

'Ah, and what's the problem?'

'Er . . . last night Paul organised a kind of spontaneous wedding on the beach. With rose petals and candles. He probably realised that I'm attracted to Leandro. Well, was . . .' Milla realised that she was getting confused.

'Why, aren't you any more?'

'No . . . yes . . . no idea. His ex warned me off him. Told me that he was a womaniser and would leave me soon, and now I'm not sure at all.'

'His ex.' That wasn't a question. Sarah smiled. 'Ah, Milla, never believe a woman who's been dumped and is hurt. I know what I'm talking about.'

'How do you mean?'

'I told my successor a similar story once. A long time ago. And I'm very much ashamed of it.' Astonished, Milla looked at her mother. 'No one is perfect,' she said quietly. 'And men aren't perfect either.'

'Well, Paul is. But maybe not for me. I simply don't know any more.'

Sarah looked at her daughter tenderly. 'Then go and find out. Or get involved with this Leandro. You only have one life.'

Milla sighed. 'I . . . got involved with him last night. On the beach. In a hut.'

'How lovely!' Sarah clapped her hands. She was taking it all very well!

'Yes, it was lovely, but Mum, I'm so afraid that I . . . we didn't use protection.'

'Ouch. But well . . . would that be so terrible at your age?'

'He might be the wrong man. At least if what Diana told me is true.'

'But maybe it's not. At least it wouldn't be so tragic as with my mother,' Sarah said thoughtfully. 'These days, you can raise a child all on your own.'

Milla wanted to know more, because she felt that it was the right moment to probe her mum. 'Eli told me about your mother's wedding. But she didn't know anything about the time afterwards, because they had fallen out. Well, Eli broke off the friendship.'

'Yes.' Sarah sighed and seemed to think. 'My mother once told me about her wedding and the time afterwards. I was sixteen then, and she was afraid I might get pregnant with my boyfriend at the time.'

Chapter Sixteen

Mallorca 1956/57

The last guests had left the wedding party. Abbi waited for Baruch, who was tossing down his whiskey. A short while ago, she had actually danced with him, because she wanted to make an effort.

Her fear of what was to follow now nearly paralysed her. Baruch slightly drunkenly indicated that she should go ahead to freshen up; he would wait for her in the bedroom. They had moved into his brother's flat, who was then living in Israel. It was to be only temporary, until they could find suitable accommodation in Palma.

Abbi, in her wedding dress, went ahead to the grubby bachelor's bathroom and looked around in disgust. In the sink were black hairs; there was a grey rim on the bathtub. Then her eyes caught her reflection in the mirror. She saw her face, the white veil pinned back, and felt sick. A very unhappy bride looked at her, when this was supposed to be the best day of her life. She couldn't do what was to come but knew that Baruch would demand it of her.

Feeling numb, she began to undress, but then stopped. The groom might want to take the clothes off his bride himself, but she didn't know. Suddenly, she felt very naive – naive and stupid. Why on earth had she consented to marry this man? How could it have come to this? But then Pomade's dark, glittering eyes came into her mind. She thought of escaping, fleeing to Johann and running away with him. But then the image of him with this other woman in the market appeared, how he had laughed with her, how cheerful and free he had appeared without her.

Free.

Her Jewish roots had wound themselves around her ankles like vines and held her tightly imprisoned. Not dead, but not alive either. She cursed Pomade, his minions and all narrow-minded people in the world.

'Abbi? Have you finished?' Baruch was calling from the bedroom, sounding slightly impatient.

'In a minute,' she replied. Soon he would take what he was entitled to as a husband. Nearly in tears now, she thought of her first time with Johann, how tender and gentle he had been with her. With so much love!

'Abbi? Come out now!' Baruch had put on some music that ought to put her in the mood, but she still felt sick.

Abbi took a deep breath and, knowing that she couldn't stay in the bathroom for ever, finally unlocked the creaking door.

Baruch had undressed and was wearing a burgundy dressing gown that showed his hairy torso. He smiled at her drunkenly.

Abbi swallowed hard and tried to smile but didn't manage it. Baruch patted the mattress next to him as an invitation to lie down. He had clearly drunk too much at the party, and Abbi hoped that at least it would be over soon and he would drop off quickly. Then she had an idea. Maybe she could manage to make him sleepy before something happened by chatting to him.

Stiffly, she lay down, still in her wedding dress, and began to ask him questions. How he had liked the party, how long he had known her parents, and so on.

Initially, Baruch answered readily, but soon he grew impatient. Without warning, he bent over, pulled her towards him and declared she was a chatterbox and that he hadn't known this side of her. Before she could retort, he kissed her. His breath smelled of alcohol and cigars, and his thick, wet tongue pushed into her mouth. It was difficult not to retch, and then he grabbed her breasts, kneaded them awkwardly and pulled up her white dress.

Abbi didn't resist; she simply kept quite still and tried to think of something nice. She imagined the almond blossoms around the *finca*, a life of freedom.

Finally, he let her go and asked with a proud smile whether she had liked her first time.

She looked at him, lost for words. 'Did you think of me for even a second?' she hissed. There she was again, the old Abbi who could never hold her tongue. At last.

Baruch frowned and looked annoyed, turned away and started snoring shortly afterwards.

Abbi went to the bathroom and threw up.

When she awoke the next morning, she saw with relief that Baruch was no longer lying next to her.

During the next few weeks, Abbi slept fitfully next to him, but he didn't touch her again.

Soon her tummy felt tighter than before, her breasts were fuller, and tender, as if preparing to nurse soon. Baruch had noticed it very quickly, because her dresses were getting tight around the chest. He sent her to a gynaecologist, who examined her and then snorted, 'You're pregnant.' That was all.

Abbi fainted and collapsed. Her worst fears had become true.

After someone had patted her cheek and held an evil-smelling tissue to her nose, she came to. Shortly afterwards, she heard Baruch's voice from the next room. They had called him, the husband, to pick up his wife. Baruch looked proud when he entered the room together with the doctor. Abbi turned her head and tried desperately to suppress her tears.

'Come home!' Baruch ordered. 'From now on, you are not going to work in that ridiculous shop any more.'

◆ ◆ ◆

'Pant! You have to pant!' the doughy midwife with the thin brown hair ordered Abbi, who was covered in sweat.

'I am panting!' she shouted so loudly the whole neighbourhood might have heard it. By now, they were living in their own flat in Palma's old town. Abbi had made sure of it. In addition, until a few weeks ago, even though she was heavily pregnant, she had continued to go to her shop, which had led to an almighty row. During the pregnancy, Baruch hadn't shown any interest in how she was feeling. Instead, he dug himself in with his books – the great publisher who never mentioned her cookbook again, which she had nearly completed in the last few months of her pregnancy.

Shortly before the due date and after some customers and locals had made comments, Abbi had had to accept that she must stop working in order not to annoy her customers or chase them away for good. She asked a young student to run the shop for the next few weeks but planned to go back to work soon after the birth. She hadn't mentioned this to Baruch, but more from a lack of opportunity, because Baruch worked until late in the office or spent his time in his favourite bar. Often, he came home drunk, and if Abbi didn't hold her tongue, she paid for it.

When this happened Abbi locked herself in the guest bedroom, which she had taken as her own space. Baruch didn't seem to mind. The main thing for him was that nobody knew about the state of their marriage. But for the birth of the baby, she had to return to the marital bed, otherwise the midwife or the doctor would begin to wonder.

'Now push! Push!!' The midwife's big hands pushed up Abbi's shift to see how close she was.

'Shut up . . . I am pushing!' Abbi shouted. The pain was overwhelming, unbelievable, ripping her apart.

Abbi remembered her father's words: 'In life, everybody gets what he or she deserves.' That had been many years ago, even before Rachel's death. Since then, Abbi had thought about it a lot. Had Rachel deserved to die? What had she done? She had been killed because she was thought to be Jewish. Had they all deserved to endure pain, be tortured or killed? Abbi remembered the words in the delirium of the contractions: *this child inside me is the reason I am suffering this pain.*

Another contraction. Abbi felt as if she had been ripped away by an almighty wave and thrown against a rock. She went under, nearly drowned, swallowed water and fought to get back to the surface.

'Now one more time, with all your strength. I can see the head.'

Abbi had given her all; now there was nothing left to give, and she didn't want to any more. She had run out of strength, but things seemed to move on their own. The child wanted to get out, wanted to live, to breathe. But when the midwife pulled the baby out, it looked blueish and didn't breathe. Abbi's heart nearly stopped.

'That was to be expected,' the midwife mumbled, and patted the back of the slippery creature. The baby winced, took a deep breath and uttered the loudest cry Abbi had ever heard from an infant. The midwife took the little bundle up and rocked it, but the baby kept on crying.

Oh, my God, Abbi thought. If this is a noisy child, Baruch will chase me out of the house. Even now, she thought only of the shame this would bring on her parents, of her poor mother with her heart problem.

The midwife announced that it was a girl, a proper *xueta*, to be precise. She said it so proudly, as if she herself had just given birth and this baby had caused *her* all this pain.

A *xueta*, Abbi realised with a shock. Then she might endure the same fate as Rachel – and her. But all she was feeling now was exhaustion, and she dropped off.

During the next few days she felt she was living in a nightmare. The baby cried continually, and Baruch went out even more to visit bars and other establishments.

One afternoon, a week after the birth, Abbi looked at her daughter in the cradle as if she was a doll. They still hadn't named her, just called her 'the child' or 'the little one'.

'What kind of a name would suit you?' she asked quietly, gently rocking the cradle. Baruch was putting pressure on her. The child needed a name, a Jewish name. What would people think?

Okay, Abbi thought. A Jewish name, but a name that sounded cosmopolitan. When her father suggested Sarah, she nodded. 'Why not, Father? If you like it.'

'Abbi, what's the matter? She's your child! Look at her, she has your eyes!'

'I know. But that's all.' She couldn't tell anybody.

After a few weeks Abbi wanted to go back to work in the shop and escape the domestic routine and drudgery but had to accept, bitterly, that it wasn't possible with a constantly crying infant. Baruch refused to employ a nanny, because, as the wife, she was responsible for the household. Esther, her mother, offered to babysit the little one every now and then, but as Abbi was nursing Sarah, she was chained to home and child. To breastfeed a baby in the shop, in public generally, was quite unthinkable.

Baruch rubbished Abbi's shop at every opportunity and told her one morning when she had broached the subject of going back to work again that they didn't need the small profit the shop was making. He, the great publisher, could pursue his career away from house and home, but not her, it seemed. The thought of staying at home with the baby filled Abbi with dread; she couldn't understand how other women endured their dreary existence as a housewife without any fuss.

Her parents were worried about her, that much she knew, but she couldn't do anything about it. Her mother had lost weight and was often short of breath – it was her heart. So Abbi did everything to hide her unhappiness and appear as if her life was fine and her marriage no different to so many other young couples'.

But Abbi's marriage wasn't normal. Rather, it was a prison with invisible bars; it was martyrdom. Baruch completely ignored her. He lived his life, and Abbi and her daughter didn't have a place in it. He had wanted a son and didn't know what to do with a girl, particularly not such a noisy one who obviously took after her mother.

Abbi withdrew more and more. She never heard from Johann again, but she thought of him every day, every minute, every second. When she ironed Baruch's shirts, she dreamed of being in their *finca*, on their beach, in Johann's embrace, so she could block out everything else.

The last time Abbi saw Johann had been a few days after the wedding when she was walking with Baruch across the Plaza Mayor. Suddenly, Johann had appeared in front of them and stared at her first, then at her husband. Then had said with deep sadness in his eyes, 'My congratulations. Eli told me you got married.'

'Eli?' was all Abbi could retort, flatly. That's why he hadn't contacted her. She had had no contact with Eli, but her former friend knew Abbi's neighbour and had probably heard all the gossip from her. Abbi wanted to say something to Johann, but her husband abruptly pulled her away, as though she was a child.

'Who was that?' Baruch wanted to know, and asked with a brittle voice.

'Oh, nobody,' Abbi answered quickly. Her knees were trembling.

Afterwards, she often wondered why Johann had looked at her so disappointedly. It had been him, after all, who after their separation had found another love so quickly.

Those thoughts haunted her. Had she made a mistake? The mistake of her life? No, surely not. She could never have married Johann. Her father would never have consented.

Whenever her thoughts became too haunting and the baby had been crying for hours, Abbi grabbed the little one, put her into the pram and went to the shop with her. The student did very well, and being there gave her comfort, the feeling of some freedom, even though she couldn't run the place herself now.

One day, when little Sarah had again cried so much that she went blue in the face, Abbi stormed out with her. What was the matter with the baby? Did she sense how imprisoned her mother felt? How lifeless, lonely and abandoned? Abbi didn't have anything to give to the little girl, no matter how much she tried. On one of her walks with the crying baby she suddenly encountered Pomade, and she nearly fainted. He seemed astonished that Abbi had a baby.

He looked at her strangely, the dark eyes flickering nervously. 'Now you know what your destiny is in life: to be a wife and a mother,' he hissed.

'That can't be all,' Abbi retorted with a cracking voice. 'Get out of my way.' All the terrible things that had happened to her flooded back like lava pouring from a volcano. She pushed the pram forward and hit Pomade's shin.

'Bitch!' he called after her. But Abbi felt a bit better.

However, that little bit of self-respect she'd recouped was crushed the same evening when Baruch came home.

'Where are my slippers?' he yelled drunkenly.

'Where you left them,' Abbi retorted defiantly.

'If you answer back one more time, you devil of a woman, I'll beat the living daylights out of you,' he threatened. She was hit by a wave of his alcoholic breath.

'Don't you dare,' she said quietly.

That provoked him even more, and he raised his arm and, before she could react, his big, bony hand landed on her cheek. Abbi hadn't expected it and was thrown against the wall, banging her head.

Her eyes stung with tears of pain and she could feel a trickle of blood running down from a cut on her head. She looked at him in disbelief. For a moment he seemed shocked, but then his gaze grew lustful and she saw a glint of satisfaction in his eyes. She rose with difficulty and ran outside. Stars were glittering in the night sky and from the open window of the nursery she could hear little Sarah crying.

In desperation, Abbi leaned against a wall and dried the blood with a handkerchief. What could she do? What if he hit the baby too? Suddenly, she heard Baruch shouting at the child to stop crying. There was a brief silence and then it started again. 'Stop it! Stop it now!'

Terrified that Baruch would harm the baby, Abbi ran back upstairs.

◆ ◆ ◆

Weeks passed, and during that time Baruch had tried to hit her again only once. But Abbi had grabbed his hand with all her strength. Drunk, he had whined in pain and promised never to do it again. But he insisted Abbi should never tell anybody because it would give him, an educated man, a bad name. Abbi didn't tell anybody and buried it deep in her heart, where it grew into a huge, painful lump, until one day it felt as though it would burst like a putrid blister. Although Baruch never hit her again, the icy atmosphere in their home, the lack of respect, hit her worse than any beating.

'I must get out of here,' she whispered to Sarah, who by now was crawling. We have to get away. A plan took shape in her head, and Abbi started to save every penny from the meagre household allowance Baruch gave her. As her husband, he had taken control of all her savings from the shop.

She planned to tell her parents that Baruch had hit her so they would understand why she had run away and not be angry with her. She needed to find shelter with them, because there was nowhere else to go with her fidgety baby. She had just packed a small suitcase with a few necessities when one of her parents' neighbours came running in.

'Abbi, quick, your father isn't well.'

'What? What's the matter? What's wrong?'

'I don't know. The doctor has just come.'

Abbi hid her small suitcase in the wardrobe so Baruch wouldn't get suspicious when he returned home. Then she picked up Sarah and ran after her neighbour, the little girl on her hip.

Her father, his face ashen, was lying on his bed. He looked at her sadly and said weakly, 'Abbi, dear, your old daddy isn't very well.'

'Don't say things like that, Father. What's the matter?

'I can't walk any more.'

'What?' She rushed to his bedside, put Sarah on the floor and took his hand.

'I had a minor stroke. But luckily, I can still talk. Only my legs and my left arm are paralysed.'

'Oh, my God . . . but that might get better again?'

'The doctor seems to think it unlikely.'

Abbi's thoughts were racing. Her father was still only middle-aged; surely he couldn't become dependent so early?

'I see it as a sign. I'll hand over the office to someone younger. We'll survive.'

'What do you mean, survive? You've always had a decent income?'

'Yes, for a while. But after Rachel's death . . . It was alright again after a while, and then you . . .'

Abbi looked at him in shock. 'What do you mean, me?' she whispered.

He looked at her sadly and said quietly, 'Do you think we didn't notice? A German man, of all people, Abbi. How could you do that to us?'

Abbi's heart seemed to stop. 'Is that the reason . . . I mean, did you have fewer clients because of that?'

'Of course. You know how people are. But then everything went well again. You're married to a good man now.'

He turned away awkwardly. Abbi was beside herself. In this condition, she could never tell him how cold and rejecting Baruch had become: Baruch, the educated man who initially had appeared so sensitive.

'Abbi?' She heard her mother's voice behind her. Esther waved for her to come over. Abbi, in a trance, took her child and followed her mother to the kitchen. She put Sarah back on the floor.

'Abbi,' Esther began hesitantly. 'I'm afraid it doesn't look good.'

'Father doesn't look well,' Abbi conceded.

'That's not what I mean.'

'What *do* you mean?'

Esther wiped her flour-covered hand on her apron. She hesitated, before bringing herself to say, 'Your father hasn't been paid by some of his clients.'

Abbi was so shocked she had to sit down. Could people really be that brazen? 'And he hasn't done anything about it?'

'No.' Esther's voice was very gentle now. 'Your father is simply too good for this world. It has upset him very much. But you know how people talk and harass us. Your father has lost the will to fight it.'

'I understand. And all of this because of me?'

'Ah, my child.'

That was all she said. Abbi stared at little Sarah, who was sitting on the floor, looking at her with her dark eyes. She felt so detached from her, so indescribably estranged.

'Abbi, do you think that Baruch, maybe . . . I'm embarrassed to ask, but as Father can't work any more, could Baruch now help us a bit?'

Abbi swallowed and nodded straight away. 'Of course, Mother. I mean, I'll talk to him. I'm sure that's possible.' This meant she had to stay. With him.

She stared at Sarah, who was just about to stick a pea she had found on the kitchen floor into her ear. Abbi didn't react at all, but her mother did. 'Sarah, darling. No! Let go!'

Esther quickly bent down and just about managed to take the pea from Sarah's little fingers. Then she turned to Abbi, who was sitting on the kitchen chair like a statue.

'Abbi, why do you treat the little one like that?'

'Like what?'

Esther didn't reply, just stroked her daughter's shoulder and sighed.

In Abbi's head an idea was growing. 'I want to support you too, Mother. I can earn a bit as well with my shop. If you could look after Sarah during that time? What do you think?' Abbi needed some time away from her child.

Esther thought about it for a moment. 'A child should be with her mother.'

'Please,' Abbi urged her, sounding desperate.

'Alright,' Esther sighed. 'If your husband agrees.'

I hope so, Abbi thought. She could get back to her shop, away from it all!

As she had expected, Baruch was not enthusiastic about the prospect of supporting his in-laws and allowed Abbi to go to work again so he didn't have to pay as much for his wife's annoying relatives. He wasn't particularly fond of the little girl either. All she ever did was cry.

When he reluctantly agreed to her going back to work, Abbi let out a deep breath. From now on she could get away every day for a few hours, to her haven, her shop.

Chapter Seventeen

Mallorca 2016

Lost in thought, Milla walked through Palma's narrow streets, passing souvenir shops, bistros and cafés. What a blessing the shop had been for her grandmother. She must never, ever sell it. The tale of Abbi's marriage to Baruch had shaken her, but still Milla felt that this alone couldn't be the reason why Abbi had felt unable to love her child. There must be something else, but what?

Milla sat down outside the café where she was to meet Paul. At the table next to her a young couple were kissing tenderly. Milla averted her eyes. Soon she'd be sitting opposite Paul and having to hide the fact that she'd slept with Leandro. The guilt made her feel sordid, but at the same time excited and alive.

'Good morning, or rather good afternoon,' Paul's familiar voice said behind her. Milla took a deep breath, turned around and smiled at him apologetically. Last night she had declined Paul's romantic proposal. How on earth was he feeling now?

She got up and hugged him. 'Paul, I'm so terribly sorry for yesterday.'

Hope flickered in his eyes. Oh no, maybe he had misunderstood her!

Quickly, she withdrew from his arms. 'I mean, at the moment, there's so much happening that I need some headspace, if you know what I mean.'

'Hmm, yes, I think I do.'

There he was again, her uncomplicated, good-natured Paul, who'd always understand her no matter how turbulent her thoughts were. He was a gem of a man.

'Just finding out about my Jewish roots has changed so much. Mum was right, it *is* important. It's our family's history. And a big responsibility. All my ancestors' sufferings . . . we, the children, must keep that history alive. I just don't know how.'

They sat down, and Paul took her hand. 'I'm here as well,' he said quietly. 'I'll tell our children and grandchildren. And maybe Dave – you know, the one I play tennis with who works for a newspaper – can write an article about it.'

Milla looked at him, overwhelmed. For a moment, the world around her disappeared and it was just the two of them. But then the memory of last night returned. Carefully, Milla withdrew her hand and suggested ordering something to eat.

'Yes, please. How's your mother?'

'Better, thank goodness. The whole episode seems to have triggered something positive in her. I hope it stays like that,' she added with a smile.

'Sure. But you know how stubborn she is.' Paul laughed. 'Do you know what I read somewhere today?'

'No, tell me.'

'The governments of Madrid and Lisbon regard the decision of their then royal houses to expel the Jewish population as a "historic mistake". They want to remedy it, but that's impossible, of course. Now Spain and Portugal are granting the descendants of expellees Spanish or Portuguese nationality. In addition to their other passport.'

'Ah, well. Late, but still . . . It's a very good gesture.'

'Exactly. Do you fancy some fish?'

Her mobile beeped. *Oh no, please don't let it be Leandro.* She had kept it switched on in case something was happening with her mother. She looked at the screen. It was from her mum. 'All tests went fine. Have discharged myself. Where are you? Will you show me the blossoming almond trees? Can it be just the two of us?' Milla read out loud, stone-faced. 'She can't have discharged herself!' Milla stared at the message.

'You should be pleased that she feels so well . . .'

'Discharging herself against the doctor's advice doesn't mean she's well.'

'She's a grown-up. It's *her* life.'

Milla thought about it. 'Would you mind if me and Mum go to Johann's on our own?'

'Of course not. I'll explore the island a bit. There are so many beautiful places on Mallorca. I'd love to have come here in the fifties, when everything was still unspoilt and quiet.'

'Me too!'

Milla texted the address of the café to her mother while Paul read the menu.

'Mhmm, Mallorquin *bacalao* pie. Or Catalan red mullet?'

Another text message, this time from Leandro. *I miss you terribly.* Milla's stomach tightened.

'What is she saying? Are you picking her up? Then I'll wait with the food.'

'Umm, she can't decide. You know her.'

Paul smiled. 'You two are very much alike. Making decisions isn't exactly one of your strengths.'

If he only knew how right he was!

'Mum, why have you discharged yourself?'

'Because I'm feeling very well, and you have an excuse not to have to spend the day with Paul.' Sarah smiled, proud of her mischievous plan. She had taken a taxi to meet them, and when they'd finished eating Paul had left them alone. Milla smiled at her mother gratefully.

'And also because I finally want to support you in your research and I definitely want to come with you to see Johann. I've left it all to you for too long. The same goes for your wedding preparations. I'm ashamed, Milla.'

'Oh, no, Mum, there's no need for that. I'm just happy you're here. That alone counts. But I would have preferred it if you'd stayed in hospital.'

'Who knows how long I still have? And because of that, I'd love to see the sea of almond blossoms and meet the man my mother loved so much. She talked of him so often I think her love for him lasted a lifetime. That really is rare. Between your father and me, it was special too. But fate took him from me much too early.'

Milla swallowed hard. Had her parents' love been equally strong? She hadn't known that.

'And you?' her mother asked carefully. 'You haven't told Paul of your night with Leandro?'

'No.' There it was again, Milla's guilty conscience.

'Good. You've done the right thing.'

'Good? And what if there are consequences? I don't think I've done the right thing at all.'

'But I do.' Sarah smiled again. They were walking towards their car. Milla took her mother's arm to support her.

'Milla, honestly, it would be very unlucky for you to be pregnant after just one time, so try not to worry. I don't think it's bad that you slept with him. You're young and need to find out what you really want. "*So test therefore, who join forever, if heart to heart*

247

be found together . . ." Sometimes you can learn something from the oldies,' she teased. 'In any case, you can learn how *not* to do it.'

Her mother's good mood cheered Milla up. Sarah was being surprisingly tolerant about her fling with Leandro! She was right, though. Unlike her grandmother, Milla could decide freely whom she would marry, and she should use that freedom. Hopefully, she wasn't pregnant, because that would constrict her choices.

In the car Milla turned on the radio and 'La Bamba' by Los Lobos rang out and they sang together, whatever lyrics they could remember. Outside, the sky was blue, and the sun was shining, and Milla realised she had never seen her mother so carefree and happy and knew that she would remember this moment for ever.

But as they got closer to Santa Maria, and the pink and white flowering almond trees started to appear across the landscape, the mood in the car became more thoughtful as they each considered what was to come. What else would they learn about their family? Would the old man, who only a few days before had discovered the love of his life had died, want to talk to them at all?

Milla steered the car further up into the mountains and soon they could see the Mallorquin *finca* in the distance.

'Look, Mum, there it is. The *finca* Johann bought and renovated for Grandmother and himself. Isn't it lovely?'

'Oh, yes!' Sarah was visibly moved.

There seemed to be even more yellow, red and purple flowers around it than when she had last been here, Milla realised. Springtime was beginning to show itself in all its glory.

'That he only came back here at his age . . . it's really lovely,' Sarah mused, and put on her sunglasses. 'Why not years ago? My father has been dead for a long time. She would have been free . . .' Sarah said as she pulled out her red lipstick and refreshed her make-up.

'Something must have stood between them, and we'll find out what,' Milla replied determinedly. 'In any case, Grandmother must have been a lovable person after all, Mum. If he kept loving her for all these years.' She looked at her mother sideways.

'For him she was lovable, definitely,' Sarah answered quietly, but with less bitterness than usual.

Milla parked the car and they got out.

'Looks like there's nobody here.'

'Oh, I hope he didn't go back to Germany or wherever as soon as he heard she had died.'

'No, he hasn't,' they heard someone say in Spanish behind them. Milla and her mother turned around. A Spanish man of about sixty with dark curly hair and brown eyes smiled at them. He was holding an empty wooden box.

She had seen this man somewhere before. But where? Sarah seemed to recognise him straight away and began a lively conversation in Spanish with him. When Milla saw her mother flirting with the man, she remembered. He was the friendly man who had delivered the almonds to Leandro's café – Jesús Fernández Jiménez. Did he work for Johann?

Milla interrupted her mother's conversation. 'Sorry, but what do you mean? Is Johann – I mean, Herr König – coming back soon?'

'I think so. He just went to the doctor to pick up a prescription. I recommended our old doc in the village.'

'Is he ill?' Sarah looked worried.

'Not as far as I know. He wanted something to calm him down,' he said. Abbigail's death had probably hit him quite hard, which wasn't surprising.

'Do you work here?' Milla asked curiously.

'Yes, I've been looking after the almonds for years now. Before, it was my parents, who lived over there. I only met Señor König last week. Until then, we had only spoken on the phone, when he would tell me what to do here.' Then he added thoughtfully, 'It seems that for years he had been waiting for a woman. That's what my parents told me. Which is why he wanted everything here to be looked after properly, and my parents were to contact him straight away if she turned up. But she never came.'

'Yes, he's been waiting for my grandmother, Señora Fuster.'

'Ah!' Jesús seemed genuinely surprised. 'Señora Fuster, who had the shop next to Leandro's?'

'Exactly.'

Jesús nodded, looking a little misty-eyed. 'It's a small island, after all.'

And sometimes it's very large, Milla thought. So big that two lovers could never find each other. Milla looked at the planters with the colourful flowers. How sad. All these years, Johann had the *finca* and all the almond trees looked after, always in the hope that Abbi would come back to him at some point.

Milla noticed that her mother looked weary. 'Mum, how are you? Shall I take you back to the hospital?'

'No way,' Sarah replied, slightly embarrassed that Jesús might have noticed her little dizzy spell.

'Would you like to sit on the terrace until Señor König is back? I could make you some tea in my house over there.'

'That would be lovely.' Sarah smiled at him and slumped on the bench on the terrace, looking exhausted. Milla sat down next to her, while Jesús hurried towards his *finca*, to the right of Johann's property.

The view the two women were enjoying from the terrace was breathtaking. Blossoming almond trees as far as they could see, and in the distance the sea.

'How beautiful it is,' Sarah breathed, her expression dreamy.

Milla's mobile rang. It was an unknown number, and she answered the call. It was a nurse from the old people's home, El Castellot, asking to speak to Señora Milla Stendal.

'Yes, that's me,' Milla said.

'I have a message from Señora Bescha Baum. You remember her?'

Milla hadn't forgotten the petite Jewish ex-dancer. 'Of course. How is she?'

'Unfortunately, she's not very well. She's in palliative care now, you understand.'

'Oh, I'm sorry to hear that.'

'And she would like to talk to you again to tell you something very important. Are you still on Mallorca?'

'Yes.'

'Please come as soon as possible.'

'Right now?'

'I'm afraid, yes. It could be too late if you leave it any longer. Her voice is quite weak already.' Milla was shaken and promised to set off straight away.

'What's the matter?' her mother asked when Milla ended the call.

'Bescha Baum, the old Jewish woman from the old people's home, Grandmother's last friend. I told you about her . . .'

'Yes, yes, what's the matter with her?'

'She's dying and wants to tell me something important.'

Sarah looked at her, startled. 'What could it be?'

'I'm hoping to find out.'

'Then hurry, Milla. I'll wait for you here.'

Milla hesitated. 'Wouldn't you rather come with me and have a rest afterwards in the hotel?'

'No. Jesús will be back soon. I feel safe with him. Please go! We'll be alright until you come back. Hopefully, you won't be that long.'

Milla still hesitated. Could she leave her mother, who should really be in hospital, in this faraway place? But she didn't have a choice. She had to hurry if she wanted to find out what Bescha had to tell her before she died.

◆　◆　◆

Milla ran to the car and with trembling hands tried to put the key into the ignition. Eventually, she managed to start the vehicle.

Was this finally the moment she would find out what had happened to her grandmother? Please, Bescha, stay alive, she whispered to herself. Why had the old lady not told her at her last visit? Was the secret that terrible?

She waved to her mother on the terrace, who was talking animatedly to Jesús, who had just returned. *What a pretty couple they make*, she thought with a small smile.

Milla put her foot down and raced the car down the narrow road. A flock of goats suddenly came out in front of her and Milla had to brake hard and wait while they crossed the road, her fingers drumming nervously on the steering wheel until the last kid had followed the herd. It was all black; the other goats were white.

Milla drove fast towards Palma. There was a traffic jam on the coastal road, tourists on their way to the beach or back to their hotel, and they seemed to have all the time in the world. Some drivers slowed down to take photos; others simply stopped by the roadside to get something from the boot of their car.

For God's sake! Milla was getting increasingly nervous. She couldn't be late, as she had been so often in the last few days. She had missed her grandmother's last days, and then her funeral.

At last the traffic was moving, and Milla drove towards El Castellot, the little castle, where Bescha Baum was waiting for her. Sadly, Milla thought that this wonderful woman would soon die, but tried to comfort herself with the fact that she was very old; older than many.

Quickly, she parked the car and ran to the reception. Aina Garcia, this time in a beige skirt which emphasised her slender legs, came towards her with a serious look on her face.

'Señora Stendal!' she greeted Milla in a neutral voice.

'Am I too late?' Milla was out of breath.

'No, not as far as I know. But she could go any minute now, I'm afraid. Come with me.'

Aina Garcia walked ahead of her over the path to the care centre. Because of her high heels and the skirt, she could only take small steps, so they made slow progress. Milla was getting agitated. What would she have to face now? She had never seen a dying person, let alone someone who had just passed away. Her hands were getting sweaty.

The palliative care unit didn't look like a hospital ward, but rather like an elegant, stylish hotel.

'Her room is over there.'

'Thank you. Is she on her own? I mean, are none of her family with her?'

Aina Garcia shook her head regretfully. 'She has no family. But I'm aware that a good friend from here is with her. Franz-Xaver Schuller.'

Of all people, this ex-Nazi officer was sitting at the Jewish woman's deathbed! Milla managed a little smile. Her grandmother must have worked wonders. It was possible, after all, to change people.

Aina Garcia accompanied her to the door, stopped and looked at Milla questioningly. 'Are you ready? I hope it's not too much for you.'

'So do I,' Milla said, then apologised.

'You don't have to apologise. I think it's always good to talk about feelings; not to do it might damage the soul.'

Milla smiled at the woman gratefully and knocked gently. Nothing. Was she too late after all?

'Try again. Señor Schuller is a bit hard of hearing.'

Milla knocked again, louder this time. She heard a sonorous voice: 'Come in.'

'I have to go. If something happens, call a nurse.' Aina Garcia left her then.

'Okay. And many thanks.' Milla pressed the door handle and carefully entered.

Franz-Xaver Schuller looked at her, his expression grave. 'At last.' He got up awkwardly.

Only now did Milla spot Bescha Baum in her bed. She had her eyes closed and looked fragile, thin and quite ethereal.

'I'm sorry I couldn't make it earlier.'

'It's alright. She's asleep.'

Milla sighed in deep relief.

'I'm a bit jealous that she wants to see you in her last hours, and not me. I'll leave you to it now.' He gave her a little smile. People of his age obviously dealt with death in a more matter-of-fact way.

Milla tried a smile too. 'Maybe it won't take long and you can come back to her. On your own, I mean.'

'Oh, no, no. We have said goodbye to each other, just in case.' Then he added with a little grin, 'We'll meet again soon up there. At least she's sure that I'll be up there and not down there with the horned one.'

Milla didn't know what to say, and the old man just smiled, touched his forehead in farewell and walked to the door. Reverently, Milla stepped towards Bescha's bed. The old woman was breathing calmly, but with a rattle. Her cheeks were sunken, and she looked grey.

'You have to wake her up. Otherwise, I'm afraid, she won't come to again.'

Milla looked at him fearfully. 'Really?

'As I say. Just shake the old girl a little. She really wanted to tell you something. A bit late, I think, don't you?'

'Yes.' Milla felt totally overwhelmed now. Her heart was pounding. Franz-Xaver Schuller left the room and only now did Milla notice how welcoming and cheerful it was. From Bescha's bed, there was a view to the sea. The rattling of her breath was getting louder, and Milla stepped closer.

'Frau Baum,' she tried gently. But Bescha didn't open her eyes. 'Frau Baum, it's me. Milla Stendal. Abbigail's granddaughter.'

Again, no reaction. The old woman's breathing was very shallow now. Milla touched the bony shoulder and shook it gently. 'Frau Baum. You wanted to tell me something about Abbigail, my grandmother. Please, it's so important to me . . .'

A ray of sunshine fell through the window onto Bescha's face. It seemed to tickle her nose. Slowly and painfully, she opened her eyes and tried to focus.

'Franz, you old charmer,' she breathed.

'No, he's gone out briefly. It's me, Milla Stendal. You wanted to tell me something about Abbigail. Something important.'

'Abbigail, well, Abbigail,' Bescha Baum whispered, concerned, and Milla had to bend down to understand her. 'It had happened . . .' she whispered, 'before she agreed to marry this *xueta*. This Baruch . . . otherwise Abbi would never have married him. Never . . .' Bescha coughed, got it under control and continued quietly, nearly inaudibly, 'She never even told her friend Eli what had happened, only me, before she died . . .'

Chapter Eighteen

Mallorca 1956

Pomade suddenly appeared one evening when Abbi had dragged herself to the shop despite her high temperature. He stood at the window, staring at her with burning eyes. What else did he want? Abbi thought in desperation. She felt miserable. Her father wanted her to marry a man of Jewish descent whom she didn't know, and just a couple of days before she had seen Johann with this other woman in the Plaza Major.

Pomade stepped into the shop and looked at her greedily. 'Come with me,' he ordered, and nodded to the door.

Was it the fever that dampened Abbi's spirit, or the memory of Johann with that woman? Feeling empty and exhausted and utterly incapable of fighting any more, Abbi followed him like a lamb to the slaughter. Outside, Pomade took her arm and led her along the streets.

The plaster on his ear had slipped, and Abbi could see the festering wound she had inflicted on him. The ear wasn't growing back properly and would always hang down like a piece of skin. Suddenly, she became fearful. What did he want? Would he take a late revenge now? His eyes were restless, a bit crazy, but when he looked at her she could see lust. He fancied her; she was sure now.

'What are you looking at?' he barked.

'Do you like me?'

'You'd like that, eh?'

She realised that she was right. He had fought it, because in his eyes she was only a *xueta*. But his desire seemed to have the upper hand.

'Please let me go back to my shop.'

'Shut your dirty gob!' he hissed. 'Why don't you ever keep your mouth shut!'

'But that's what you like about me,' she dared to say. 'Admit it.'

'To hell with you.'

'Please let me go. You aren't allowed to be with a *xueta*.' When she dared to look at him, she saw his eyelids twitching. For a while he didn't say anything and only stared at her, his eyes spitting fury and hunger. His breathing was shallow and irregular. Eventually, he pulled her into a house and pushed her into the dark hallway. Abbi started to shout, but he frantically held his hand over her mouth. 'Be quiet,' he hissed. 'I only want to show you where we will be living.' Abbi bit him, and, cursing, he pulled her towards the cellar, where Abbi knew no one would be able to hear her scream.

Abbi struggled with all her strength to get free, aware that Pomade's eyes were becoming more and more frantic. In the cellar he kicked open the wooden door to the coal bunker with his boot, shoved Abbi onto the cold floor, then threw himself on top of her, one hand over her mouth to stifle her screams, while the other roamed roughly over her body.

◆ ◆ ◆

After what seemed an eternity Abbi's eyes blinked open and stared into the darkness. She listened. Was she alone? She was in shock, felt sick, couldn't move. Her whole body was aching, particularly between her legs, where only one man had touched her before now – Johann. She was overwhelmed by disgust: disgust at Pomade and what he'd done. She'd known he fancied her, but to do this . . . He too had seemed shocked by his actions, as after he'd finished he'd got up and fled without another word.

Abbi had no idea how long she'd been lying on the cold cellar floor. She must have passed out; her whole body was hurting. The air smelled musty and damp; her eyes only slowly got used to the darkness and she could make out an old chest of drawers and the heap of coal next to her, a worn old shoe, a coal bucket and a leather suitcase. She tried to move but couldn't; she felt paralysed. But worse than her physical pain was how tortured her mind felt. Abbi felt utterly humiliated and dirty. She felt the urge to wash and tried to sit upright. Gritting her teeth, she slowly got up and staggered up the cellar steps.

The front door was closed but, luckily, not locked. Abbi pushed it open and, blinded by the bright beam of a streetlight, closed her eyes tightly.

She staggered out into the street, not knowing what to do or what to think and feel. It was dark now. Some pedestrians coming towards her stared curiously at the dirty young woman. But before anybody could ask her whether she needed help, Abbi rushed on. There was only one person she could go to now. No matter what had happened between them, she was the only person she could trust right now.

◆ ◆ ◆

'Oh, my God! Abbi, what's the matter?' Eli had put a dressing gown over her nighty and stared at Abbi in horror. Abbi's face and clothes were grubby from the coal dust. 'What on earth has happened to you?'

Abbi told Eli in a flat voice that she had been attacked in a dark alley but had managed to escape. Eli slapped a hand over her mouth and quickly led her into the house but indicated with a finger to her lips to be quiet. 'My parents are entertaining visitors, luckily. They're in the living room and shouldn't see you like this. Come upstairs.'

'Eli, who is it?' Eli's mother called from the living room.

'Just Abbi. We're going to my room.'

'At this time of night?' Eli's mother sounded surprised. 'But not for long, okay?'

'Alright.' Then, whispering to Abbi, 'Come on.'

In Eli's room Abbi slowly sank onto a chair. Her head felt as if it had been bashed, but she looked at Eli apologetically. 'I didn't know where else to go.'

'It's alright.'

'Thank you.'

'Tell me what happened.'

'There's nothing to tell.'

'Are you saying they haven't done anything to you? You know what I mean . . .' Shyly, Eli pointed to Abbi's skirt.

'What? No . . . I could just about get away.' Abbi was overwhelmed by shame.

Eli looked at her friend sceptically but saw no reason to doubt her words. They had always been open with each other.

'My God,' Eli said compassionately. 'Get changed. You can have a wash here and then put on one of my dresses.'

There was a sink with a mirror in Eli's room. Abbi shyly stripped to her underwear and scantily washed her aching body, arms and neck with a sponge, while Eli chose a green dress with a petticoat from her wardrobe. Their eyes met. No word was spoken.

'Abbi, it was Pomade with his gang, wasn't it?'

'No.' Abbi tried to sound convincing. 'It was some other guys.'

'And what did they look like?' Eli asked quietly, suddenly close to tears.

'No idea. It was very dark.'

'But . . . how many was it?'

'I think . . . four.'

'What? That many? Didn't you know any of them?'

'No.'

'But . . . you must have seen their faces. Would you recognise any of them?'

The memory of what she had just experienced hit Abbi like a fist in the stomach. She shook her head and stared at her dirty face in the mirror over the sink, then rubbed her cheeks hard to wipe away the terrible memory. But it remained – unrelenting, cruel.

'Abbi, you must have been very courageous and strong . . . that you could escape . . . I'm very proud of you, and so should you be. Do you have any idea why they did that to you?'

'Well, you know . . .' Eli understood and lowered her eyes.

Abbi rubbed her face harder to remove the grime, but it didn't wipe away her thoughts. Had she provoked Pomade in any way? With her skirt, with a look which could be misunderstood? Her forthright, insolent way? Her father always said that women had only themselves to blame when they became victims of sexual attacks. Abbi felt like a whore: ashamed and helpless. She couldn't tell anybody how tortured she felt, and time and again she saw his face, his desire.

She slipped Eli's dress over her head, hesitated for a moment and then tried to do it up. It fitted but was a bit tight around the hips. Eli was slenderer, more boyish. Had it been Abbi's female curves, her not exactly small breasts, that had taunted him? Should she have worn a different bra that didn't emphasise her breasts, as was the fashion? Abbi stared at her dirty clothes. 'What shall I tell my parents?' she asked in a trembling voice. 'I mean, about the clothes.'

'Is that your only worry, dear?' Eli commented, amazed. 'Won't you tell them about the attack?'

'No way. They're always so worried about me anyway. After what happened to Rachel.'

'Ah, yes, your sister. I'm sorry, sometimes I forget about it.' Eli pulled up a chair opposite, took Abbi's cold, lifeless hands and looked at her friend intently. 'Abbi, those men are dirty pigs. I'm sure Johann will find them and then . . .'

'Stop!' Abbi whimpered. 'You know that there's no more Johann. He's found another woman. I've seen him.'

'What? What has he done?'

'They kissed. In the middle of the Plaza Mayor.'

Stunned, Eli hugged her friend, and the two young women held each other in a tight embrace for some minutes.

◆　◆　◆

Time went by, but the memory stayed vivid. Whenever Abi thought about the hours in the coal cellar, she felt sick. This got worse, so that soon she had to throw up every morning.

Soon Abbi realised with a shock that she might be pregnant. It had to be Pomade's, because Johann had confessed to her before their first time that he couldn't have children, as he'd had mumps as a child. He had asked her seriously whether she could envision a future with him despite this. Of course she could, she was sure of it. She would have loved to have a child by him, but what couldn't be, couldn't be. She cared for him too much.

A child by Pomade! The thought hit her like a hammer blow. She went to a doctor straight away and begged him to examine her without telling her parents. He promised, and her suspicion was confirmed. Abbi, shaken by a crying fit, implored him to get rid of the pregnancy. He declined. 'I'm not allowed to do that. It's God's child, like every other child.'

'This one isn't!' she cried in desperation, got dressed and ran out. She was utterly disgusted by what was growing inside her and tried to get rid of it with toxic teas and other terrible measures, but the child stayed inside her.

What could she do? To have this child without a husband – she could never do this to her parents. Abbi was completely overwhelmed and alone, and finally she realised there was only one thing she could do.

Soon afterwards, Abbi came home one evening, pale as a sheet. Her mother was cooking.

'Abbi, what's the matter?' Esther asked, and offered her daughter a cup of tea.

'Mother,' Abbi croaked, staring at the floor.

'Yes, darling?'

'Mother, could you please tell Father something from me?'

'Of course. What is it, sweetheart?'

'To tell Baruch Bonnin . . . that I will marry him.'

She could only hope that Baruch wouldn't notice she was already pregnant.

Chapter Nineteen

Mallorca 2016

Bescha Baum haltingly finished her tale and looked at Milla with sad, tired eyes. 'Abbigail told me all this shortly before she died. She had kept it to herself all her life.'

Milla stared at Bescha, shaken. 'Which means that this ghastly Pomade is my grandfather . . . Mum's father?'

Bescha nodded imperceptibly. She seemed to feel very sorry for her. Telling the story had cost her nearly all her remaining strength.

'I wasn't sure whether I should tell you,' she said, 'but you desperately wanted to find out why Abbi couldn't love her daughter. Can you understand your grandmother a bit better now?'

'Of course,' Milla answered quietly. Her poor grandmother, how much she'd had to suffer!

Then the door opened and a nurse came in. 'I think Frau Baum needs some rest now,' she suggested gently.

Milla put her hand over the old woman's. 'Thank you, Bescha. Thank you so much!' The thought of all her grandmother had suffered moved her in ways she'd never felt before. 'It was a terrible secret, but I'm very grateful that you told me.' What else could she say to this brave woman who was halfway to heaven? Presumably,

Bescha herself had had to suffer unspeakably in the war, like so many others.

Bescha looked at her sadly and said, 'It happened to many of us. The worst thing is that history repeats itself all the time.'

'It's so wrong!' Milla exclaimed, upset.

Bescha trembled. 'Then do something about it. You're young.' Milla nodded. 'Send Franz in, please,' Bescha breathed. 'Quickly.'

'I'll get him,' Milla assured her, and rushed out.

Franz-Xaver Schuller was sitting in a rattan armchair in the corridor and looked up knowingly. 'Is she getting ready, the poor soul?' Awkwardly, he rose to his feet, clearly finding it difficult. 'So she beats me to it. Well, at least she can say hello to Abbigail from me, and once I've gone too, I'm the cock of the walk again.' He shuffled towards the door, gave Milla another encouraging smile and disappeared into Bescha's room.

Milla stood rooted to the spot as she tried to digest the terrible story she had just heard and, compounded by the fact that Bescha was just about to die in that room, it made her gasp for air.

Outside in the grounds, she took a few deep breaths and looked up into the sky. She saw a little bird, and for a moment Milla thought it was singing to her. Deeply moved by Abbigail's story, she decided not to tell her mother under any circumstances that her father had been a rapist. It would be too much for Sarah's heart, and she didn't want to trigger another attack.

Milla's fingers went through her hair. Her grandfather was a rapist. What would she give now not to have been told!

She came across Aina Garcia, who was pushing a patient in a wheelchair. 'Did you make it in time?'

'Yes, thank you.'

'Very good. Bescha Baum has just peacefully passed away.'

Milla swallowed hard and didn't know what to say. 'She . . . was a wonderful woman. At least she could see the sea in her last moments.'

Aina Garcia smiled, then bent to help the old lady in the chair to sit more upright.

Milla thanked her and said goodbye, wishing that everybody could be looked after in a place like this. It was good to know that her grandmother had spent her last months being cared for so well. Abbi, the Jewish dancer Bescha and the ex-Nazi officer seemed to have formed a very special friendship.

Slowly, Milla went back to her car and drove to Johann's *finca* to her waiting mother. Presumably, she wasn't really waiting for her, being in the company of this Jesús. 'Life goes on,' Milla thought, feeling a little more relaxed as she drove. Jesús seemed to have had a good influence on her mother; Sarah had perked up considerably when she saw him. Why should she burden her mum now with this story about Pomade? But what could she tell her instead? What could have been so important that Bescha had to tell her? By the time she arrived back at the *finca* she still hadn't thought of anything.

Walking up the path, Milla could see how comfortable her mother was in Jesús's company. The two were laughing together, looking only at each other, and they only noticed Milla when she had come closer.

'Oh no, were you too late again? Had she died already?' her mother greeted her.

Milla nodded quickly, grateful that she didn't have to explain anything. 'Yes, unfortunately.'

Sarah gave Milla an apologetic look and sighed. 'It's probably for the best. Maybe our family secret should rest in peace too.'

Milla swallowed.

'It's always sad when a person leaves this earth,' Jesús commented. 'Even though I never knew the lady.'

'Well, Bescha Baum was over ninety years old.' Milla thought of her mother, who already had a sick heart at the age of sixty. She must never tell her why Abbigail hadn't been able to love her.

While Jesús started another conversation with Sarah, Milla sat down, exhausted. What had this Pomade done to her grandmother? How could anybody do something like that? No wonder Abbi couldn't love her little daughter as most mothers love their children – unconditionally, from the moment they are born. No wonder Abbigail had kept Johann at bay for the rest of her life – out of shame, guilt, love. Her grandmother, the brave but broken woman.

Jesús's mobile rang. 'Señor König? Yes, of course. I'll be there right now.'

Johann! Milla and her mother looked at each other expectantly as Jesús rang off. 'I'm going to pick him up in the village. He went to the restaurant for some food.'

'Well . . . we'll wait for him here,' Sarah suggested, and smiled at him. He returned her smile with a captivated look, as if he couldn't bear to part with her.

'Mum, I'm so happy for you,' Milla said after he'd gone.

'What? It doesn't mean anything. He's probably married and has a family.'

'Haven't you tried to find out yet?'

'Of course I have. But I'm not sure whether he understood what I was asking. You know how men are . . .' She laughed.

Milla joined in. It was a relief that her mother was so cheerful, after everything that had happened. Since the health scare on the beach Sarah was a changed person. Or was Jesús the reason? Or was it the sun, Mallorca, her home island or the scent of the almond blossoms?

Whatever it was, Milla was enjoying it. She breathed in the beautiful scent. Maybe Sarah was right. She should stop digging in the past. That was it then, her family secret, why her grandmother hadn't been able to love her daughter. It wasn't surprising. Milla considered how it must have been for Abbigail to bring up a child conceived in such a traumatic way and sighed. The thought of being a descendant of this brute was horrible.

What was she still doing here anyway? Soon Johann would arrive, and of course she wanted to hear from him how this unhappy love story had ended. But it didn't really matter any more.

Her mobile beeped. It was Leandro. *Would you like to come to my mother's birthday party tonight?*

His mother's birthday? That could mean it was serious. And Paul? She had arranged to meet him later and couldn't possibly take him to Leandro's parents' house. Milla's heart was racing. What could she tell Paul?

She closed her eyes, like her mother next to her, and felt the warm sun on her cold face. She was the granddaughter of a rapist. Why had she made all those enquiries?

In the distance she could hear the deep humming of Jesús's Jeep. He parked in front of the *finca*, so the old man didn't have to walk too far, while Milla and Sarah watched in anticipation.

Jesús walked around the car to help Johann, opened the door, assisted the old man out and passed him his walking stick.

Milla tried hard to push aside what Bescha had told her, but it was difficult. She got up and walked towards Johann, who used his stick like a blind person to feel his way on the ground. 'Hello, Herr König. It's me again, Milla Stendal.'

'I know,' he muttered. 'Jesús warned me.'

'And she brought, as I said, her mother,' Jesús explained. 'Two beautiful ladies. They really look like the lady in your photo.'

Lady in the photo? Milla heard with a shock. Of course. Johann must have a souvenir of the time when he and Abbigail were in love. She needed to see it, because her mother didn't have a single photo of Abbigail.

'Herr König?' Milla dared to ask. 'I hope we aren't bothering you?'

Johann mumbled something and stared in her direction. How much he was still able to see, Milla couldn't tell. It must be a little, because he turned his head to Sarah, who reached out her hand to him, somewhat timidly.

'Hello, Señor König. I'm Sarah, Abbigail's daughter. She talked a lot about you. She loved you so much.' Milla gave her mother an astonished look.

'Did she?' he whispered, visibly moved. He seemed to soften, and his eyes moistened, but he managed to hold back the tears.

'I loved her too,' he whispered, nearly inaudible.

'Why don't you sit down, Señor König?' Jesús suggested tactfully. Johann nodded and let himself be led to the terrace, where they could all settle down.

Johann continued, 'But she didn't want me enough. Her love was not strong enough, she said. Even when her husband died, so many years ago, she didn't come back to our *finca*.'

Milla swallowed past the lump in her throat. Should she tell this man why Abbigail hadn't felt able to be with him, even in her old age? That her grandmother had felt incredibly ashamed until the end?

She cleared her throat. 'As far as I know, Abbigail was very shocked when she saw you with another woman so briefly after your separation.'

Johann's head went up. 'Me? With another woman?' He shook his head. 'Absolutely not. It was many, many years before I could get attached to another woman.'

Milla looked at Sarah in amazement and then turned back to Johann. 'Abbigail saw you in the Plaza Mayor kissing another woman. At least on the cheek, we've been told.'

Johann stared ahead of him, frowning. Maybe the old man was dredging the depths of his memory.

Then he seemed to remember and brightened up. 'Oh no, it can only have been my Spanish teacher. I didn't know any other women in Palma. And we always greeted each other with a kiss on the cheek and said goodbye like that, but there was definitely nothing more.'

Milla thought of Paul and how she had suspected him of having an affair with his guitar teacher. She and her grandmother seemed to share some traits. Johann was beside himself. 'And that's why she . . . never wanted to see me again?'

'Not just because of that,' Milla couldn't help saying, but immediately bit her tongue. Luckily, Johann couldn't see that.

But her mother squinted at her questioningly. 'Milla, is there something you're not telling us?' she whispered, breathing more heavily.

'No, nothing, Mum,' she said quickly. She couldn't tell her mother that she was the product of a rape. 'Are you feeling worse? Shall I take you back to the hospital?'

'No, Milla, don't worry. I'll enjoy life from now on and look after myself.' She looked at Jesús, who returned her smile.

Reassured, Milla turned to Johann again. 'After all I've found out, you really were Abbigail's true love, but because she was a *xueta* . . .'

Suddenly they heard a Vespa, and a man wearing summer clothes and a black helmet was racing up the track. Milla immediately thought of Leandro but was relieved to see it wasn't him; instead it was a nice-looking man in his fifties with black hair and light blue eyes, who greeted Johann and Jesús cheerfully.

'Hola, Jesús, hello Papa. You seem to have some charming visitors?'

Milla and Sarah watched the men with interest. He had called Johann *Papa*.

'Hello, Samuel,' Johann replied in a tired voice.

'Don't you want to introduce us?'

'Of course. These are . . . Abbigail's daughter and granddaughter,' he said sadly. Milla's thoughts were racing. Bescha had told her that Abbigail had been sad about Johann's inability to have children. That was the reason she had been so sure the child was Pomade's.

'Hello.' Milla shook Samuel's hand. 'Excuse me, but are you really Johann's son? I mean, the son of Herr König?'

'Yes, of course,' Samuel smiled. 'Pleased to meet you. And my condolences. My father rang me straight away when he heard of Abbigail's death.'

Milla nodded. An important question popped into her head, and she just came out with it. 'Abbigail had always thought that you . . .' Now she looked at Johann. 'Well . . . that you, Herr König, would not be able to have children.'

'What does that matter now?' Sarah interrupted.

'It's important.'

Everybody looked at Milla in surprise.

'Yes, Abbigail was upset that I was infertile,' Johann explained at last. 'The reason was that I had mumps when I was sixteen. But miraculously, my late wife became pregnant, so the prognosis of my paediatrician was clearly wrong.' Then he looked at Milla anxiously. 'Was that the reason . . .? Had it put her off so much, that we wouldn't have children?'

'No, no, that's not the reason,' Milla said haltingly.

'Milla, what's this about?' Sarah asked. 'Darling, please say what you've discovered.'

All eyes were on Milla now, and she stared at the ground, kicking the gravel with her sandalled feet while she tried to figure out what on earth she could say. Abbigail had clearly thought little Sarah could only be Pomade's because she thought that Johann couldn't have children. But could she have been wrong? Was it possible that

Sarah was Abbi and Johann's love child? Milla's thoughts were on a rollercoaster. The chances were fifty-fifty.

Samuel looked at her searchingly. 'Why don't you just say what you're thinking? For me, it always works best.'

He was right. She needed help with this. Her thoughts were in a tangle. 'Okay. Abbigail was constantly harassed by this guy, Pomade, a very nasty man. He believed that he could put her under pressure because she was of Jewish descent, a *xueta* . . . and . . . he hurt her very much, this Pomade, and she thought it was him who made her pregnant. Because Johann couldn't sire children.' After the words had tumbled out, she halted again.

The others looked aghast. 'No!' Sarah cried, and Jesús immediately took her hand and stroked it gently.

Johann looked even paler than before and clung to his stick with trembling fingers. 'My God, why did she never tell me?' he breathed.

'Because she felt ashamed and guilty, as women often do . . . after something like that.'

Sarah shook her head, still in shock. 'Then I might be the daughter of this disgusting . . .'

'No, wait,' Milla interrupted her quickly. 'Maybe not! It doesn't have to be like that. Not any more. Don't you understand? Now that we know Johann has a son, that he's not infertile, it could be that you're Johann's daughter, Mum. The daughter of Abbi's true love. The tragic thing is that Grandmother never knew and couldn't love you because of that . . .'

Sarah and Johann looked at each other speechlessly, and then Sarah turned to Milla again. 'And if not, I'm the child of that rapist? No wonder she treated me like that.'

'Yes, and that's the reason. I understand her now. But please don't be so upset, Mum. Just stop it. What if what Abbigail believed all her life isn't true? Then you still have a father and a half-brother. And I have a grandfather and—'

'Dad, you have to do a paternity test straight away,' Samuel interrupted her excitedly.

'Maybe that's not necessary.' Johann squinted and bent closer to Milla's face.

'Is your father of Asian descent?' he asked Milla.

She shook her head. 'No, he was German.'

'Why are you asking that?' Samuel wondered.

Johann smiled. 'Because she's my granddaughter.' He pointed to Milla's eyes. 'Those beautiful almond-shaped eyes, they are from my family. An ancestor of my mother came from Vietnam. Mine are not shaped that way, and not my daughter's either.' He looked at Sarah, full of emotion.

Sarah laughed. 'What? That can't be true! We've always wondered who Milla got those eyes from.'

Milla too had often asked herself as a child why she had almond-shaped eyes, unlike her parents. Sarah had told her one day that a magic fairy had come and given her those beautiful eyes because she was a very special girl.

Overwhelmed and deeply relieved, Milla first hugged her mother then her grandfather.

'Grandfather!' What a lovely, homey word. Johann trembled slightly as she held his bony frame in her arms. But he seemed happy too. She could see it when she let him go again, slightly embarrassed. They looked at each other, and Johann's clouded dark blue eyes suddenly seemed to shine.

'Abbigail,' he said, visibly moved, and swallowed.

'No, I'm Milla.'

'I know, I know. I'm not that senile.'

Milla smiled. 'I never said that. Herr König, how much can you . . . ?'

'Call me Johann,' he interrupted her, smiling.

'How much can you still see?' she asked him.

'Unfortunately not very much, but almond-shaped eyes and Abbi's nose I can just about make out. Samuel, please get the photo.'

Samuel nodded and ran into the house. Johann wiped his forehead and smiled at Sarah and Milla. When Samuel returned, Milla took a step towards him.

'Here, that's Abbigail. The photo was on our mantelpiece for years, and I gave in to Father's last wish and brought him here to Mallorca so he could look for her.'

'But we're too late,' Johann sighed.

Milla stared at the photo of her grandmother. They were not that much alike, but she noticed certain similarities, particularly the nose. Milla beamed happily. That was Abbi then, her courageous grandmother when she was young.

Sarah had come to stand next to her and was staring at the picture. 'My God,' she whispered. 'How different would she have been with me if she had known all this.'

They all looked at each other, concerned. Jesús put his arm around Sarah's shoulders and pulled her close to him.

Samuel interrupted the heavy silence. 'What am I to you now?' he asked Milla cheerfully.

'Well . . . my uncle?'

Samuel confirmed it with a nod and turned to Sarah. 'And you're my sister!'

'Half-sister,' Sarah corrected him with a smile. 'Who would have thought?' Then she turned to Milla. 'Thank you for never giving up.'

'Giving up is never a good idea, Mum.' Milla grinned.

'There are more family members living in the north of the island, and I'm sure they'd love to meet you,' Samuel said with a smile. 'My wife, my two boys and another half-brother.'

Sarah was visibly moved. 'This is . . . I don't know what to say any more.'

'Fantastic! Brilliant! Unbelievable! I've always wanted a large family,' Milla said joyfully.

Sarah took Milla's hands, but then turned serious again. 'Milla, will you please forgive me that I was distant with you so often?'

Milla was overwhelmed. 'But of course, Mum!'

Sarah pressed her hand in relief.

At last. She was reconciled with her mother – and after all these years it felt incredible!

Her mobile beeped then and reminded her that she had to make another important decision. And maybe it was her heart that had to make it. Leandro had texted, *Where shall I pick you up? The party will start soon.*

What was she to do? Paul would be waiting at the hostel, as arranged.

◆　◆　◆

Milla followed Leandro into the kitchen, where his mother was rolling out some pastry. She was a slightly rotund, dark-haired woman with a welcoming smile. 'How lovely that you could come. Leandro has spoken so much about you.'

Before Milla could respond, the woman gave her a hug. She smelled sweetly of aniseed and spice.

'Oh, sorry.' She stepped back. 'I can't help it. Now you have flour on your dress!'

'Not to worry.' Milla wiped away the flour. Her mother would never have hugged one of her friends like that. It was so sad, but it was only because she had never experienced much love from her own mother. Milla let go of the thought, because she only wanted to live in the present from now on.

'Milla, this is my mother, and she's always like that,' Leandro introduced them. 'Mother, this is Milla.' He pronounced her name like some rare delicacy, as if tasting it on his tongue. 'My mother makes the best almond cake. Would you like to try a piece?'

'Oh, yes. It looks delicious.' Milla thought of her grandmother, who certainly would have included a recipe for almond cake in her cookbook. Presumably, it was never published. But maybe it had been after all?

'Leandro?'

'Yes?'

'Do you happen to know whether my grandmother ever published her cookbook with the almond recipes?'

'She talked about it a lot. But no, it never happened. It was always in a drawer in her shop.'

Milla looked at him excitedly. 'Are you sure?'

'Yes, pretty sure. She showed it to me a few times. Everything was handwritten. The paper was a bit yellow with age.'

Milla beamed. She wanted to look after her grandmother's inheritance and find a publisher for it.

Leandro's family was noisy and cheerful. His tall, large father had immediately hugged her; his sister, Judith, a petite woman in her late twenties, greeted her with a friendly smile. A few more friends of the family and aunts arrived. Milla wondered fleetingly whether they were all *xuetes*, but it didn't matter. She felt at home, surrounded by these cheerful people, eating delicious food. She pondered how to have her grandmother's cookbook on almonds published. If she couldn't find a publisher, she might do it herself. Unlike in the fifties, these days everything was possible. With sadness Milla thought about Eli and Bescha's tales of the hostility and harassment young Abbi had had to bear; of how women had lived at the time and how her grandmother had tried to rebel against it.

Milla had told Paul on the phone that she needed more time, and as he had probably thought she meant time with her mother he had been understanding. She felt guilty, but also happy. Her period had started, so now she really was free to make her own decisions.

Throughout the events of the past few days she had kept in touch with Tine via WhatsApp. But today her friend was on her mind more than usual, because she had just had the operation. The myoma would have been removed, and Milla hoped with all her heart that everything would be alright now.

Soon she got the news she had been waiting for. *Op went well. Can have as many children as I wish, said the Doc. Kisses and hugs, Tine. Love you.*

Milla broke into a wide smile and replied straight away. Then Leandro rose and raised his glass for a toast. Everybody smiled at him and raised their glasses, and when Leandro pronounced a warm welcome to Milla, she blushed deeply.

'What are you doing?' she whispered, embarrassed. But then the friendliness of these people, of being in a family, overcame her self-consciousness.

'Can you feel it?' whispered Leandro.

Suddenly she knew exactly what he meant and she was flooded by a feeling of belonging, of having arrived.

'Let's go outside for a bit,' Leandro suggested. While the others carried on partying, Leandro and Milla got up. He took her hand as if he'd done it for ever and led her outside. 'Come on, I want to show you something.'

Leandro's parents lived in the old part of Palma, not far from her grandmother's shop. His hand felt soft and warm, and he never let Milla go. For a moment she thought of taking her hand back, but something in her refused to do it. What if Paul saw them like that?

'Where are you taking me?'

'Trust me,' he said quietly.

She followed him silently through a few alleyways until they were in front of her grandmother's shop.

'Let's see whether the recipe book is still there.'

Excitedly, Milla opened the padlock and rushed inside. Again, the slightly musty smell of many years surrounded her. She went to the drawer and opened it. There it was, hidden among other papers. Why had she never noticed it before? Because one only sees what one wants to see. She browsed through it. Grandmother's handwriting was familiar from her last letter but looked younger and less spidery. Eli had told her that Baruch had done everything to prevent other publishers taking on the cookbook.

'Take it and come with me,' Leandro said, interrupting her thoughts.

'Where are we going now?'

He smiled like a teenager in love and again took her hand. 'To the sea. You love it just as I do, don't you?' He was right.

They stopped by the water. Ships were silhouetted against the horizon and closer to shore; a few sailing boats were gliding by. Milla briefly looked at Leandro, then back at the water. Her heart was pounding. She loved the sea just as he did, and he had remembered. Did he too feel they had known each other for years? With Paul it had been so different . . .

Leandro pointed to one of the enormous cruise ships. 'Those ships come from Israel, America, from all over the world. Many Jews are in search of their roots.'

'Really?'

'They visit Palma's Jewish quarter and are grateful for everything they can learn about their ancestors.'

Like me, Milla thought. We need to know where we come from. At least, she saw it like that now: it was good to know that she was the granddaughter of Johann, Grandmother's true love.

Her thoughts expanded, like the sea in front of her. She could stay here and take over Grandmother's shop, as Abbigail had hoped for her. She could open a small goldsmith's atelier, in cooperation with Tine, making gold and silver rabbi figurines for the tourists, and maybe persuade Mother to stay with Jesús. And Tine would have to visit often.

'Milla.' Leandro interrupted her thoughts. 'Stay here with me. I love you like crazy. We belong together.' It was as if he had read her thoughts.

She didn't answer; only knew that it was the right thing to do, that she was no longer the woman who would move into a loft with Paul, that she had dreams and longings like Abbigail, and that she wanted to realise them – for herself and for her grandmother.

'You're as courageous as she was,' he whispered.

Milla smiled confidently, pressed his hand and looked out to the sea, watching as the ship sailed past.

ABOUT THE AUTHOR

Anja Saskia Beyer studied dramatics, communications and advertising psychology in Munich and has worked successfully as a TV scriptwriter. Her debut novel became an instant e-book bestseller in 2013. Since then she has published eleven novels.

She lives in Berlin with her family – husband, children and a dog.